Rebel Angels

TOR BOOKS BY MICHELE LANG

Lady Lazarus
Dark Victory
Rebel Angels

Rebel Angels

Michele Lang

A TOM DOHERTY ASSOCIATES BOOK
NEW YORK

REBEL ANGELS

Copyright © 2013 by Michele Lang

Edited by James Frenkel

Map by Rhys Davies

A Tor Book
Published by Tom Doherty Associates, LLC
175 Fifth Avenue
New York, NY 10010

www.tor-forge.com

Tor® is a registered trademark of Tom Doherty Associates, LLC.

ISBN 978-0-7653-2319-4 (hardcover)
ISBN 978-1-4299-4783-1 (e-book)

First Edition: March 2013

Printed in the United States of America

0 9 8 7 6 5 4 3 2 1

For Steven

*Every blade of grass has its
angel that bends over it and
whispers, "Grow! Grow!"*
—The Talmud

ACKNOWLEDGMENTS

As always, words seem inadequate to the task of expressing gratitude for all of the help, seen and unseen, that has made my writing possible. I can never thank all the people who made this book a reality. There are simply too many of you!

I'll thank some of you here, anyway, with apologies for my inevitable lapses. Let me start by thanking Beth Negri, for reading the early drafts of this book, sharing her knowledge of witchcraft and mysticism, and being my beta reader extraordinaire.

Again, my thanks to the fine writers of the LIRW, who so generously share their talent, enthusiasm, and friendship. Bianca D'Arc, thank you for your encouragement, vision, and heart. Thanks also to Alexandra Honigsberg, for being such an inspiration. A special thanks to author D. B. Jackson, for your eagle eye and historian's skill.

Thank you, once again, to everyone at Tor—for all that you do, and for the graceful way you do it. Thanks as always to my editor, Jim Frenkel, for his editing skill, his enthusiasm, and his kindness.

Thank you to all of my friends from and in Azerbaijan, for your generosity, warmth, and for introducing me and my family to a magical world.

To my family, thank you all so much for your example, for putting up with me when I go insane over my writing, and for loving me as I am, with all my passions and flaws. None of my books could have been written without you.

Rebel Angels

✕ I ✕

I did not plan at first to record my memories of the last time I saw Gisele in Budapest. I had wanted to tell only of Churchill's brave letter to me, his admonition that I turn my sights to the East, where all of us hunted a superweapon that could end the war.

But I find that I cannot soldier on, and write my tale of battle and blood without starting it with my little sister's farewell. I cannot begin my tale in the East before ending the one in Budapest, the home I had to leave behind. And so I tell you how we said good-bye.

The angel Gabriel towered over our heads, his sightless marble eyes gazing over Budapest. It was a glorious fall afternoon, but Heroes' Square was deserted.

My little sister Gisele gazed up at the gigantic statue perched upon his narrow Doric column. "I'm going to miss that fellow," she said, trying for a joke, but her voice was filled with such a sad finality that she all but broke my heart.

"Forget the angel, I'm going to miss you," I forced out. "We've said good-bye too many times."

"This won't be the last time," she replied. Gisele's voice sounded faint and far away, as if she spoke from another world.

It was, I realized with foreboding, her voice of prophecy.

A chill wind blew through my thin cotton suit and I shivered. The cold made me think of Gisele's impending journey, so far away. Into the terrible cold . . .

"Raziel and Knox should arrive at any moment," I said. "The trip to England is long, and it is freezing on the plane, mouse. Make sure you bundle up. You always forget your jacket."

"I can hardly feel a thing, Magduska. I already feel . . . gone."

I peeked at Gisele out of the corner of my eye, bracing myself for her tears. My little sister cried rivers over little hurts, things it was safe to cry about.

Her eyes were bone-dry now.

She began pacing the perimeter of the enormous paved square, and I trailed behind her like a silent shadow. The heroes of Hungary past posed before us, frozen statues preserved like mastodons in ice. The marble Gabriel presided over the fossilized heroes.

"I've never been the one left behind," I said, just for something to say. I did my best to keep my voice light, but I had to clear my throat to speak, it was so tight. "It's always been me bounding into the unknown, leaving you and Eva to fend for yourselves."

Gisele winced at Eva's name. "Poor Evuska," she whispered. "Look out for her if you can, Magda. She is in terrible, terrible danger."

Eva had become a partisan for the Hashomer, going undercover to spy on the local Fascists. She had chosen her mission over our life together, and I for one was grateful. As she was a spy, Eva's life was in constant danger. But still I hoped that Eva would outwit our enemies and emerge victorious at the end of the war. Like a cat, Eva had always landed on her pretty feet. And I had to believe that this war would end someday.

The time for watching over Eva was done. I still had Gisele to protect if I could. But the danger—for Gisele, and for all of us—kept changing and growing, faster than I could match it. I didn't need Gisele's gift of prophecy to see we stood in death's shadow.

Gisele and I, and my darling Raziel, too, had cheated death for a solid month, escaping from Poland and somehow making it out of that Nazi war zone alive. But who knew how long our luck could hold? Or Eva's, either?

I said nothing about that. There was no point in troubling my little mouse even more than the circumstances demanded.

Gisele picked up speed in her progress around the statues. The wind picked up, too, sending a rolling cascade of dead leaves dancing a tarantella around our ankles.

I shivered again, and chased after her, to both warm my blood and cheer her up. "Nineteen thirty-nine is almost over, mouse. And we're still alive, despite the Witch's prophecy. Nineteen forty has got to be better than this."

Gisele stopped walking, faced me. She shook her head and laughed—a mournful little sound. Her gaze pierced me straight though the heart. "Sweetheart," she said, suddenly sounding older than me, "we might well all be dead by nineteen forty, despite our luck so far."

I knew she was right, that the ancient Witch of Ein Dor herself had warned us when we had summoned her through séance to appear in our parlor. But I couldn't admit the truth aloud, as if speaking my fears would bring them into being. Besides, I didn't want a deeper shadow over Gisele's journey to the West.

"You'll be safe as can be in England," I said, more to reassure myself than anything else. "Winston Churchill himself will be looking after you."

Gisele blushed at the mention of the great man's name. "That may not be enough, not even the great Churchill's protection. But I'll go. I promised you I would."

I steeled myself against the misery in her voice, reached for her hands, and looked her right in the eye. "I can take you there myself, my dear, if that will make it easier. Nothing matters more. I'll go with you to London and settle you, pretty as you please. And Raziel will come with us, too."

For the first time a flash of tears sparkled in her eyes, burnishing their brown almost into gold with that trapped light. The wind caressed her hair like a mother's gentle hand.

"No," she said, her voice sounding offended. "There's no time for coddling me. You've got to keep fighting now—it's war."

I hated to admit it, but she was right. We both had our parts to play. I had almost killed Hitler in our last encounter at the

Wolf's Lair in Prussia. But he had recovered from his wounds and regained his strength. No matter how physically maimed, the Führer would not wait long before striking Europe again. Especially since his demon, Asmodel, goaded him incessantly to the attack.

But the thought of Gisele alone in a strange country, unable to make her way, made me half-frantic with worry. "Nonsense. I'll get you settled quickly, my dear, and then I can go east with an undivided heart."

She shrugged and sighed. "It's no use, Magduska, you'll have to fight with a shattered heart," she said, and turned her face away from me. "Today is another day for good-bye."

I hugged her close so that she couldn't see the tears escaping from my own eyes. "You were always the brave one," I said, careful to keep my voice from wavering. "I'll go east, you go west. I'll stop Hitler for good somehow, I swear it, or die trying. And I'll see you through; Eva, too."

It was my old promise to protect them, the promise I had first made after my mother had died, years before the war began. And I had repeated it to Gisele a hundred times or more over the last few, terrible years, as if it were an Indian swami's magical mantra. As if saying it a hundred times aloud would somehow make it come true.

It was the promise I had renewed to her, every day since the war had come. Gisele's awful visions had haunted us, and Eva, too, our dearest friend and sister of the heart.

But this time, Gisele stiffened in my arms as I recited my old promise.

I hugged her harder, and swallowed the bitter tears. "I swear it!" I whispered fiercely. "I swear it on my soul!"

She hugged me back then, and for a few minutes neither of us could say a word. I silently vowed to remember the feel of her in my arms, little and round, the sweet smell of her hair, the sound of her husky little voice.

Oh, she used to laugh, my Gisele, but I hadn't heard her really laugh in over a year. How I loved her, even burdened with her visions, even in despair.

Her jacket was scratchy under my fingertips. I kissed her cheek, tasted the salt of her tears. "I'm sorry you have to go so far away," I said.

She pulled back, still wrapped in my arms, her smile watery. "I'm crying for *you,* my poor Magduska. Your road ahead is long and hard. My poor sister."

I drew myself up to my full height, head and shoulders over Gisele. "I am a Lazarus, an eldest daughter. I mean what I swear—I will protect you! And I will never take it back. Never."

She chuckled at me, her sad little mourning dove song instead of one of her old easy belly laughs. "You are so fierce! I am not a dragon, you don't need to roar at me. I'm just your little mouse."

Before I could reply, a sleek black Mercedes limousine pulled up around the circular drive at the edge of Heroes' Square. Autos were not ordinarily allowed along the square on the weekends, but my dear Count Gabor Bathory, vampire lord of Budapest and my employer, enjoyed some special dispensations from the Hungarian government. And now, as the new Chief Vampire of the Budapest Vampirrat, he could expect even more deference, from both the human denizens of the city and the magical.

The sky seemed to darken as the limousine pulled closer. Knox and Raziel sat together in the backseat; Janos, Bathory's molelike driver, sat silently behind the wheel. With the limousine's engine still humming, Raziel shook Knox's hand and emerged from the backseat.

Knox, Churchill's spymaster, looked at me and nodded. And for only a moment, I saw it. A death's-head, superimposed over the man's bland, rounded American features.

I started, rubbed hard at my eyes, and just like that the image of death's angel had disappeared. But a shadow remained over Knox's face. I tore my gaze away, blinded my second sight. Death ruled over everything in 1939. Gisele was in no more danger with Knox than she was with me.

"Okay, Gisi, this is it," I said, keeping my voice light. I couldn't fall apart in front of her. "Not even a valise for you to pack—it's a pleasure to travel light, you will see. Go now, there's a good girl. Don't look back. Good journey, and write to me when you can, sweetheart."

Her tears had also vanished. She leaned in and kissed me on both cheeks, then reached for my hands and kissed them, first on the knuckles and once on each palm.

She folded my hands over the kisses. "These are some extra kisses for when you need them. God bless you, Magduska."

And before I could say another word, she slipped into the open door of the limousine, the door closed, and they hushed away along the cobblestones, Knox and Gisele now in the backseat. Raziel put a strong arm across my shoulders and squeezed me hard as we watched the shiny black Mercedes slip away.

When he saw the condition I was in Raziel wanted to call me a taxi, but I waved him away. Better to walk the pain away if I could.

As the light failed we walked across Budapest, all the way to the river, past the gigantic Parliament building as we watched the sun set behind the Buda hills.

After all of our travails in wartime Poland, losing Gisele now would be almost more than I could stand.

"She's safer in England," Raziel said, his voice smooth. Gently, he chucked me under my chin and smiled, one of his irresistible, lopsided smiles. His gentle strength poured into me, but it just wasn't enough. "We made this plan for a reason, you know," he said.

"I do know," I whispered, my voice hoarse. "I can't understand why I'm being such a baby."

"Knox will take care of her," Raziel said.

I could only laugh when he said it. Knox, Churchill's spymaster, had a job to do, just as we did. His mission was to get Gisele to England, not to protect her from all harm. Nobody could do that—not even, though it hurt me to admit it, me.

The sun continued its descent, and the Danube below us flowed like molten gold. "It's a luxury you have, to be sad that Gisele has gone away, even if it is for her safety," Raziel said, and his almost unbearable kindness sent me over the edge. "So go ahead and grieve the separation, drop the burden for a bit. Then back we go, into the fight."

I nodded miserably. The wind gusted up from the river, cleared my head a little. "So Gisele's out of harm's way. And so are we, for the moment. Bathory has prevailed."

Raziel's eyes darkened as he studied the hills beyond the

river. "For now. His enemies are formidable. It's something of a marvel he won, to be honest."

"He's going to want me in Budapest, to stay."

"Maybe. But if he's done so well without the need of you, he will most likely accept your leaving Budapest again, to fight the Nazis some more. After all, Bathory is a patriot."

The Budapest sarcasm in his voice could have come from a native. My beloved Raziel had fallen far from Heaven, indeed. But I was selfish, I was glad he had fallen. I loved him so much as a man.

"Patriot or not, Bathory's a pragmatic creature. He'll want me to serve as his assistant as I used to. But it's too late for that now."

I wasn't the girl I had been when I had started out on my journey west, in search of my family's inheritance, bound into an ancient book called *The Book of Raziel*. I had found a version of it, and it had been subverted by the Nazis into a terrible, evil source of magical power. Only the original of the Book, a primordial gem called the Heaven Sapphire, could overrule the Nazi perversion.

Raziel and I had sworn to hunt the sapphire in the place where we believed it was hidden. Hitler's demon, Asmodel, lusted after the sapphire, and if we didn't find it first, he would claim it for his own.

It was because of the hunt for the sapphire that I sent Gisele away. I could not both chase the gem and protect her. The war had decided for us: the gem came first. And not even the specter of death itself could stay either of us from our separate paths.

I wrenched myself from thoughts of my sister, to thoughts of my husband, my man, Raziel. "We're going to have to tell

Bathory about us," I said to change the subject. I couldn't bear to think about Gisele anymore.

Raziel smiled at that; he saw right through me. "He won't mind that I didn't ask for your hand, you know. He's your boss, not your father."

I didn't blush often anymore, but I knew that I was blushing now. "Former boss."

"You can't quit a job like you had with him."

As usual, Raziel was right, but that didn't make it easier to accept. I could not simply untie my loyalties to Bathory, or to Gisele, and coldly slip away. Alas, I was no vampire, and though a witch, I was all too imperfectly human.

My thoughts strayed again to Gisele, no matter how hard I tried to turn my mind to other subjects. Her plane had surely taken off for London by now. "Gisele was my mother's favorite, that's no secret. But I was my father's. Papa. Did you meet in the second Heaven the day he died?"

Raziel's smile was sad. Undoubtedly he was thinking of his all but eternal time as an angel, now past. He had sacrificed his wings to join the human fight against the Nazi menace on earth. Out loud, he insisted that our love made up for everything he had relinquished. In his heart of hearts I was not so sure he was telling the truth, to himself or to me.

But all he said was, "Your father was one of the finest men I ever met in the afterworld. I was your family's guardian angel, but he did more to guard you than I could from up above."

"Do you think Papa approves of us, from up above?" I was joking, mostly—Papa wanted only my happiness, and how could he object to a primordial angel of the Almighty?—but Raziel's smile faded.

"I'm not an angel anymore. I earned my mortality in Krueger's prison in Kraków, good and hard."

I winced at that. "Krueger's dead, my love, and we are still alive. We have to get the Heaven Sapphire, or all that we've done so far will be for nothing."

"It's lost," Raziel said, his voice soft in thought. "I brought it first to the Garden of Eden, when the world was young. And long the daughters of Eve guarded the gem, until the First Temple of Jerusalem was destroyed. And now . . . who knows."

I drew back and looked at my beloved. His thick dark hair rippled in the wind coming off the river, his hat clasped in his hands. All of us are ancient in a certain way, I suppose; we are sparks thrown off by the Maker of the world at the time of the creation.

But Raziel remembered. As a man he was new, raw, in a strange world he still hardly knew. But he remembered, all the way back.

He did not speak of it often and I respected him enough not to demand he reveal his secrets, not when they were so painful to remember. But just knowing he carried these secrets inside of him filled me with awe.

"Can I summon it out?" I asked.

"No," Raziel replied. "Your magic is in words. This gem is invested with great power, but it is not translated into human or even angelic speech. It is pure."

The thought of the gem, the Heaven Sapphire, in my hand made me shiver. With it, I could destroy my enemies. But I had been unable to capture the bespelled *Book of Raziel* from Hitler and Asmodel. What made me think I could master the gem itself?

It didn't matter what I thought. I had sworn to Gisele and myself that I would do everything in my power to fight the evils arrayed against us and all of our kind, and no matter how slight the chance, I had to try.

And Raziel stood by my side. I might have lost the Book, lost my beloved sister, even lost my best friend, Eva, to the war. But Raziel, now my husband, walked with me.

Night had fallen over Budapest. Soon the vampires would be out, hunting, and though I walked under Bathory's protection and could protect myself in any case, I had to get inside.

We had an impossible dream to pursue.

✳ 2 ✳

For the moment we were staying above the flower shop on Ferenc Körút, where Eva had once hidden from the Fascists. We returned from Heroes' Square, and tidied ourselves up as best we could.

Once night had fully fallen, I prepared myself for my first audience with Bathory since we had returned. I was determined to go alone—the Café Istanbul was a dodgy place for mortals at the best of times.

Raziel got undressed, washed up at the basin in the corner, then started putting on his clothes where they lay in a crumpled heap by the bed. I loved to watch Raziel dress. He did so many things masterfully, but buttons and clasps still got the better of him. He had not been human for very long.

He slipped his shirt on, studied the buttons upside down,

then gave me a piteous look that drew me to him at last with a laugh.

"I'll save you, archangel," I said as I joined him near the nightstand. "Buttons are easy, once you've got the trick of them. One, two . . ."

His buttons distracted me from thoughts of Gisele, and I welcomed this kind of diversion. I buttoned my way up his chest, half-breathless. When I reached his collar I looked up into his eyes, warm as a sunset, and all my levity melted away.

"We have to get out of Budapest," he said, his voice gentle, his eyes full of wariness. "Bathory will have to help us get out of here alive. You were right to send Gisele away, my love. Since war has come, Budapest has changed. Too dangerous for us, too."

I am a tall girl, but my husband towered over me. I laced my fingers together behind his neck, raised up onto my tiptoes, and kissed him breathless. "It was hard to get here," I murmured, pulling back from our embrace to look him in the eyes. "It will be harder to leave."

Now that war had come, crossing the border had become a high-wire act, and without Bathory and his network of supplicants and fanged cousins we would soon be lost in the East. In our battles with Hitler and his resident demon, Asmodel, we had decimated Hitler's stronghold, the Wolf's Lair, and its forces. But Hitler had over a million men in his army, with a cohort of magical warriors besides.

Despite my every effort, Hitler still held Poland. It was the false peace of the fall and winter of 1939–40, and the world held its breath, waiting for the Reich to make its next move. France and Britain had declared war against the Axis, but so far they had attempted no offensive against the Reich. And the Reich had not attacked the West, not France nor Britain, either. Not yet.

The world hung by a single thread. Something as small as a gem, an ancient sapphire of primordial power, could tip the balance. Plunging the world into war or vanquishing Hitler's army for good.

I had my theories of where to find this hidden gem. And so did Hitler's demon, Asmodel. Both Raziel and I suspected that the gem was hidden deep inside the territory of Hitler's reluctant ally, Stalin.

"You will talk to Bathory," Raziel said. "And he will help us."

"He'll help us because he thinks we will succeed. Bathory is nothing if not practical," I said. I had to steel myself against Bathory's ancient, predatory charms. Over the centuries he had perfected his avuncular, elegant persona.

But he was a vampire. Created for murder, dismemberment, and war, he performed all of that mayhem without turning a single well-groomed hair. Oh, Bathory was loyal, loyal unto death.

Not for the first time I realized how strange were my feelings about him. I loved the old duffer. All the more reason I had to protect myself from my softheartedness for him.

Raziel didn't bother replying to my anti-Bathory ravings. He knew my feelings for the dapper old vampire were dark and tangled. He was counting on these ties to persuade Bathory to invest in our venture.

But I didn't know how or whether to tell Bathory about our marriage. How would he react?

❧

I left Raziel to pace the little room alone, and met Bathory that night at, of course, the Café Istanbul, Bathory's unofficial place of vampire business, where he received human supplicants of an evening, and where one could eat lovely pastries and sip strong coffee. As I entered the café and ran my fingers along the length of the smooth wooden bar, I felt a sharp twist of nostalgia, though I had left Budapest for Poland only a few short months before.

Now that I was married, my allegiance had shifted. I had been and always would be Bathory's loyal, mortal assistant— one cannot give one's notice for that sort of position—but my first loyalty, now and forever, was to my family. My little sister Gisele, my sister of the heart Eva Farkas—and now my husband, my beloved soul mate Raziel, the once but no longer king of the angels.

By day, the sleepy café was all but deserted, with only an atmosphere of gloom to suggest how dangerous the place could prove to ordinary people. But now, at night, the vampires came to roost, warming their cold bodies with Turkish coffee, rumballs, and perhaps something more illicit before they swooped into the night, seeking their prey.

Bathory was surprised to see me. "So you have returned! With no fanfare, and alone. But it is a Wednesday," he murmured. I was shocked he did not say hello. My count was always the soul of good manners, no matter the circumstances.

"Yes, my dear count, I know," I said, peering over the side of the mezzanine railing. The lights were still dim.

"And tonight is the floor show. The special entertainments

presented on the Wednesday nights." His nostrils quivered ever so slightly, I guessed in anticipation.

I could not suppress a sigh. "My troubles force me here tonight." Before this night, I had always refused to work on Wednesday nights at the café. And Bathory, knowing I did not ask for much otherwise, acceded to my request.

Before I could explain myself, a set of spotlights shone on the main level of the Istanbul, which had been cleared for the night's performance. A beautiful girl, slender and blond, was bound in silken cords and seated backward on a chair, head tilted back. She wore only lingerie and silk stockings.

The band started playing "J'attendrai," slow and sinuous.

"Where is your handsome Raziel?" Bathory asked, smiling just enough to reveal the tips of his fangs.

I sank into the seat next to where Bathory held court in the corner so I could hear him better over the trumpets and the snaky oboe. "Are you kidding? I wouldn't bring anybody mortal in here on a Wednesday night. Raziel has come back with me, too. He's hidden away, for the moment at least."

Two young male vampires drew close to each other and met over the bound lamb's head. They started in on each other, snuffling at their bared necks, licking their exposed wrists. These young males, too, wore next to nothing.

"Is that really why you kept Raziel away?" Bathory asked. His nostrils flared now, a little wider, as if he could scent the blood coursing through the young vampires' veins.

I could never hide anything from Bathory. "We have something important to tell you, but now is not the time to tell it. Even I might not be safe in here tonight."

The bloodlust rose in the veins of the denizens of the Istanbul like a collective tide. I kept my witch's sight reined in tightly so that I could sense the edges of it but keep from getting swept in. There are certain things about the vampire way that I had no interest in experiencing.

The larger of the two males yanked at the hair of the younger, more delicate one, and dark, almost purple blood dripped down the submissive's bare chest. The first vampire licked it clean and kissed the bound girl roughly, deeply. I could hear her whimpers from way up in the mezzanine.

"You like the floor show, little chicken!"

I shifted uncomfortably in my seat and kept my opinions to myself. Instead, I tore my gaze away from the violent seduction playing out below and stared my dear Count Bathory right in the eye.

"I came tonight because I need your help. We've just come back from Poland as you know. Gisele is safely away thanks to you, but I need a place to hide Raziel. I've given up my flat, and we're staying one night here, one night there. Budapest is just too dangerous for us now."

There, I had spat out my request. I hated to ask Bathory for anything, for a vampire's gifts always came with strings attached to them. But I had barely gotten Gisele out in time, and needed to hide Raziel until we left, probably for good.

I was good luck to Bathory: now that my witch's magic had manifested, helping me would enable him to call upon my services later, and help him hold on to the position of Chief Vampire. I hoped that my magic counted for enough with him.

Budapest's charms had faded upon my return from the war in Poland. The things I had once thought so important—the physical gorgeousness of the city, its cosmopolitan air—rang hollow and false to me now, after all that I had seen in the war so far. They say that travel broadens your worldview, and I suppose that is true. But no one had ever warned me that knowing the world might tarnish my vision of Budapest, my golden home city.

Bathory looked different to me, too, both larger and smaller than he had before I had gone. He had saved Raziel's life in Kraków, and his courage and loyalty had proved a lifeline out of the horrible nightmare of Nazi-occupied Poland.

But here, in the Istanbul, I finally understood that Bathory was a vampire. Stupid and slow, I know, but I had always seen Bathory as a singular phenomenon, one of a kind. Now that he was risen to the position of chief, I finally saw that he served as the leader of his people, as a distinctive and different member of the vampiric tribe. He enjoyed the floor show at least as much as any of the other vampires who had come to the Istanbul.

When you love someone, it is easy to overlook their flaws up close. And I was stupid enough to love Bathory despite the fact he was a vampire. Bathory had proven braver and more honorable than a dozen ordinary vampires. But the fact remained—he was still a vampire, through and through.

The count shrugged and dabbed at his mustache with a linen napkin. "Of course you must protect your Raziel. He is your witch's lamb, is he not? He feeds your magic like that little blonde down below feeds her masters. If he is in danger, I will protect you both. It is my duty, and my pleasure."

The girl's cries grew louder, as if to punctuate Bathory's words. Both vampires had now attached themselves to her neck.

Even after Poland, I blushed to see this display. "Now, what would our glorious leader Regent Horthy have to say about such vulgar entertainment?"

Bathory's lips twitched with amusement. "He'd be horrified, of course. Yet, Horthy still allows the vampires to live openly in Budapest. We act as something of a check upon the Arrow Cross and their wolves, who answer only to the German Reich and not to Horthy's government. And Horthy will use even vampires to keep the Arrow Cross from seizing power here. For now, my position as Chief Vampire is secure, but I need not remind you, my dear, that these remain perilous times."

He turned away then to watch the floor show, and delicately licked at the corners of his mouth, like a cat watching a bird bathing in a fountain. I cleared my throat, but he was intent on watching the girl's defilement to the end.

I leaned in to whisper in his ear as he watched. He wasn't getting rid of me so quickly. "I need your protection, sir, not just a place to stay. For Raziel."

Bathory chuckled under his breath, even as he kept watching the goings-on down below. "Oh yes. I will protect him. He is a precious prize, my dear. Mark my words, better than that ancient gem you've been hunting for high and low."

He took a slow intake of breath, his eyes lidded nearly closed. I glanced down at the floor show; the girl was limp now, the vampires frantically slashing at her body and at each other. Her face was transported by a terrible bliss.

"Is she dead?" I asked in a horrified whisper.

"Not yet. But she wants it," Bathory whispered back.

The girl arched her back and screamed. Cries and applause

rippled through the café, and I was careful not to look too deep into the shadows to see what was going on in the audience. Bathory as always maintained superb control, but the younger, weaker vampires succumbed to their own bloodlust all around us.

"Why would somebody want to die as a vampire's sacrifice?" I whispered.

I didn't expect an answer, was only thinking aloud, really, but Bathory encircled my wrist with his cold fingers, startling me.

"You don't understand the meaning of surrender, the glory of it," Bathory murmured. "The ecstasy of release, of passionate submission to a stronger force. You only know resistance. Your ignorance of surrender is where your power lies, little chicken. And it is also your folly."

I turned my head and looked at him, tried to pull my hand out of his grip, and failed. His eyes were dilated, his deadly fangs fully extended.

"Surrender to me," Bathory growled.

I stared into his eyes, the way that no mortal could and still evade his thrall, just to show him I could do it. "You know I will not," I replied, my voice calm, steady. Once Bathory had frightened me more than anything else in my nightmares or in my existence in the night of Budapest. But after what I had seen in Poland, no longer.

"I worked for you once, but I won't bare my neck to you," I continued. "I am not Gisele."

That cruel little barb snapped Bathory out of his bloodlust. His eyelids fluttered, then his fangs abruptly disappeared back behind his lips. "Your sister is gone to England. Of course."

"Yes, she and Knox are safely out of Hungary now. Nothing holds me here, dear count." *Not even you,* my silence whispered. "I have to find Raziel a temporary haven, or else I will have to fight here. And if I fight here, I'll never get out of Hungary to hunt the gem. My enemies will prevail as long as I battle them in Budapest."

"I suspect you would handily win any battles you fought here," Bathory replied, his voice sounding under control once more. "I cannot say the same of your fight to claim the gem, in some faraway land."

"But that's my trouble, dear Bathory. I must get that gem, and I must leave Hungary to find it. Nothing would please my enemies more than keeping the battle here, in Budapest."

He pursed his lips together, considering my reasoning. But a thunderous roar of applause distracted us both from our clash of wills.

The girl now sprawled in a heap on the floor, lips blue, eyes sightless and open, staring into the dim light of the sparkling chandeliers. The male vampires were collapsed on the floor with her, one on each side of her, heads thrown back in ecstasy. All three of them were covered in blood.

"Ah, she's dead," I murmured under the screams and applause.

"No, my dear," Bathory replied, a note of surprise and delight in his voice. "They have turned her instead. Usually this is all for show, the pets are saved for next time. But this night . . . those young creatures forgot themselves."

He raised a sardonic eyebrow and leaned back in his chair with a world-weary sigh. "She is a bloodlust vampire now,

Magda. Watch your back on the way to your hiding place. A newly turned creature like her is starving for blood. Unless she feeds, she will not last the night."

He shifted in his seat to look at me. "Hide for a few more days, I have some business to conclude. Check here next week and I will have a place for you and your Raziel."

Without warning, he leaned forward and grabbed me by the shoulders, most unlike him in his lack of propriety. I saw his dilated pupils, his own gargantuan bloodlust, now held barely in check. "You may stay with me," he said, slurring slightly over his words.

I swallowed hard. I was sworn at one point to Bathory's service, and he had released me to hunt *The Book of Raziel* to Amsterdam. But now that I had returned to Budapest our relationship was blurred, and therefore dangerous.

My former role as loyal subordinate was too small to fit me now, and both of us knew it. I could not take orders from a vampire lord while wielding a thing as dangerous as the Gem of Raziel.

But I as yet did not possess the gem. And there was the not inconsiderable matter of Raziel. I could not swear service on behalf of someone else, and this little technicality was why I had come alone to make my request for protection.

The blond girl began sobbing and moaning as the bloodlust took her. I watched her passionate suffering, and could not help imagining Raziel turned that way. My stomach did a sick, slow flip.

Her travails convinced me. Despite the murky implications of accepting Bathory's protection, I had little choice. My power, strong as it was, still wasn't enough to hide Raziel from the magical denizens of Budapest. I was banking on the fact that Bathory's temporal power as chief would be enough.

I held out my hand for Bathory to shake. He licked his lips and squeezed my hand hard. For the first time, I worried that the bloodlust would overtake him and that Bathory himself would attack me.

"Good," he said, his voice short. "Consult with Imre. And go now. I will see you in a few days. Hopefully we will have news of Gisele's safe passage to England by then. Hide, stay safe."

I had never heard the bloodlust choking Bathory's voice before. He held himself in check now only with great difficulty.

"Go now," he repeated. "And ask Imre to see you safely to your hiding place. The city will be crawling with bloodsuckers tonight. The floor show this evening was so marvelously . . . stimulating."

✳ 3 ✳

Raziel and I hid with various allies and enemies until we met with Bathory the following week. When we met, Bathory read us the following letter, which I have mentioned before:

October 22, 1939
Café Istanbul
Budapest, Hungary
10 P.M.

By Hand Delivery
To Magdalena Lazarus
c/o the vampire Bathory, chief vampire of Budapest

My dear Hungarian witch,

*Brava, and brava again. I cannot call upon the an-
gels the way that you do, but whispering spirits tell
me that you have put quite a dent in the Nazi war
machine. Oh, the papers put about that Herr Hitler
was burned in a curious electrical fire, but I know
the truth. He is recovering, but from all reports the
Führer will never be the same.*

*I am, to be frank about it, quite pleased. You have
bought Britain time, time to arm against the Hun.
Every extra day we gain before Hitler turns his ambi-
tions westward is another day to build munitions, call
upon our soldiers, prepare our fair island to defend
against Nazi attack.*

*And there is no honor amongst thieves. There are
rumors that Stalin and Hitler have already fallen
out. Stalin, too, buys time, but Hitler grows impatient already, I hear. This is an educated guess, but
one that I believe you will make good use of: Hitler
will make a break for the Caucasus oil fields, and
sooner than I had thought. Hitler needs oil to run
his war machine, however much you have dented it.
Once he seeks to invade the Caucasus, Hitler will
enrage the Russian Bear.*

*And you will be ready, dear Lady Lazarus, won't
you? Knox, who has delivered this letter for me, believes that what you seek is also in the Caucasus.
And he wanted you to know this fact, particularly.*

*Most importantly, know that your sister has ar-
rived safely to our shores, with the assistance of both*

Knox and Bathory. She will stay at Chartwell until we have found her a more suitable place. She is very quiet, and very sweet, your little sister. But she is possessed of your family's dark and terrible fire as well. She is not such a dreamy little mouse as you described at our dinner at Chartwell.

Please find enclosed a small token of my esteem. I had Knox take the trouble of changing it from British pounds to Hungarian pengoes, as those will be more useful to you. I would have sent you gold, but Knox would not have been able to carry this much so easily.

I bid you well, my dear. Your former employer has reportedly been restored in Budapest, above his former position, so I am hopeful this letter finds you in fine fettle.

With all good wishes,
Your obt. servant,
Sir Winston Churchill

I lingered most over the section about my little sister, Gisele, now lost to me in Budapest. I had to trust in Churchill to keep Gisele safe, now . . .

My employer, Bathory, took the news of my secret marriage to Raziel better than I could have hoped. Cheered by the great Churchill's letter, Bathory insisted on a hotel suite for a honeymoon, a real night of passion to celebrate our wedding in Poland.

After I reminded him of the dangers, he instead offered us his own lair, a gorgeous, crumbling mansion high on Rose Hill, so that we could consecrate our union, a single night of love, not war.

That night, our honeymoon, was a mistake.

Marrying Raziel was not a mistake. It was the smartest, bravest thing I had ever done. But that night of indulgence, that single night devoted to celebrating our love alone, led to a world of troubles. The world shouldn't be like that, but alas it is, and there is no point resisting the world's way.

Bathory's protection was not enough to save my life, but at least it saved Raziel's. I am a Lazarus witch, capable of summoning my soul back from the dead. By my honeymoon night, I had died so many times I made it look easy. But every death exacted a price. Oh, a heavy price. I never let my enemies know how much it hurt to die, that was just another of the world's hard truths.

But that night alone with Raziel . . . it was worth dying for. For a single night we did not run, we did not fight, or scheme or worry or foretell. We had cheated death, and for a single night we dedicated ourselves to celebrating our love, and life.

And celebrating Raziel was easy. Angel he was no longer; now he was a man, a magnificent, fierce, passionate man.

He was powerful enough to open me, the defended one, the lonely one. I loved Raziel enough to surrender to him, to allow him inside my defenses to love me.

Bathory had abandoned his quarters for haunts unknown for my and Raziel's night together; in any case, he hunted the night and ordinarily went abroad by moonlight. He left his trusty factotum, Imre, to guard the doorway against intruders, and I knew there was no place safer for us in all of Budapest.

There was no truly safe place for us in Budapest. No safe place in all the world.

Once we retired to Bathory's guest room, which was musty and filled with enormous pillows and ancient Persian carpets, we spent a moment looking at each other. Alone at last.

And then like two waves crashing against each other, Raziel and I met, standing beside the low bed piled with blankets and pillows.

With great gentleness Raziel removed my hat, placed it on the nightstand. He ran his fingers through my hair and lowered his lips to mine.

We kissed each other hard, bruising kisses filled with desperate passion. We kissed as if every touch were the last.

Raziel's hands had grown rough in the forests of Poland. But his callused fingers were gentle against my skin, and he undressed me with tenderness.

My heart pounded as he lowered me onto the pillows. As above, so below. A cosmic truth my teacher, the tzaddik Yankel Horowitz, had taught me in the forest. Would that it were simply so, for my joining with Raziel was the most perfect connection to another soul that I have ever known.

It was one night. It cost me nearly everything. And it was all worth it, it was so glorious.

When I came back to earth long enough to think, I glanced at the alarm clock tick-tocking away on the bedside table. Three thirty A.M. In my life before this war, this love, it was the hour of my employer's court, my time as well, the witching hour. The hour when the dark mystery of night prevails.

I rolled over in the bed, all tangled up in the slippery satin sheets, and I studied Raziel's profile as he dozed. Ah, that nose. I caressed the line of his jaw, and his smile widened, and his eyes opened.

"Awake?" he asked, and he rolled onto his side.

Darkness is attracted to light, a dusky moth to the flame. And my Raziel, even fallen, shone with a pure and righteous light.

I basked in that light, surrendered to it.

And right then, all hell was unleashed around us.

Over Raziel's shoulder, hidden in the long shadows along the walls, a hideous creature climbed out of the darkness and slashed my husband across the face with his long, curved claws.

Raziel sprawled across the bed, his hands grappling with the creature's ropy forearms. I leaped backward with a hoarse yell and fought my enemy, as naked as the day I was born, unashamed, clothed only in my elemental fury.

The smell of Raziel's blood drove me crazy. I gathered a ball of witchfire in my palms and threw it as hard as I could into the creature's leering, hideous face.

He toppled back, cursing and screaming, and a horde of similar creatures rose up in a mob out of the shadows with unholy yowls.

"Imre!" I yelled, though I despaired of his life, too. "Imre!"

I stood steady on my feet and took a deep, shuddering breath, the power rising up from deep inside.

"No," I said, and the power in me poured from my center out along my limbs, sizzled to the very ends of my hair.

Raziel crawled off the bed, wiping the blood off his face.

"I'm all right," he said, choking on the blood still pouring from his nose. He reached under his pillow and retrieved his Mauser pistol, a gun that he had taken off of a German soldier in our journey south from Poland.

Without hesitating, Raziel slid back the safety and shot his attacker in the face. Whatever the creature was, he could not survive a point-blank bullet. Magic notwithstanding, the creature had manifested on our plane, could bleed and die like us.

The supernatural being that had slashed Raziel was dead. It was maybe ten seconds since the attack began. No magic among this mob other than what they were, nonhuman creatures invested with inherent magic. And even if they had some kind of spell-casting skills, these attackers had not yet wielded magic strong enough to match mine.

I didn't have time to weave a spell, so I simply whispered a ward onto Raziel and blasted the rest with witchfire. They retreated to the wall, burned by that slashing blue light.

"Parley," the largest of them gasped, in German.

"Go parley in Hell," I snarled back, and gathered up another ball of crackling witchfire. But Raziel's hand on my shoulder stayed me.

"Stop," he said, and wiped at his bloody face again. "Listen to what he wants to say."

"He attacked you," I said, still half out of my mind with fury.

"Magdalena. Listen. No harm in a moment's truce."

Slowly Raziel's calm, reasonable words seeped into my brain. Of course he was right. I could perhaps learn why they had come by speaking to these creatures.

I wrapped myself in the now-bloody bedsheet; now that I was more in my right mind I remembered my naked state. "Speak your piece," I said.

"Thank you," the head thug said, and he clumsily bowed.

His manners made me laugh. "How nice and polite you are now, Herr Monster, now that your fellow is dead." I tried my best not to taunt them, but my best wasn't very good at all.

"You come from Berlin," I continued. No need to ask: an attack of this magnitude, violating the wards of the Chief Vampire of Budapest, was obviously the work of the German High Command.

The head of the mob nodded and licked at his nose nervously: he had failed in his prime directive, to kill me.

"What are you?" I asked.

"Wood trolls. From Bavaria, we come."

My curiosity faded into an uneasy dismay. Wood trolls, though bad tempered and meddlesome, are not known for their magic or their ability to violate wards. The foul Teutonic magic that Hitler commanded in concert with Asmodel had augmented the trolls' natural power. But had the trolls attacked alone, or with other magical allies?

"So what is your parley?" I asked with a sigh. All the while knowing I would not accede, so confident in my magic that I could not imagine compromising with my enemies.

"If you will not die, surrender," he said, sounding like he didn't even believe in his parley himself. "Stop fighting and we will spare Raziel's life, and Gisele's. If you surrender your person, they can live their lives in peace. Isn't that what you really want?"

When I had first started fighting, it was. When Gisele first received the awful visions of what 1939 would bring to Europe, Budapest, and our own little lives, all I had wanted was to see Gisele through the war alive, and Eva, too, to ride out the storm, and afterward life would go on as before.

But everything had changed since then. I had found my inheritance—*The Book of Raziel*—and my power within it. I had fallen in love with the author, the source of my true magic, my soul mate. I could not turn my back on that power and simply walk away; my conscience would not allow it. Of course I could not stop the war, no matter how hard I tried. But I could fight. I had to fight. And the fact my enemies saw my potential retreat as a victory only confirmed my conviction that I had to fight to win.

Victory or death. No other choice. No matter the price I had to pay.

But my girls, the ones I loved . . . and Raziel . . .

I hesitated, considered the wood troll's words. Really I did. But it was too late to heed them now. .

"I will not surrender," I said.

"Then die," a woman's voice said from behind me.

And a white-hot poker pierced me between the shoulder blades, and clean through the heart.

Ah, the pain! Brutally sharp, slicing through my spirit as well as my body. That pain struck me down, struck me dead.

I was dead.

And Raziel, surrounded by murderous enemies, would soon be next.

✳ 4 ✳

Into the second Heaven I fled, shooting into the gray nothingness like a sparrow fleeing a hawk. By now, I knew the second Heaven like the backstreets of Budapest—another bad neighborhood, to be sure, but mine.

In my astral form I came to a stop in the ether and took a long look around, hoping to see my dearly departed mother, Tekla, here to welcome me. My mother died when I was only sixteen, but since then I had not let her rest in peace. I needed her help again now, as always. And as usual, my need was urgent. I had to return and save Raziel, without getting killed again if I could help it.

"Mama!" I called, unwilling to risk her wrath by compelling her soul to appear. I had once believed I did not have the power to work magic in the astral. But after many desperate battles in this fateful year of 1939 I had learned better, by sheer necessity.

The last time I had seen my mother's spirit, she was leading a cohort of murdered ghosts back to Heaven. I still desperately needed her help, but the better part of my nature hoped she had found a more peaceful corner of the afterworld than this one in which to rest.

A dark shower of sparks exploded on the horizon, tiny at first, then growing larger. I braced myself for a visitation of a creature of air, most likely less than friendly. The second Heaven used to be a kinder place when Raziel presided over it.

I expected a spirit of air, out hunting, hoped it might be Viktor, my newly appointed guardian angel. But my visitor was none of these, and when I saw who it was I almost died again of shock.

It was Obizuth, one of the three demonesses I had set free from the terrible Nazi wizard known as the Staff. My first murderess—she and her sisters had killed me in an Austrian field, the summer before.

I braced for a fight. At least this time, she couldn't kill me again. And unlike the Bavarian trolls, Obizuth swore fealty only to herself. Self-interest can usually be reasoned with.

"Daughter of women," Obizuth said, her voice tart. "How like a demoness you have become."

Here in the realm of air she revealed her true aspect: her teeth, long and pointy, gleamed pearlescent in the dull, gray light of the astral plane.

I ignored the needle prick of her veiled taunt, and crossed

my arms against the flutter of fear under my ribs. "I have become cruel like you, I suppose. But our bargain still holds; you have no claim upon me."

"I warned you, Lazarus. Beware of me. Of my sisters."

I sighed with impatience. "I know that. I am your sister of the air, and your sisters have never fared well in league with you. Warring sisters we will be for always."

Because of Obizuth, I had learned of my demonic lineage: fallen angels had lain with my foremothers long ago, in time out of mind. And because of this, death did not consign me to the next world with the ordinary finality. My gift—the ability to return from the dead—was at least in part bequeathed to me by my line's fallen patriarchs.

Obizuth's laugh was low and scratchy, a hoarse little growl. "I have come to warn you again."

"Warn me? Why?"

She shrugged and stared away into the middle distance. "Perhaps I am not as neutral in this war as I like to pretend. Perhaps freedom is not all I crave, but also revenge."

I considered her cryptic-as-always words. "Go ahead. Explain."

"Can you not guess?" she said, so low I could barely hear her. "The Ancient One has finally discovered your whereabouts. He has seduced my sisters back into his service, to destroy you and everything you fight to save. Your safety is all illusion."

Not even Bathory could keep me hidden, not when Asmodel and his minions hunted me. Raziel and I had managed to evade them for an entire month, in our escape from Poland. But we could not remain invisible forever.

I drew closer, and Obizuth's yellow reptilian eyes widened. "Safety is not what I am after," I said. "Do your sisters not realize that I will not let them destroy me? Killing me is not enough to stop me."

"But that is not what I mean, witchling, not at all. My sister demonesses are not the danger. You are. You rely on your power and your magic to sustain you, Lazarus. That is an idolatry. And a desperate illusion."

Anger flashed through my astral body—how dare Obizuth accuse me of idolatry when it was her sisters who had thrown my gift of freedom away.

I kept my voice level. "No. I know my gift and I use it. And I remember always that it is a gift, nothing of my own to claim credit for. I never earned my magic."

Obizuth squinted and pursed her lips. "You are a fool. Do you not understand?" She looked uneasily over her shoulder and shook her head. "You all but killed his host, Hitler, and the Führer is now scarred and twisted, burned almost beyond recognition. Their grasp on the Reich is slipping away. Every day now, another traitor is caught and punished. But that is not enough to stop the rebels, now that the Führer is maimed so terribly."

Obizuth looked down at her bare scaly feet and bit her lower lip. Sighed. "Beware the cornered beast, witch. The Ancient One is most dangerous now that he grows desperate. The old ways fall away," she said, her grief and longing now audible in her voice. "Your magic never was infallible. Even the Witch of Ein Dor died at last."

"Asmodel wasn't the one who killed the Witch of Ein Dor," I said.

That did it—I had made a terrible mistake on the plane of souls, to speak of my nemesis by name. And I knew it was a mistake, the second I made it.

Obizuth's eyes widened and she drew away from me with a sharp gasp. "You disdain my warnings. You do not even bother to guard your own words. So be it."

She rose into the air as the gray clouds surrounding us billowed in the sudden astral winds. "I came to warn you to get the hell out of Budapest. But obviously I came too late. Well, here's another warning: Get your little sister, the vampire's lamb, out of London. Before that warning is too late as well."

Obizuth hesitated, looked down from where she now hovered, far above my astral head. "There is no safe, and never was." And with that, she sailed off like a shot, not bothering to say good-bye.

Before I could answer her, or thank her, I saw a great, black shadow move over the horizon, like a hole opening in the world. I watched it come, knowing I had done the unthinkable.

Summoned Asmodel by name.

He already had known my whereabouts, I reminded myself. It didn't matter that we met here, now, in the astral. I might even have a chance now to destroy him.

None of my desperate rationalizations made any difference. My nightmare trampled through the second Heaven, and soon the ancient demon and I stood at thirty paces, a good distance for a duel.

"Your host, Herr Hitler, has not made much of a recovery, I hear," I said.

"Never mind him," The ancient demon snarled. He hovered

in the air, like a thundercloud with a twisted mouth full of fangs.

"You cannot harm me here," I said, though I wasn't exactly sure I was right.

He laughed at that, a cruel, echoing laugh that shook my courage. "I don't need to, witch. That is not why I have come."

Only my curiosity stayed my hand from hurling a ball of witchfire across the ether at his face. "Oh? You have sent your minions to kill me if they can. Is that not harm?"

He laughed again and shook his massive, ugly head. "You think you are so wise, little gnat. Why do you think I had you killed?"

I hesitated, crossed my arms against his voice. A part of me agreed with every word that Asmodel said, and I had to keep that wayward remnant in check.

Instead of replying I shrugged, and secretly worried about Raziel, who was still embroiled in battle in the world below.

"I know killing you makes not much difference in your magic," Asmodel said. "I had you killed so that we could speak again."

"Parley? It didn't work with your Bavarian troll offering it to me below, I don't know that it will work up here, either."

"Your bravado is shit, child. Do you not understand?"

I shrugged again, not willing to admit my ignorance any more overtly than that.

"My host, the Führer, is maimed. He is not dead, he will not die. But his physical body must withstand the terrible rigors of war."

I smiled at him. "That's the best news I've had for a month. Thank you, Asmodel."

He snarled again. . . . I had yanked at his soul with his name like a massive silver chain. "Insolence!"

"Yes, that is me, all around. Obnoxious brat. Ungrateful child. Idle dreamer. My mother called me all these things and more. Hearing any of it from you isn't going to change me a bit."

"I am here to offer you a choice, witch."

I stood in the clouds, absolutely still.

"Take up the mantle of the Führer when he succumbs to his wounds at last. I will hurry him on his way should you agree. Or waste your magnificent talents on fighting me. Don't you understand? You can turn aside the Witch's curse, the prophecy that dooms you and your sister. You can undo everything that Hitler has done."

"There is nothing more to discuss," I said, sincerely disappointed that the demon only offered me the same tired temptations he had dangled before me in our last encounter. "You are the Prince of Lies. I will never bow to you, never join forces with you."

He gnashed his great tusklike fangs and rolled his eyes to the hostile heavens. "You throw away your only chance to deliver your people from destruction, all for the chance to defeat me with your magic. You think your magic will destroy me in the end. It can only serve me. Do you not understand from where it flows?"

"From the Fallen Ones. Perhaps directly from you. But I still have the power to choose."

"So you want to believe." His tongue lolled out, as if the effort of restraining himself from attacking me had utterly exhausted him. "But you must consider your other choice. If

I cannot have a witch, I will have the nearest thing to serve me; demonesses of the air. Perhaps you will not meet your doom tonight. But if you do not join me, you will pay a terrible price."

I thought of Obizuth's warnings and shuddered. "Go. You are well warded, I sense. There is no point trying to fight each other here. This is not our final battle. Let's fight that battle in the flesh."

I had summoned the ancient creature by accident, and now I turned away. I was half-convinced I had made a mistake somehow. For something in his words troubled me, revealed a flaw in my magic.

But as in a dream, I could not solve the puzzle both Asmodel and Obizuth had put to me. I only knew that now the ancient demon knew my whereabouts and his minions would hunt me no matter how fast I ran away.

Obizuth's warnings, and Asmodel's futile temptations, weighed upon my thoughts, sparked new worries for my mouse, and I began to sink down, with no ministering soul to raise me up again. In any case, Raziel needed me to return to the mortal plane. I had no idea how long I had been dead, or what battles Raziel fought in my absence . . . and I had no more time to lose.

Instead of returning blindly to my body I sent my witch's sight ahead . . . and almost tumbled altogether out of the second Heaven.

Raziel stood athwart my bloody body, fighting off the mob

of trolls doing their best to steal my corpse away. He had shot another two of them, but Raziel was still terribly outnumbered. I searched the perimeter for my murderer and found her outside the room. . . .

It was another demoness, Onoskelis, the youngest and weakest of the trio that had first killed me outside Linz. Obizuth was right—she had returned to the command of the Reich, and sought to rise in her masters' good graces by murdering me.

The world turned red with my rage. I swooped down upon her and instead of returning to my mortal form I struck her with pure magic, pure vengeance.

"Onoskelis! I bind you thus!" I began. The great courtesan of Amsterdam, Lucretia de Merode, had first taught me my spellcraft, and I wove her Bane of Concubines into a baleful spell that I hurled at Onoskelis's blond hair like a bomb.

The demoness staggered back, hair aflame. She had manifested in her physical form and was vulnerable to death, as I had been.

Her blond earthly guise was innocence itself, rat poison baked in a tea cake. I recited the malefaction and choked her hard, and she scrambbled away, clutching at her throat.

Her eyes widened as my spirit wavered into visibility, as translucent and insubstantial as a ghost but capable of harming living, animate creatures like a demoness incarnate.

The first time we had met, Onoskelis and her sisters Obizuth and Enepsigos had an easy time of murdering me. But I had died half a dozen times since then. I no longer hesitated to inflict the ultimate punishment on my enemies with my witchcraft.

She tried to speak, but no air could pass through her windpipe. Onoskelis's eyes bulged as she sank to her knees, and she entreated me with a stare that I am sure had disarmed the many human males she had entrapped and destroyed over the centuries.

It didn't work on me. I wove my spell tighter and tighter until the ancient demon Onoskelis was dead. Or more precisely, until I had forced her from this plane onto the astral, for a demon cannot, strictly speaking, die. I sent her spirit into a noncorporeal, lower level of being. She could stab me in the heart no more. When I was done, all that was left of Onoskelis was a smoking little pile of clotted goo, bound together with scorched tufts of blond hair.

I had no time to bask in my triumph. I had exacted a quick revenge, but Raziel was still in danger of his life.

With no time to waste, I shot back to my body, and saw that Raziel was taking care of the trolls one by one. But where was Imre?

I stayed near my body, unsure whether I was better off dead or alive in this battle. Not for the first time, I determined to return, despite the pain such magic demanded.

But as I hovered over my body, crumpled by my honeymoon bed, I thought of Asmodel and hesitated. If I could fight just as well dead as alive, why did I bother coming back at all?

I ran from that whisper of doubt back into my body. With a hiss, I whispered my family spell and returned to life with a needle-hot pain I knew well by now, as if the thread of my life was thrust back through the needle.

The pain between my shoulder blades punched into me

once again, now that I was back in my body to feel it. I reached behind me and yanked out the blade Onoskelis had used to murder me, a Teutonic-spelled knife strengthened with Nazi sorcery.

The trolls staggered back with a cry when they saw me stir. "You're surprised?" I spat low, furious with pain. "Curse you."

The trolls stumbled back out over the threshold, sneezing furiously—my spells are worse than pepper sometimes.

Raziel lunged after them, then paused in the doorway when he saw the trolls had truly fled.

He whirled and returned to my side in an instant, kneeling by my body. "You're bleeding back to death," he said, his voice low and steady as a heartbeat. "Heal, or you'll die again."

The world was turning gray and my lacerated heart twisted in my chest, trying desperately to beat. I whispered the healing spell I used most often, and the wound began to knit itself back together.

Slowly the pain receded. I stared at the ceiling, concentrated on the effort of taking breath, and again I chose to live and fight on the human plane.

I blacked out, then awoke nestled in Raziel's arms. When he saw that I had managed to stay in this world he scooped me up and settled me gently on the bed.

"I put the dead trolls in the hall," he said.

I nodded and looked at the door, still ajar, where weak morning sunlight was streaming in.

"Imre?" I asked, my voice a tiny puff of breath. "We have to find him. It might be too late . . . the sun."

I only barely managed to get up—the Teutonic knife had harmed soul as well as body. We could not find a trace of him, no blood, nothing. Almost fainting, I sent my witch's sight in search of Bathory's factotum.

I saw with my second sight Imre's crumpled body, dragged by wolves. My sight caught a flash of yellow eyes, of gray slashing teeth, and I gasped in surprise. "By my creed," I sputtered, "it was the werewolves that took him. Didn't kill him, either, that I can tell. They're the ones who have taken Imre away. They attacked him while the trolls attacked us. But why? The vampires and the weres declared a truce. Officially, they are both allied with the Fascists."

"Both the wolves and the trolls answer to Berlin," Raziel observed.

My mind scrambled to find an explanation that made any sense. "Maybe we have tilted the balance." I spoke my thoughts aloud, trying to solve the disastrous mystery like a puzzle. "We are the variable here. The Arrow Cross wolves must be acting in concert with Bathory's enemies." I thought of the former Vampirrat chief, and winced. "Erszebet Fekete—she will not give up her power easily, and perhaps the Reich itself will restore her to power here."

Raziel shook his head. "But this is Bathory's stronghold. They have violated his lair. How is this not war?"

A wave of dizziness suddenly overtook me, and I tottered on my feet. This was my doing. "My darling, it is Asmodel. He has found us, his minions must have been watching Bathory's haunts for any sight of us. And I obliged him. How stupid of me. I am sorry."

Raziel steadied me and guided me back to the bed. "It was only a matter of time until he found us, you know," he said.

"But he came to me just now, in the second Heaven. And he . . . I think he was warning me, Raziel, that I was making a big mistake."

"Asmodel, with his words of honey," Raziel murmured with a sigh. "He may speak true, my love, but his words are twisted by his lust for power, and their meaning is a mirror image of the truth at best. Ignore his words, for they are meant to wound."

I resolved to follow Raziel's advice, and let the ancient demon go so that we could look after Imre. "He told me that I was throwing my magic away."

Raziel laughed at that. "He covets your magic like treasure. If it's not his, then it's wasted. Never mind Asmodel."

He spoke his name so freely, knowing that we could not hide from the demon's spies and his evil machinations. There was no point in worrying about what Asmodel did or didn't know. We had more immediate worries to consider.

I racked my brain for a plausible explanation for why the wolves had let Imre live, even as my battered, bone-tired body screamed in pain.

"They want us to follow Imre," I finally said. "The wolves didn't even try to cover their tracks, they knew I'd be able to track him, or that Bathory himself would be able to smell them once he discovered their crime."

"Can the wolves be so subtle? The ones in Poland only lusted to kill."

"Most are mad dogs, it is true, the turned ones. The wolves of the blood can be wily, the born wolves like Krueger. Aside from Asmodel's battle with us, the wolves have their own local position to secure."

We exchanged a stare and a mutual shudder, remembering the late, unlamented Gestapo chief of Kraków. Krueger, the alpha dog of the greatest free wolf pack in Europe, had been bloodthirsty, but wily, crafty, and brave, too.

Imre now was the prisoner of that terrible wolf's kin. We had to rescue him without starting a war between the wolves and the bats—Imre had always been true, and had gotten into trouble on my account before. I had to find him before it was too late.

"I'm rested enough," I said with a low gasp. "Let's go. It's better to hunt the dogs by day. By night their power only grows, as the moon rises."

I dressed slowly, my muscles quivering with the effort. Haunted worse by the specter of the demoness's disgust with me, and Asmodel's taunts, sowing doubts no matter how I resisted his words. I could not erase the image of Imre, dragged by wolves along the ground like prey, from my mind, and I considered the possibility that Raziel and I could be the spark igniting a war between the vampires and the werewolves of Budapest.

We had to get Imre out alive. And, much as I hated to concede anything to my sister enemy Obizuth, we had to leave Budapest, fast as we could. Ever since we had returned, I had only meant to stay long enough to get Gisele safely away. And now I worried that I had only sent my little sister into even greater danger, given the demoness's strange warning. A third sister, Enepsigos, still lived, and I worried that she could get to Gisele despite all of Churchill's protections. In order to save Gisele as well as fight my enemies, I had to get that gem, quick. And that meant saving Imre if possible, then getting out of town. Somehow.

I could not speak to Bathory now—with daylight, he slept in his native soil as was the way of his kind, and I didn't dare disturb him. As we emerged from Bathory's lair, I blinked hard in the dappled autumn sunlight. It had been so long since I had walked in the daylight that I felt half vampire myself.

Instead of rousting Bathory, I had telephoned the head of the Budapest Hashomer to find out where his archenemies the Arrow Cross operated. He could tell me where the Arrow Cross headquarters was located, but not where the local wolves made their dens.

"The wolves hide in the Buda hills," I said to Raziel after I hung up. We hiked up Bathory's street, away from the Danube behind and below us. "The Arrow Cross is settled here, and the wolves must hide in the Buda caves when they go to ground."

I didn't know the werewolves' names, and could not summon their souls without their true names at hand, or use spellcraft against them in any particularly effective way. But then I was struck by an inspiration.

"Eva," I said, and I stopped trudging along the cobblestoned street. Raziel raised an eyebrow.

If my dearest friend Eva's cover as Szalasi's girlfriend still held, she wouldn't be far away from Martin and his pack brothers. And I knew Eva, true name and soul, as well as I knew my own.

I sent my witch's sense after her name, and I looked for her soul, though I didn't intend to summon her. And before a minute had passed, I had found her, soul still bright and sharp like a little knife.

Her heart beat in the vicinity of the Arrow Cross headquarters . . . a confirmation of my hunch. She was either with the human Arrow Cross or with her werewolf paramour, Szalasi.

We were close. Very, very close.

"We need to surprise them," I said to Raziel after I explained what I now knew. "They'll smell us out if we hesitate. And daylight is to our advantage."

"But do werewolves turn men by day, like Krueger? When the world was young, werewolves did not hunt men, or turn into men, either."

"Turned werewolves are slaves to the moon," I replied. "At the full moon, they turn, whether they want to or not, and when they turn they are wolves, incapable of communication or even human thought, it seems. But the wolves of the blood . . ." I shuddered, thinking of the great Eastern Werewolf Pack. "They can change at will, any time, the stronger ones. They can speak and reason like men, no matter their form. They live as a pack, as both men and beasts."

We were almost there. I had to slow down; my poor body was not up for even a stroll, much less a battle of magics.

Raziel's eyes narrowed. "Are you all right?"

I nodded impatiently, my lacerated heart pounding, too out of breath to speak.

Raziel reached for my hand and I leaned on him as we went along. "What about the females? Could Eva have been . . . turned? Like Martin?"

"Ugh. No, thank goodness. She is still herself." I thought of the leggy blonde at the Istanbul, who resembled Eva in looks, and swallowed back a wave of nausea.

The headquarters waited around the corner from where we stood, in front of a medieval bakery built half into the ground. I had once bought hot cross buns there, what seemed like a million years before.

"Did you bring your gun?" I asked.

"Of course." Raziel hardly got dressed now without bringing his revolver, and a silver-bladed knife, too.

"Don't show it. We'll go in, demand Imre, and see what we can get without magic or bullets. If it gets too dangerous, we'll have to fight our way out, but even now I don't expect things have come to that. Not yet."

Raziel nodded, and once again I realized how much I loved him for accepting my bossiness as a necessary evil. We turned the corner, and now we stood in front of the elaborately carved and beveled wooden front door. It had the kind of careless, almost excessive beauty you could find all over Budapest.

I took a deep breath and rang the doorbell. The plate over the buzzer read: THE BAVARIAN UNDERTAKERS' ORGANIZATION. A clumsy, but apparently effective, cover.

The door swung open, and I took in a sharp breath. One of the wood trolls filled up the doorway, a survivor of last night's attack.

He stiffened at the sight of me, and growled under his breath.

His crenellated nose wrinkled in disgust. "You cannot pass," he said in German.

"I've come to speak to your masters about your visit last night," I replied, affably enough.

A female voice interrupted the rising growls emanating from the hob as well as his compatriots in the shadows. "Let them in, you imbecile."

He backed away, revealing the threshold and allowing us to enter. I exchanged a long, silent look with Raziel, took a deep breath, and pushed by the hob in order to enter the hallway.

The headquarters was nothing so dramatic as the title implied. A single room, with a surprising number of windows, scuffed wooden floors, and a low, shiny tin ceiling. A single battered wooden desk stood at the back of the room, with folding chairs set up in rows facing the desk. The back wall was festooned with maps, pushpins, a portrait of the unsmiling Führer, and yellowing newspaper clippings in both German and Hungarian.

A worn-out-looking man with a receding chin and blood-shot eyes sat behind the desk, papers like dead leaves scattered over the cheap-looking cardboard desk blotter. And a little blond woman perched on the corner of the desk, dimpled arms crossed, pretty legs dangling.

"What do you want?" she said.

"Bathory sent me," I replied.

The troll slammed the office door behind us, and Raziel and I drew closer to the desk, and to the unlikely couple behind it.

"Bathory? Who's that?" snapped the little blonde.

"Shh, Kati," the man behind the desk murmured. "Don't

trouble your little head about this business. Go, make me some coffee. There's my flower."

The blonde leaned over and kissed the man's receding hairline. She straightened and hopped off the desk, flashed the man a dazzling smile.

And it was only then that I realized this gangster's floozy, this nasty Aryan creature, was in fact my beloved friend Eva, as dear to me as a sister.

So thoroughly did she own her role as the lover of Szalasi that I hardly even recognized my dearest friend in the flesh. That was how powerful my nonmagical friend's acting abilities ran, how deep her cover. She had forgotten herself altogether.

She tottered away in her stiletto heels and I gulped for air. "You are Martin Szalasi of the Arrow Cross, yes?"

He looked surprised that I knew him by name. "Why, yes."

"And of the Arrow Cross werewolf pack as well, yes?"

It was Martin's turn to gulp at that—very few mortal Budapest denizens knew the werewolves had such human loyalties.

"I come in Lord Bathory's name, to seek his servant Imre." I used the vampire honorific for the Chief Vampire of Budapest, to imply I was also a servant of Bathory. The less I said about my own identity, the better.

Martin's lips pursed into a little asshole. "We have some questions for Master Bathory. And we assume this servant will give us the answers. He has been less than forthcoming so far, but we have our methods."

I took a deep breath. Time to get to the point of our meeting. "What questions do you ask of Lord Bathory? Perhaps I can be of service to you, sir."

"We have reason to doubt Bathory's loyalty to the glorious Reich." And for the first time, Szalasi smiled.

"What are your doubts, sir?"

Szalasi's smile widened. "Are *you* an enemy of the Reich?"

He bared his teeth, forgetting for the moment that he was a man, not a wolf. But at that moment, "Kati" returned with a tray of coffee in a small metal carafe, and coffee cups.

She put the tray on the desk, on top of the sliding pile of papers, and took a folded white linen napkin off the tray. She patted Martin's sweaty forehead most lovingly, poured his coffee while leaning forward, her chest almost in his face. By the time she had straightened up again, Martin had forgotten everything but the scent and shape of her curvaceous little body.

She wiggled her shoulders and a vacant smile played over Martin's lips. "Give them the vampire back, sweetie," she murmured. "They already gave you the proper respect. You got Bathory in your pocket like you wanted. Now, get them to back you up, give you power in Budapest in exchange. Or . . ." She growled low in her throat and smiled at him.

He growled back, sounding much more like an actual wolf than Eva. Without looking away from Eva's chest, Martin snapped his fingers at the troll. "The servant's more trouble than he's worth, anyway."

The troll glared at me, as if I were the one insulting him instead of Szalasi. "You heard what I said!" Szalasi shrieked.

The troll growled and snorted, but evidently he had his orders not to interfere too deeply in Budapest affairs. Grumbling under his breath, the Bavarian hob shuffled out of the room, clearly disgusted with the Hungarian mob of us.

"I trust you haven't damaged him, sir," I said, my voice smooth, neutral.

"Well, the idiot put up a terrible fight. We had to knock a bit of the stuffing out of him. But I am sure your master will understand."

Before I could reply, Imre himself appeared in the doorway, his face and hands hideously burned by the sun.

But I could also see they had beaten him, badly. Two black eyes, and his oft-broken nose was broken yet again. A vampire's body heals fast; they must have worked him over more than once.

"*Now* you're quiet, tough guy," "Kati" taunted him, but Imre refused to be drawn out.

Her cruel words crawled on my skin like lice—how could Eva sound so very convincing? It was masterful, it was necessary, but it was an awful thing to see.

"We'll give him back," Martin snarled, his nose running now. "And Bathory will publicly acknowledge his debt to us, yes? The last Chief Vampire had no problems with our secret pact between the magicals of Budapest. We want to make sure that Bathory, also, respects the wolves. And we don't want filthy, foreign influences like you in the way."

"Certainly you can tell I am Hungarian," I said, using my most formal, correct speech.

"You are a Jew!" Martin spat. "You stain the glorious motherland with your existence."

I shrugged, refusing to confirm or deny what Martin saw as an accusation. "I am Hungarian," I repeated, with a bit more steel in my voice than before. "And I wanted my master to bless my fiancé before we leave Hungary forever."

Eva's eyebrows shot up at that news; for a fleeting moment I could see behind her Fascist façade to the true Eva, hidden way inside, almost lost, even to herself.

"You are leaving Hungary?" Martin's nose crinkled, as if he could smell out the truth if he only tried hard enough. "Will Bathory honor your parley with us?"

"Yes." I could not bear to say "forever" again; it seemed too much like a prophecy and not a self-serving bit of embellishment to my story.

"So you came back just to get the old vamp's blessing?" Eva drawled. "Are you two going to get married?" She glared at Martin and he glanced away and shrugged his shoulders. It occurred to me that "Kati" wanted very much to be married to Szalasi, herself.

My eyes narrowed. My own marriage had to stay a secret from these murderous thugs. Who knew what they would do to Raziel if they understood how closely he was bound to me? "We're going abroad. Far away, not within the Reich at all."

"Well, if there's going to be a wedding, where is the party?" She batted her eyelashes, and her jaw set mulishly. "I mean, who gets married without a big old party? And why wasn't the pack invited? It's an insult!"

I didn't have to pretend at my panic. "Oh dear, Bathory hadn't invited you? No wonder you feel slighted."

I glanced at Raziel, who shrugged—whatever I had to do, he was behind me.

I thought fast. "The party is imminent, in fact." I thought fast. "At . . . the Café Istanbul."

Everyone in the room but me and Raziel gasped out loud. I had just offered up the central vampire social spot for a party including the werewolves, the eternal enemies of the fanged ones no matter what temporary alliances they made.

"The Reich has brought us together, don't you see?" My voice was bone-dry with the Budapest sarcasm. "Now, you give us Imre, and there will be peace between Bathory and the wolves. And you, Martin, will get all of the credit."

Imre snuffled through his broken nose—the old duffer hadn't missed a thing.

"Ooh, Bathory will be furious," Imre said. We all looked at him and he coughed. "He will be furious that the invitations somehow went astray, I mean."

"Well, consider this personal visit an effort to make amends, Mr. Szalasi. In every way. Would you please come?"

Martin cast a glance at Eva, who smiled and fluffed her hair, looking suddenly like a little toy poodle presented with a new chew toy. "Let's celebrate, Martin," she said. "Maybe it'll give you some ideas."

"Maybe," Martin said, his voice neutral.

The German troll snarled at me—I don't think my story fooled him for a single second.

"Sorry, trolls from Bavaria are not invited," I said.

When dusk fell and the Chief Vampire arose from his coffin, Bathory was not amused by my ruse. "The Istanbul is not your private playground, Miss Lazarus," he said.

I blushed to the roots of my hair—you could fry an egg on my forehead, it flushed so hot. "Don't be mad at me, dear count. And you forget, I'm a married lady now."

His eyes narrowed and he looked me over shrewdly. "Oh, so that's the way it's going to be. You want your old vampire uncle, your dear count, to throw you a wedding party to get your ass out of hot water, but you won't even tell me your married name? Why, what will I engrave upon the invitations?"

He sat up in his coffin and brushed the dirt from his sleeves. Imre drew forward to ease him from his place of repose, and Bathory tut-tutted when he saw his factotum's mangled face.

"Ah, my dear old bruiser, you were no beauty before, but now the dogs have dug new scars into your face, yes?"

Imre shrugged. His breathing was loud, clogged by his broken nose. "Magda saved me, boss. She cut a deal with the wolves, made you look good. And that's just the simple truth."

Bathory studied Raziel and me from under his furrowed eyebrows.

"Thank you for saving Imre," he said, his voice affable, his face even paler than usual.

"Imre is a special favorite of mine," I murmured, politely glancing away from the coffin and the dirt sprinkled inside. "He watched out for me when you were gone to Berlin and we thought you were lost. The least I could do was defend him now, when his very existence was at stake."

I heard the creak of the oak coffin as Bathory eased out of his bed. When I returned my gaze to him, Bathory was staring at me, a curious expression on his face.

"You hardly sound human," Bathory said. And though I knew he meant it as a compliment, I got a little sick at the thought of it, for I knew he was right.

All this dying and returning, the wielding of spells and

crushing of enemies, was leaching the humanity out of me. My mother had warned me; as usual, I hadn't listened.

I mostly didn't mind: it was the price I gladly paid for power. It was still disconcerting to realize it was so obvious to those who loved me. For despite his cold, still vampire's heart and his unending thirst for human blood, Bathory loved me in his vampiric way.

"It is good you have sold your soul away," Bathory continued, to make sure he drove home the obvious. "The places you will have to go now would fell a more congenial human spirit."

I sighed and thought as always of my sister Gisele and suspected Bathory thought of her, too. And why not? She was his lamb, and he had tasted her blood in the not too distant past. He had imbibed enough of her to be bonded with her, though he had refrained from turning her vampire, for which I was forever grateful.

"Boss, she got me out alive, and tricked the wolves, too," Imre said, pressing into the silence, misunderstanding it.

Bless him. Honest as the day was long, that Imre. Never enough of a courtier to lie in order to feather his own nest. He was grateful enough to me that he gave me all of the credit. But Imre never even considered his own position in the matter, how it looked to Bathory that the werewolves had been able to overpower him in the first place.

"Imre saved Raziel and me last night," I hurried to add. "He fought so hard we had time to save ourselves. And it was my poor Imre who paid the price."

He smiled at me for that—one of his fangs had been snapped off, and the effect of his smile was rather more fearsome than before. But Imre was beautiful to me.

Bathory muttered under his breath, clearly exasperated by his subordinates conspiring to protect each other from his wrath. "I loathe parties," he said.

I knew now that I had won. "So just have a little reception," I replied. "Don't announce the purpose. Outsiders will think it is a peace offering . . . nobody will have to be told it is a wedding party at all. Hell, have another floor show for all I care, as long as the werewolves are allowed to come."

Bathory brushed the last vestiges of the grave off his suit jacket, and he smiled, not with the terrifying display of his ancient fangs but with a tiny mysterious grin, the smile of the *Mona Lisa* by night, in a coffin.

"Ah, well, that is a different matter. And it solves another problem for me. We will have a fitting celebration for you. But don't get angry at me, not after all that I have done for you."

Something in the way he spoke made me uneasy, but I couldn't say a word—obviously he had just made a big show of granting my crazy request. All that I could do then was thank him.

"Have you heard from Gisele?" he asked, interrupting my own train of thought. "Any witchly sendings from London?"

"No," I replied with a sigh. "I don't want to draw attention to the fact she's tucked away in England. It's not an especially magical populous country these days, not compared to here in the East. Better to hide her away in plain sight and let Churchill look after her. Albion's wards should hold."

Even as I dutifully recited my intentions, I could hardly bear our separation, and only the thought of her safe away from me kept me from bolting to London to say good-bye before I turned east to hunt the Gem of Raziel.

She and I had our own witchly bonds, those of Lazarii, and though we were untrained in the finer points of astral travel and in sendings, I was determined to figure out these arts for myself. For by then I had learned that boldness is its own magic and nobody will give you permission to throw a spell except yourself.

Raziel broke our gloomy silence. "Sir, you know what we must do next. Seek the Heaven Sapphire, my gem of knowledge. It was lost to time, but Magda and I have our suspicions as to its hiding place. The soiree will provide cover for our escape, you see—all of our enemies will be at the Istanbul, enjoying your beneficence, and we shall slip away in the night."

Bathory smiled, a terrifying sight to the unprepared mortal. His long, ivory-colored teeth gleamed in the garish artificial light of his sleeping chambers.

"If anyone can retrieve the Heaven Sapphire, it is the intrepid pair, Magdalena and Raziel." And Bathory bowed his head to Raziel, a singular honor when so bestowed by the Chief Vampire of Budapest.

I fumbled for the proper words of thanks, suddenly all out of fierceness and grandiosity. "My dear count," I said, "I believe the gem is in the Caucasus. Our friends, the carpet merchants from Azerbaijan, know more than they told us when Ziyad came here to ask for your help. It is time I paid them a visit in their lands."

Bathory tucked away his ancient fangs, wandered aimlessly to the open window, curtains now wafting in the evening breeze. "But Ziyad fears to return to his native land," Bathory said. "He conducts his business from Istanbul. You must visit him immediately and gain passage into the Socialist Republic."

He raised a sardonic eyebrow and plucked at the sheer white curtains with his long, bony fingers. "It will be just like home for you, my dear girl. The Café Istanbul is only the city of Istanbul in miniature after all." And he chuckled to himself at his little joke as he nibbled at his lips with the very tips of his terrifying teeth.

Considering how dangerous the Café Istanbul could prove to nonmagical mortals, this observation was less than reassuring. But as I peeked at Raziel and he warmed me with one of his fierce, open smiles, I determined to pretend that the Istanbul would be delightful to visit, as safe as my front parlor on Dohány Street.

But we had to get through the party at the Café Istanbul first. Public displays like the one I had forced Bathory to make were dangerous, for all kinds of reasons. But Bathory had evidently decided the risk was worth it, for reasons he did not deign to share with me.

Bathory decided to hold his soiree the following night. That gave me another day to heal from my own murder wounds. Raziel dined with Bathory and Imre, while I retired to bed, dozing. Now that Bathory had placated the wolves and Onoskelis was dead, I was as safe as I was going to be in Budapest. I warded the place well, and finally at leisure, I considered the mystery of Obizuth's warning, and her little sister's appearance as my murderer.

The night of rest and the long, languid morning after gave me plenty of time to consider our predicament. In the light of the new day I lay with my head resting on Raziel's chest, listening to the steady beat of his heart.

"We're lucky to be alive, my darling. But I'm afraid of what Asmodel will do now. He can't touch me directly, not all the way from Berlin. But his minions will cause as much harm as they can."

"I'm not so sure about that. The Reich is allied with Hungary, but does not control it. There is only so much they can do outside their master's domain. As for us, our love is here. We'll make do with the rest," he replied.

I sighed, still too tired to protest. Raziel slid out from under my embrace, and I watched him rise from our bed and pace the room, as tense and coiled as a panther in a cage.

"This is what we are going to do," Raziel said, pacing and pacing. "You are going to rest some more—nothing magical will dare attack us by daylight. And then we'll organize an escape from Budapest."

I held my breath, pretended to be dead again as I watched those corded muscles, those long legs eating up the room as Raziel stalked.

No. I couldn't stay dead, not even as part of Asmodel's grand plan, because Raziel, my husband, was still alive. And so far he had seen precious little of the world's ordinary beauty. I wasn't going to abandon him to mortal life, oh no.

I planned to live.

"Bathory," I said, my voice weak. "I've had time to think about him. It's precarious at the top, isn't it? What can he do to hold his position? He cannot fight Berlin—not with the vampires in formal alliance with the Reich. This little party will strengthen his alliances. I hope. But I'm afraid it's only a matter of time before he is deposed, before Horthy himself is replaced by a Nazi puppet."

Raziel stopped pacing. I couldn't stop staring at him, all of him, and rational thought flew out the window. Good riddance.

"Bathory will deal with the creatures who violated his wards," Raziel said. "Punishment is swift and severe among his kind. He wants you to find the gem. He will cover you for the sake of that mission. He had better."

I watched Raziel pace some more. Evidently watching me die yet again had gotten under his skin . . . his angelic perspective on death, his serenity, had gone into retreat.

Gone was the otherworldly, impartial angel who had only encouraged me from Heaven. Instead a mortal man paced next to my bed, an enraged, deadly, scarred man.

My man. My husband.

"All right, Raziel," I said meekly, my voice still wavering. "You can stop pacing like a caged tiger and come stay by me here."

He smiled at that, a ferocious, carnivorous smile. "I thought you needed rest."

"I can rest when I'm dead and decide to stay that way."

He laughed at that, and lowered himself onto the tangle of sheets and blankets, next to me in the bed.

And the world left us alone for a few precious hours.

✳ 5 ✳

Gently Raziel coaxed me awake at dusk.

"Everything has been arranged," Raziel said. He tangled his fingers in my hair, kissed me fiercely on the lips, and let me go.

"How did Bathory announce the party?" I asked.

"Imre told me. He declared an armistice among the magicals, and all manner of creature is guaranteed safety inside the Istanbul this night."

"Even mortals?" I thought of Eva as I asked.

"Mortals must travel under the protection of a present magical. That covers us, and it covers Eva, too, if she comes along with Martin Szalasi."

"How could she not come? We concocted this whole party as a way of mollifying her and her nasty boyfriend."

Raziel laughed at that. "Bathory issued no written invitations at all, only sent messengers throughout the city. He invited all the magical factions, the demons, the vampires, and the wolves. And he promised special entertainments."

I gulped at that, thinking of the previous Wednesday night. "Such as?"

"I don't know."

I saw Bathory before he left his mansion on Rose Hill ahead of us—he looked every inch the dapper vampire around town, with white tie and tails.

"You're not doing another floor show again, are you?" I asked.

"Do not fret, little chicken. No mortals will be maimed to commemorate your union. This will be a celebration of the Grand Alliance of magicals in Budapest. It will send a message, all the way to Berlin. And you will see, the other guests will be delighted by my entertainments."

His eyes glittered a little too avidly during his speech for me to lay my worries completely to rest. After putting Bathory into this spot, I had to trust he would make the most of it. But I could not shake the fear he planned to solve his problems in a savage, vampiric way.

Since I only had the clothes on my back after our battles in Poland, Bathory opened his closets to me before he left. I discovered finery inside. Delicate lace frocks from a more innocent age, floor-length gowns sewn with genius and patience by long-dead human seamstresses. Who first wore these nowforlorn creations? I wondered as I sifted through the satins and chiffons.

Raziel suited up much more easily. Bathory had some tuxedos in his size, and men's fashion goes more slowly out of style. My husband selected old-fashioned cutaway tails, with spats, suspenders, and all.

"It looks like you are marrying the Queen of Romania tonight," I said with a wink.

"No, I am already a married man," Raziel said in a low voice, pulling me close.

"Where did all these clothes come from, do you think?"

His body tensed, pressed up against mine. "Bathory has lived for a very long time, Magduska. And I don't suspect he has ever married within his own kind."

I sighed and with a heavier heart returned to my tour of Bathory's closets. Of course. These were the costumes of his victims, his willing pets. Even his protégées and assistants, my predecessors. All dead now, their finery left behind to molder in the dark.

"What shall I wear, darling? Tell me."

He rummaged around for a while, and emerged with a lilac frock, flimsy and sheer, with an empire waist.

"Once upon a time, I think that was a princess's peignoir, my dear."

Raziel smiled. "I think you could wear it abroad, in these degraded days."

I flashed on a mental photograph of the blonde writhing at the Istanbul, all but naked on the marble floor, and I blinked hard. "I'm sure you're right."

And I stripped down to my own underwear, looking at Raziel all the while. Hearing my pulse pounding in my ears like the tides.

"Get dressed," Raziel whispered. "Quickly. Or we'll end up very, very late."

I was tempted to delay, but forced myself to focus on my dress instead. It smelled of dried flowers and a very faint, faraway scent of French perfume. A bit melancholy, but lovely, too.

"What do you think of it?" I asked once the dress was settled over my hips.

His kiss was all the answer I needed.

The Istanbul was full to bursting when we finally arrived, tucked in the back of Bathory's limousine, driven by the faithful Janos as always. A crowd had gathered outside the café and the people erupted into wild applause when we emerged.

Raziel looked all around, plainly confused by the ruckus. "It's all for Bathory, darling," I said, a little breathless despite the fact. "They are showing the Chief Vampire of Budapest the proper respect."

I felt rich, with my bonus from Bathory tucked into my bejeweled clutch. The lilac peignoir was really too sheer, but it was perfect for this decadent affair.

And it was unprecedented, for never in my lifetime at least had such a blanket truce been declared in the center of the city. Budapest was a metropolis divided, with clearly demarcated domains for the three largest magical populations: the weres, the vampires, and the demons. You crossed those lines only at great peril—and if you were an ordinary mortal without any magic, all the domains meant danger.

But this night, Bathory staged a marvelous pageant, a showcase of magical unity. And if that Grand Alliance of peace among the magicals was all illusion, I still preferred it to the hideous reality of the war, hovering like a pestilent cloud over all of us.

Imre, still bruised and battered, nodded unsmilingly in my direction. He checked the entrances and exits, then nodded for us to enter.

"What a dazzling farewell to Budapest," I murmured in Raziel's ear as we emerged from the limousine. He smiled and tucked my left hand inside the crook of his arm. I pulled close to him, and felt the loaded Mauser strapped on his left hip.

"It's all nothingness, vanity," he said. "All that matters is getting out of here."

His muscles corded under my hand, and I realized only now how much danger the two of us faced inside. Both the vampires and the weres had chosen to align themselves with the Reich. If they only knew what Raziel and I planned to do this very night—leave town in search of a magical weapon to wield against Hitler himself—our lives would end. With violence.

I gulped and drew up to my full height. I planned to at least look magnificent as we entered the lions' den.

The scene inside the Istanbul was surreal, demons, vampires, and slavering dogs all overrunning my former workaday home in Budapest. As we crossed the threshold and made our way up the massive curving stairway, I turned halfway up and looked behind me at the scene, an enormous Bosch painting, strange as a fever dream.

But then a solitary figure on the main floor of the Istanbul shocked me back into reality.

The other guests, bedecked in all of their glittering finery, were all careful to avoid the naked creature chained to the floor.

No, this was no floor show, no illusory entertainment. The spectacle tonight was all too horrifyingly real.

My heart pounded double-time and I tightened my grip on Raziel's arm. "Do you see?" I managed to choke out. "It's Erszebet Fekete."

Fekete. The former Chief Vampire of Budapest, who had sacrificed Bathory to a seemingly gruesome fate in Berlin and who had been ousted upon Bathory's return. Bathory had punished her for her traitorous alliance with the wolves. She had been stripped of the silken robes I had last seen her wearing, and now Erszebet Fekete, distant cousin of Count Bathory and disgraced unto death, shivered as she squatted, naked, on the marble floor where the young male vampires and their blond lamb had so recently writhed in ecstasy. The chains binding Fekete were bolted securely into the floor.

She was pitifully skinny and her skin was marble pale from blood starvation. A few times she snarled at the guests who ventured too close, but the gesture was for form's sake only. Erszebet Fekete had resolved to die.

I could smell her stink from far below, of sweat and fear and waste, and I shuddered. So this was what Bathory had done. My old vampire uncle, so loyal to his minions, his manners so impeccable, his passions always so admirably controlled. My dear count was capable of, indeed reveled in, publicly torturing and humiliating his vanquished rival.

"What did you expect?" Raziel asked, reading my mind. "He is a vampire. This is the way of his kind. Cruelty is their currency, the only thing they truly understand."

I shifted my gaze to watch Bathory circulating through the crowd, a jocular poison flowing through the magical bloodstream of Budapest. And my heart sank.

I had served this creature loyally, done his bidding, saved his life, and he had saved my life in turn. He had raised me in the magical world, much as my own father had watched over me as a tiny child. I owed him my survival, and my sister's life as well.

Bathory had been careful not to offend my all-too-human sensitivities, shielded me from the unpleasant realities of vampire society, its merciless rules.

He shielded me no longer. Considering all the horrors I had seen mortal men inflict on my people, Bathory must have thought such things no longer could shock me. That instead, like him, I would find such revenge and cruelty exciting.

The little blonde from the other night, now a wild-eyed bloodlust vampire, stepped forward on the crowded marble-tiled floor and dashed a glass of wine in Erszebet Fekete's face. The chained vampire's fangs flashed dangerously, but the thick irons kept her pinioned, unable to retaliate.

The little blonde laughed, one of her twin vampire masters at her elbow. I blinked hard and forced myself to keep ascending the stairs to the mezzanine, until I reached Bathory's customary table in the corner.

It was out of the way and quiet, the only remnant of the Istanbul that I recognized. I sank into my usual seat, Raziel taking Bathory's. "Nobody will see us tucked away here," I said, my throat tight.

"Not hardly," Raziel replied. He sighed and leaned his elbows on the table, such poor manners, so beloved for his lack of artifice. "You are Bathory's girl in this place, you know. You are part of tonight's sensation. And I am your ornament."

Our discreet escape was going to be more difficult than I had hoped.

A flash of gold by the entrance caught my eye, and my breath was again caught in my throat. Ah, Eva. The best friend a girl could ever have, attending the same gala affair, but further away from me than when I was in Poland.

She was the Arrow Cross girl now, and that was how it had to be. Eva walked in on Martin Szalasi's arm, sparkling in the dusky swirl of magicals, dazzling, apparently unafraid though she was almost the only mortal in the room.

She wore a tiny black dress that showed off her curves, bloodred nail polish, and blue-red lipstick to match. She looked up at Bathory's table as if from habit, and when she saw us perched up there she flashed us a dazzling smile and winked. It was as much of her true self as she could dare to show me.

"Oh Lord, she's a dead duck," I murmured to Raziel, never taking my eyes off of Eva as she sparkled and chattered away like a little nightingale in flight. "They'll figure her out in the end. . . ."

Eva leaned in and whispered in Martin's ear, those brilliant blue eyes narrowing. She pointed up at us, and Martin nodded, his lips pulled back in a canine snarl.

If I weren't bone sure of her loyalty, I would have gotten pretty nervous by this point. "What is she doing?"

When I looked at Raziel, he was pale as marble. "Maintaining her cover," he whispered, so softly I could barely hear him.

"We've got to get out of here." Imre had booked us passage on the eastbound Orient Express, scheduled to make a ten-minute stop at Keleti Station at 2:30 in the morning before departing for Romania. It was already well past midnight.

For this night *I* was Bathory's girl. Any odd behavior or sudden disappearance would be remarked upon.

A keening wail from below jolted me from my scheming. Before I could figure out the trouble, Bathory himself swooped in to quell the disturbance, so it didn't undermine the extraordinary truce that he had called.

I watched the magical creatures swirling over the floor of the Istanbul, Erszebet chained down in the middle, and suddenly I felt terribly faint. I dug my fingers into Raziel's forearm and hung on for my very life.

For the first time, sitting in that mezzanine with my beloved, I allowed myself to see, really *see,* the world that I had inhabited for the last four years. A world filled with predators, a world where the weak could not survive.

And Eva, defenseless and gorgeous, flitted among the monsters like a brilliantly colored butterfly.

"How can we get out of here? Right now?"

Raziel looked around the mezzanine. "Only way down is the stairs, into the crowd with Bathory."

"No." That negative, my oldest source of power, steadied me, and I rose to my feet. My lilac-colored confection hid the knocking of my knees. "There's a back way. Through the kitchen." I pointed to the back of the mezzanine.

The wailing below rose to a dreadful shriek—I couldn't see through that mob to its source. Were the werewolves tearing at Fekete's throat? Was Bathory exacting some kind of ritual revenge?

I did not know, did not want to know. I had to get out of Budapest. Obizuth was right—the Budapest I had known was gone forever.

And yet it had not changed a bit. The only creature in the Istanbul who had changed was me.

Raziel, the one who had changed me, pulled me along the deserted mezzanine to the service stairway at the back. "This way," he said, low and quick. I followed him.

We slipped down the plain, unvarnished staircase into the kitchen, where Gaston, the maître d', oversaw his fanged staff. "You cannot come back here!" a young busboy shouted, one who did not know me.

"We are leaving," Raziel said.

The boy flashed his fangs at us, but without much conviction. He saw the formal finery we wore and realized we were among the Very Important Guests.

Gaston rushed up to us, sweating blood at his temples. He was too frightened to meet my gaze, instead bowed and kissed his own wrist in submission. Evidently he remembered the last conversation we had together at the café's front door. The one that had ended with me threatening to pull his soul out through his nostrils.

"Please, *mam'selle,* do you wish the fresh night air?"

"Outside, yes, please, Gaston," I replied.

"Anything for the magnificent lieutenant of Lord Bathory."

His obsequiousness wearied me, as his malevolence had angered me the last time we had spoken, before Bathory had returned to rule the vampires of Budapest. But I didn't attack Gaston this time, only followed as he showed us to the service door leading to the alleyway behind the Istanbul.

"We keep the back alley clean," Gaston mumbled under his breath. "But beware of the trash outside, nevertheless."

He did not mean the scraps from the kitchen. When we exited the Istanbul into the alley, we surprised at least a half a dozen vampires, entwined with their pets, willing men and women who bared their necks in exchange for protection, food and shelter, or even for what passed for love.

We tiptoed in the shadows, among the feeding vampires. Only an occasional gasp or moan broke the silence. By the time Raziel and I had made it to Andrássy Street, I was trembling like a leaf in a storm. None of those vampires was newly turned, consumed by bloodlust, or we would have had a battle on our hands.

And how tired I was of fighting. For the first time, in love with a man, I felt quite estranged from the world of fang and amber eye. I understood now my mother's fervent desire to hide from her magic in ordinary human family life, as I had once hidden from my own magic in teenage rebelliousness.

"We'd better hurry," Raziel muttered. "Or we're going to miss that train. And I'm not sure we can survive another twenty-four hours of Budapest."

Considering Asmodel now knew our every move, Raziel was rather understating matters. We had no time to lose.

This last time, we did not leave Budapest with kisses and valedictions. The faithful Janos did not bring us to the station in Bathory's limousine. Eva did not disguise her tears this time at Keleti Station. No, now Raziel and I fled my native land under cover of night, only managing to escape because my enemies had gathered to toast Bathory and exult in Fekete's downfall.

But I didn't care. We fled Budapest this time, but we fled free. I owed allegiance, not to Bathory, not to Asmodel, nor to my mother or even my sister; only to myself.

And to my husband. If it weren't for Raziel, I would have been doomed by my hubris, the temptations of my power. We dashed aboard the train just as it began to pull out of the station, traveling east, and I reveled in our escape.

✳ 6 ✳

Before the vampire ball at the Café Istanbul, Bathory had written to Ziyad Juhuri, the carpet merchant of Baku. He told Ziyad I was coming to see him in Istanbul, on very important business.

Bathory did not say it was vampire business, but he implied it through his silence on the matter, and I was glad for his unofficial endorsement of the journey. For one, his contacts stretched across all of Vampiredom and his compatriots in Istanbul and points east would help me at his word.

For another, I needed the cover of vampire business to obscure my own. For I knew with a grim certainty that Asmodel also hunted the Heaven Sapphire, the one object of power that could release his grasp of *The Book of Raziel*. And we both suspected it was hidden in the same place: the physical location of the Garden in Eden, somewhere in the upper Caucasus.

The trip to Istanbul was long, deceptively peaceful, and much more of a honeymoon than our night in Bathory's lair. Bathory sent us via the Orient Express, and insisted most particularly on paying our passage. Not because we went abroad on his business as well as our own, but because he wanted to share in our joy by subsidizing it.

It did not occur to me until later that Bathory, denied such human connections by virtue of his existence as a vampire, must have vicariously enjoyed our union. An exotic, mysterious union, superficially similar to a vampire's thrall, but utterly foreign to him in its essence.

Vampires devour. They do not know the human trick of merging and yet becoming something more. It was an homage to human love that led to tickets on the train to Istanbul. But I did not fully understand Bathory's motives until much later.

Such luxury, that train, as we outran Asmodel's minions and moved out of the realm of the Reich, to the East. Such opulent silence, such deceptive peace as the wagon-lits gently rocked on the tracks leading to Istanbul.

We passed through Bucharest, through Sofia, through the day then night again. And Budapest faded away like a dream.

My thoughts turned from the West, from Asmodel, Hitler, and the world they sought to conquer, to the East, to the intrigues of our contact, Ziyad Juhuri, Azeri carpet merchant turned revolutionary.

Ziyad sought a superweapon to counter the slaughter of magicals under Stalin's rule. But could we help each other achieve our respective objectives?

6

Raziel and I pulled into the final stop, Istanbul, in full day-light. Istanbul was shockingly foreign, a blur of unfamiliar sights and sounds. The Istanbul station filled with voices rising in a cacophony of Turkish, the garish colors of the ladies' clothes and the multicolored carpets everywhere, even on the floor of the station; the stench of bad tobacco; the delicate scent of rose petals and roasting sesame seeds.

Raziel and I were met by a strange, furtive little man in a black Western suit and bowler hat. His eyes were hidden behind dark glasses: a veritable twin of Bathory's intrepid, near-silent driver, Janos.

He bowed and motioned for us to follow him. I had packed only a single valise for both Raziel and myself, knowing we faced rugged travels despite our luxurious start, so we did not have to grapple with the issue of porters and baggage fees.

I held Raziel's hand tightly and he carried the valise, refusing to give it up to Janos's doppelganger. We moved silently through the enormous crowd, absorbed into the teeming humanity of a new city, at once foreign and mysterious and yet somehow utterly familiar.

I suppose it had something to do with the fact that the Ottoman Turks had conquered Hungary and ruled it for a century or more before it was recaptured by the West. Something of the languid decadence had remained behind in Budapest, along with the mineral baths done in the Turkish style.

Now Turkey itself sought to emulate the enlightened West by becoming a modern state. The women were not veiled here, and many of them looked Western, with suits and high heels, even walking alone in the throng.

But Turkey is the great pathway from East to West, and everywhere I looked as we crossed the central squares of the city I saw the influence of the East, layered over the West in a hodgepodge. Pagodalike houses, gorgeous silks, porcelain teapots on vendors' carts.

An echoing cry reverberated over our heads.

"Blue Mosque," our molelike guide muttered under his breath. "Call to prayers."

Raziel stopped walking and scanned the sky, as if he could see the air crowded with the gatherings of his brother angels. I could have followed his gaze with my witch's sight, but I wanted first to see this place as a mortal woman would, take the same impressions from it that anybody would.

The muezzins' cry was beautiful in an unearthly way, echoing through the enormous square. The Blue Mosque rose before us, wide and low and Byzantine.

For the first time, I stood in a Muslim land. And the sense of slipping free of the Christian world intoxicated me. Free of the Inquisition, the blood libel, the ghetto. Instead, a world of sultans, Christian slaves, janissaries, and Silk Road merchants.

Not better or worse. Just completely, refreshingly different.

Janos's twin cleared his throat. "Inside, please."

We stood beside an exact replica of the Mercedes limousine Janos drove in Budapest. It was a good omen, an echo of Bathory's assurance that Istanbul was part of the world that I knew, mysterious as it was. I had made my way in Paris, in

Amsterdam, and in Kraków. I would make my way here in Istanbul, as well.

The little man opened the door and Raziel slid inside first, drawing me in after him and the valise. Our driver shut the door with a solid click, arranged himself behind the wheel, and we were off.

More people, carts, and donkeys than automobiles filled the streets. I had imagined camels, but of course not a single camel was to be seen. Instead, our car snaked through back alleys, grand boulevards, and ancient squares that did not look like they were made for vehicular traffic.

We swept into view of the Golden Horn, and the sight took my breath away. Countless ships of every size, from tiny sailing boats to enormous Western yachts and merchant ships, all bobbed in the golden water of sunset. The road rose away from the shore and we began to climb into the hills outside the city's center.

The crush of humanity had thinned, and the road perversely got smoother as we left the city proper. I stole a glance at Raziel, and he smiled reassuringly at me in reply.

So we swept through Istanbul in Bathory's style, and our own style, too, in something of a triumph.

But then we arrived at Ziyad's place of business.

I had expected him to meet us at the Grand Bazaar, where Bathory told me Ziyad's Istanbul carpet emporium was located. I had imagined throngs of Turks sweeping past the open alcove, a single splintery chair, and, most of all, the same furtive, submissive, eager-to-please man I had met at the Café Istanbul so many months ago.

Our actual meeting could not have been more different.

We met in an elegant, remote building on the promontory
of the Eyüp, high above the Golden Horn that shimmered far
below. It sat next to the famous Pierre Loti café, where the
French poet once sipped tea and watched the caiques skim-
ming along the water. The building was square, of marble,
reminiscent of the expensive crypts in the cemetery where the
wealthy Ottoman dead of Istanbul rested, along the same
street.

Ziyad Juhuri met us at the doorway after our driver rang
for entry. The skin on my forearms puckered into goose bumps
at the sight of him. One glance told me how much everything
had changed since the night I had first met Ziyad the previous
summer in Budapest.

Gone was the terrified, desperate man who had darkened
the doorway of the Café Istanbul. Now, Ziyad looked mild,
wary, but self-possessed, on his own ground.

Fear still clawed at him, but it was on a leash, underground,
under his control. He was a much more dangerous man here, as
our host, welcoming us to his finest showroom.

From the outside, the building looked like a giant mauso-
leum, or perhaps a private mansion. On the inside, it looked
exactly like what it was—an import/export house for carpets
from Azerbaijan. We walked into a world of carpets.

Carpets as rolling countryside. Hanging carpets, brilliantly
colored, as the sky. And a single carpet, emblazoned with a
beautiful, tragic-looking woman's face, as the sun.

Ziyad bowed and waved us into a second room, while our
faithful driver waited outside the front door. I scanned the
room for magic, did not find something like my own . . .

And yet the place hummed with a magical presence,

something exotic and yet familiar, something similar to my own power. I glanced long at the woman's face in the carpet before we passed into another room.

The next room was almost completely bare, with a stack of smaller carpets piled next to four chairs bunched together, no table. Ziyad ushered us in and arranged us in the chairs, even as he remained standing.

"Fräulein, good to see you again," he said in halting German, polite in a reserved, shielded way. "May I offer you some apple tea, some refreshment?"

I knew enough about the Eastern way to realize that he would take an answer in the negative as an insult. "Thank you, yes," I replied, also in German. When Ziyad's back was turned, I flashed Raziel a wink so he would know I wasn't too worried, at least not yet.

I was surprised that Ziyad himself soon returned, laden with a tea service. "We have private business to discuss," he explained. "I trust my men, but I wanted to serve you myself."

I inclined my head in thanks. "You have received Bathory's letter?"

"Yes." Ziyad paused to pour us each a cup of tea in tiny porcelain cups gilded all along the edges; he placed the teapot and the tray he carried upon a low, ornate table along the wall and joined us where we sat.

The tea was scorching hot and sweet: apple tea, the color of amber, almost syrupy with sugar. I sipped it slowly, savored it as a condiment to Ziyad's words.

Ziyad's words did not go down so easily.

"So at last Bathory seeks to help us in our cause."

He did not sound unpleasant, exactly, but Ziyad no longer was the supplicant. With a start, I suddenly realized the supplicant was me.

Of course, I could not let him know that. I needed him to show me into Stalin's land, his birthplace, the Caucasus, but I would find some other way if I had to.

I cradled the hot little demitasse in my palms. "Bathory was never sure of what you wanted from him. The vampires have no interest in superweapons."

Ziyad's smile was wide, and not unpleasant. But Raziel leaned back sharply, as if a snake had reared its head up between the three of us.

"You are either naïve, fräulein, or deceptive. A creature like Bathory seeks to become the superweapon. But the thing we seek could snuff a creature like Bathory out like a candlelight."

I nodded, studied my now-empty teacup. "Why do you seek such a powerful weapon, then, sir?"

When I looked up, Ziyad was staring at me so intent I felt the space between my eyebrows grow hot. "Because nothing less than this will stop Stalin from destroying us."

"Us?"

Ziyad hesitated, then swallowed hard. "Yes. My people."

"What will you do with the superweapon once you have found it?"

Ziyad smoothed his mustache with his fingertips, trying to hide their trembling. "We will find the means to use it, pay for it in any necessary currency."

I nodded slowly, and leaned toward Raziel. "His greatest

enemy is Stalin," I said in Hungarian. "But I don't know whether to trust him."

Raziel studied him intently as he considered my words. "He is a good man, Magduska. But under a terrible strain."

I placed the little teacup gently on the ground next to my chair, turned my attention to the brilliantly colored rugs piled at my feet. "These are absolutely lovely, sir," I said.

Ziyad squatted at my feet Asian-style and began to flip the carpets over one by one, faster and faster, like an old-fashioned mutoscope card reel speeding up. The different images, of horses and camels and maidens, began to blend together. "These are the carpets of my people," he said.

I pulled myself out of trance with a tremendous lurch be-fore my conscious mind had registered that it was slipping away. I rose to my feet, knees shaking, and I looked at Ziyad a little wildly, as if he were a wizard who had tried to imprison my mind.

The dizziness passed and I blinked hard, my laugh shaky but genuine. "Your people are imbued with a powerful magic. These carpets are magical."

Ziyad piled the carpets up into a stack once again, and once more they were a collection of rugs, nothing more. "We are mortals only, not adepts of any kind. But the carpets we weave, yes, there is something uncanny about them. That is what makes them valuable."

"Let us get to the point, dear sir," I said. "You need super-natural assistance to retrieve this superweapon, or you would not have come to Bathory in the first place. But I believe the superweapon in fact belongs to my family, and wielding that power is my inheritance."

Ziyad did not look surprised, but his face turned gray and he clenched his jaw as he drew up to his full height. "When I learned what you were, after our meeting in Budapest, I began to believe it was no coincidence that our paths have crossed, fräulein. I did not know that day that you are more powerful than your employer."

I didn't know what to say to that. Raziel leaned toward my chair and steadied me under my elbow. "My darling, are you all right?" he asked. "This man is troubling you."

"It's not him exactly, my love. But he has some very dangerous secrets." I kissed Raziel on the cheek and he smiled at me.

"This is what I want," I said from inside the crook of Raziel's arm, where he still steadied me. "I want to go to Azerbaijan, to the northern Caucasus. You won't want to believe this, but your superweapon is hidden where you started, in your own home. You've had it all along and never realized what it was."

Ziyad shook his head, very slowly and deliberately, like I was a dim-witted child who had just done something unspeakably naughty. Finally he caught himself shaking his head and wiped at the corners of his mouth with the tips of his fingers.

"I cannot go home again," he said, his fingers rubbing and rubbing his mouth, smoothing away the pain of his words. "The Institute for Brain Research will arrest me."

I shook my head, not understanding. "You mean the Cheka?"

"Not the secret police, not exactly. The Institute studies the suppression and the eradication of magic. Since Azerbaijan came under Soviet control, the regime has sought to obliterate magic within its borders. The Institute dissects the magic it finds in living creatures before it destroys it."

Ziyad struggled to regain his composure. "The Institute is waiting for me to return, and they will know when I come. I cannot hide, not anywhere in Azerbaijan."

"But what you seek is there, in your starting place," I insisted. "Despite the danger, we must go back and retrieve the magic before it is too late. Especially if what you say is true and the Institute is determined to hunt it down first."

Ziyad laced his fingers together in front of his belly, as if he was willing himself to stop rubbing at his face. "I am telling you, my return means death."

I shrugged, and tried my best to keep my tone respectful. "Sir, this is a war. Death is part of the landscape; none of us can avoid it. If you want the superweapon the way you say, you will have to take me to Azerbaijan to fetch it out. We will use it together, to reach our mutual ends. Both within your land, to fight the Institute, and also in the West. If you will not take me, I will find another way. But we will go quickest together."

Ziyad bent to his carpets again, as if seeking reassurance in their silken threads. He smoothed them, squared them together, lined them up like a well-worn pack of cards.

When he stood and faced me, Ziyad had regained his composure. Unlike the first time we met, I now refused to yank his soul into attention. Ziyad had to choose this descent into his country of his own volition. I could not force him.

"I will confess the truth to you," he said. "When I came to speak to Lord Bathory the first time, I thought the superweapon was some kind of bomb. Some kind of infernal death machine that I could point at my enemies that would kill them. But I have changed my mind."

With a trembling hand, he pointed right between my eyes. "Miss Lazarus, *you* are the superweapon. It is you. I do not need to return to my homeland to find it. I only need to find the key to wielding you like a weapon."

It was as if his finger injected me with an enervating poison. I pressed my lips together hard to keep them from quivering. "You cannot wield me," I said, my voice trembling. "And I cannot do what I must, not without the thing I seek in your land. So our dilemma remains the same."

We stared at each other in a standoff, as if we pointed guns at each other instead of our warring wills. Raziel wrapped his arm around my waist and said, "Magduska, the man fears for his life. Tell him what you seek, give him a reason to understand you."

I sighed and gave up. "Ziyad. The thing we seek is a sapphire stone, an ancient gem from the plundered Holy Temple. The Heaven Sapphire has the wisdom of the Maker inscribed within it. It is the only thing that can stop the Nazis."

He looked away, staggered to a chair, and sank into it with a groan. "I was afraid. But now the truth is here. To find such a thing, we must climb the Five Fingers of God. And even if we make it that far, I cannot tell you where such a treasure is hidden."

I smiled at him sympathetically; well I understood his fear, of never finding what you have sworn to discover. "All I ask is that you bring me to your people. Once we find the gem, the power will shift to our favor."

Ziyad started laughing, a low, mournful sound that still haunts me in my nightmares. "That is all you ask, you say. And yet to do that simple thing, visit my grandma in the mountains, I must die."

✳ 7 ✳

Our driver took us to the Pera Palace Hotel in the hills of the Pera district of the city, courtesy of Bathory and his vampire brethren. Ziyad had promised to meet us for breakfast in the morning, and I guessed that if he kept his word and showed up it would mean I had gotten him to agree to the journey. I wouldn't know until morning, for the people of the East did not lightly shake hands and make deals.

It was well that we did not begin the journey that evening, for a letter from Gisele waited for me at the front desk with our keys.

The same heavy, creamy paper that Churchill had used to write to me before, the same wet-looking pen strokes, the same strange, unfamiliar row of stamps.

So Gisele still lived at Chartwell. I could tell without reading even a word on the envelope.

Her handwriting looked the same as always, loopy and childish, with copious blots and flourishes when she was trying to make a particular point.

I brooded over the envelope as Raziel conducted the formalities of checking us into the room, showing a letter of introduction from Bathory in lieu of surrendering our passports (useless as Hungarian passports would soon be in our travels), and getting the keys to the bridal suite of the hotel.

The hotel manager bowed and smiled, and only the sweat shining on his bald head revealed the hidden fear that Bathory's mere name and station engendered. He took our valise and personally ushered us to the top floor of the hotel, which boasted a breathtaking view of all Istanbul.

With a bow, the fellow took his leave, and Raziel and I exchanged a long, silent glance. We had laid our heads down in various humble places, and to date only Bathory's guest room and our luxury berth on the Orient Express had been rich enough to reflect my love for this man.

This room was the most opulent I had ever seen. More fantastical than Hitler's Berchtesgaden abode, more spacious than the demoness's suite at the Gellert Hotel in Budapest, more airy than the surreal boudoir of the famed courtesan Lucretia de Merode. We stood in a pasha's fantasy of silks, low cushions, and French doors open to the night.

The bustle of the city streets of Istanbul echoed far below us in the darkness, like whispers from another plane of existence.

"Honey, we're home," I said with a lilt in my voice.

Raziel laughed and took off his hat to rake his fingers through his hair. "For a moment, I thought I was back in the second Heaven."

I remembered my last visit to Raziel's former domain and tasted ashes. "The second Heaven is nothing like it was before, my love," I said with a sigh as I sat on the edge of the bed. "This is more like Heaven than Heaven, now."

Raziel tossed his hat onto the side table by the door and paced around the perimeter of the room. "Go ahead," he said. "Read Gisi's letter. You won't be able to settle into all of this luxury until you do."

I looked down, and realized I still had her letter clutched in my fingers. "You're right, always right, my darling. Sit with me on the veranda while I see what my little mouse has to tell us."

The night air was delicious, the electric lights on the veranda tiny and remote like starlight. I opened the envelope and unfolded the sheets of paper nestled inside.

November 13, 1939
Chartwell
England

Dearest Magduska (and Raziel, too):

After a meal fit for a king, the wondrous Winston Churchill just wished me a good night, and kindly offered me paper and pen so that I could write to you, my darling girl. I trust you are with your angel, Raziel, and that together you look after each other the way we used to do.

I paused in reading the letter aloud and swallowed the tears in the back of my throat. Wicked girl—why did Gisele always make me cry? I cleared my throat and returned my attention to her words:

England is a fairy tale. No waking at dawn, no basket of shirts and ladies' brassieres to sew, no mending no market no errands or chores. It's a bit like Heaven, I suppose . . . lazy and beautiful and just a slight bit boring.

I wake up to the sun, whenever I wish, wrapped up in fancy linen sheets. A maid (!) comes to make my bed and brush my hair because I asked her to, once, when I was homesick, and now she does it dutifully every morning. She's a kind girl, but she doesn't get the tangles out the way you do, Magduska, because she's afraid to brush too hard.

A laundress does my clothes for me, and they are fresh on the hanger when I am ready to dress. Another lady downstairs makes me coddled eggs and toast with the most delicious yellow butter you've ever had. These people make me feel downright industrious, Magduska—it takes a staff of five to do what I used to do for us alone!

After my breakfast I go for a nice rambly walk in the cool leafy green of England, though it's gone from cool to cold and very, very rainy sometimes. Then a sit by the fire, ignoring the newspapers that I can't read anyway (they are all in English) and the foreign voices droning on the wireless.

I could not bear to keep reading. "She's so lonely," I said to Raziel, but he was looking into the middle distance, his lids low, his face fixed in a thoughtful expression that I could not decipher. "She doesn't have a soul to speak to, not one Hungarian like her in the wrong country because of the war."

"I don't know," he said, still staring into the night. "She's a peaceful girl, and the walks and the toast are good for her, she's been worn out so badly. But she's lonely for you, Magduska."

I swallowed hard, miserable now, but I caressed the edges of the creamy paper and soldiered on.

Churchill often comes to dinner, dear man. His wife Clemmie sometimes joins us, too. We cannot speak directly, but one night he brought a Hungarian to dinner, a melancholy round-faced man who reminded me of Papa right before he died. Oh, he was affable, and he tried to tell jokes and was able to tell Churchill for me how grateful I am, but he is no Eva. He is not even a Bathory. Just a man who wants to go home.

So I bide my time, and my days are long and quiet. But the nights, Magduska! My goodness, the nights.

Something has happened to me since Bathory drank from me. I would never have the courage to speak of this with you face-to-face, my darling—every time I even mention Bathory's name, the storm clouds come racing into your eyes, and down come your eyebrows. But his kiss was a strange gift, although one that came with a heavy price.

Yes, I am pierced with a strange hunger at times, at night, in my bed. Yes, I can sense Bathory's movements like the moon tugging on the tides.

But I can wake up from my dreams now. Do you understand, my darling? For so long, I have dreamed without surcease, I could not stop the terrible nightmare of the war from playing out before my eyes, open or closed. It has made me half-insane with grief, of course you know it.

Maybe it's because of what we did together in Poland to fight the war, maybe it's because of you and Raziel together, but now I can wake up from my dreams. And walk in them myself.

And maybe it is all of these things I have just listed, but also the fact that Bathory drank from me but then left me like I am. My blood has mingled with his, and I am not only a witch, but also the lamb of a vampire, under his dark protection.

At night, I can walk in my dreams like I said. I can visit with Mama, who braids my hair with ribbons like she did for me when she was alive. I sometimes see Papa, way in the distance, too far to ever reach, but the sadness in him is gone, Magduska, I am sure of it.

Now that I can walk in my dreams, I believe you and I can walk together. I know your nights are very busy now, for many other reasons (and I know that I have just made you blush! There is a first time for everything, even embarrassing the fell witch Magda Lazarus!).

But one night, when Raziel sleeps, find me. Walk with me. And afterward, I will happily wake up to my English bed and my kippers, and I will listen to the English broadcasts in all their gibberish, with a smile upon my face.

Until we meet again, in dreams, this world, or the next, I kiss your hands, grateful you are safe, dear sister. Hug Raziel for me, and please let me know what news you hear of Eva.

And don't worry about me, my darling. No place this dull could ever be a danger!

Love and Kisses,
Your little mouse, Gisele

My teardrops spattered on her signature, blurring the ink.

"She will be fine," Raziel said. "No matter what happens. I swear it, Magduska."

I looked up sharply. "Be careful," I said. "You're one of us, a mortal now. You don't know what's going to happen—watch what you swear to."

"I never did know, my love. And now, you should come inside and rest. You haven't quite recovered yet from that stab in the back, and it's been a long time."

Not long enough. I thought of Onoskelis, melting into gristle and shooting into the lower realms, banished from the mortal plane by my spells.

"Some wounds are more mortal than others." I said it with a grim little smile on my face.

"I suppose. Come inside now."

I sighed and obeyed. And resolved to dream.

Oh, I dreamed all right, of trains endlessly rolling into a featureless landscape; of demonesses swooping around my head like bats; of Raziel moving above me like a steady wind over restless waters.

But I could not master the trick of finding Gisele in this tangled dreamworld of fear and desire. At one point, I turned and saw a silver cord, thin and strong as a spider's web, reaching back from my spirit to my body. I remembered that I dreamed, and—

Whoosh! I slammed back into my body with an all-but-audible thump. I opened my eyes and surveyed the darkened room until I adjusted to the lack of light and could make out the contours of the ornate pasha furniture strewn all about the suite.

Raziel slept, with the mad abandon of a man fully satisfied. One arm over his head, he rested his head on an elbow, and a tiny smile played over his lips and away.

As quietly as I could, I slipped from the bed and put on the silk robe I had left shimmering on the floor. I tiptoed to the French doors of the veranda, feeling ahead for the haphazard furniture, to protect my shins.

I swung the doors open wide and stepped out, the marble of the balcony cool against the soles of my bare feet. A low, gusty wind whipped up and over the top of the building, and clouds scudded past overhead like sailboats in a gale.

It was no longer cool on the balcony, it was cold, but I gathered my robe tighter and stayed.

"Leopold," I whispered. I didn't want to summon him too roughly; I had been soul-summoned myself, and the feeling is in no way pleasant. But I needed my imp, needed him urgently. I would not be able to heal without him.

Leo was a brainchild of mine, a stray spark of my fury that escaped and shot through the elemental mists of the second Heaven to form a sentient creature, one with its own soul and the power to choose. Unlike his brothers, who contented themselves with mischiefs and the petty entertainments of lower imps, Leo for some reason had determined to cast his lot with mine. Perhaps he had inherited some of my ungodly stubbornness and ambition. Or perhaps he simply wanted to grow.

Leo was, as he so often insisted, at my service. He racked up good deeds like points in a cosmic game of bridge, and kept careful count of the celestial gains he made. In return, I treated him like what he was, a free spirit with his own consciousness and soul. I had a lot to learn from the fellow.

This evening, he looked like a little sparkler, white sparks opening like flower petals. With a graceful leap, Leo hurtled onto the marble balcony, to kneel at my feet.

"Mama!" he said, his voice bright and full of enthusiasm.

"Hello again, Leo," I said, amazed by him. He rose to his feet and I gasped. "You look like a human child today! What happened to you?"

"I do?" He looked down at his quite human-looking torso and shrieked with laughter. He did a little jig on the polished marble, and scratched under his arms.

"I hope you didn't make any unsavory deals out there in the great beyond," I said. I wasn't really any kind of mother to Leo, but I couldn't help fussing at him just a little. He had always been such a help, with no tangible way for me to reward him.

"No, I did nothing of the sort. But after our battles in Poland, with all of the ghosts, leading the other imps . . . I have felt uncommonly queer since then."

"I don't think you are even an imp, anymore. But I don't know what you are."

He looked up at me, quite abashed, and except for the longish ears he'd always had, and eyes that were a little too large, he looked quite like an ordinary boy. A naked one, wreathed in mist, who could fly around in the night.

"What am I then?" he asked, his voice a bit panicky.

"I am sure there is a name for you, Leo, but I don't have the learning to tell you. If you can possibly find the watchmaker Yankel we knew in Kraków, well, he could tell you everything you need to know."

I sighed, thinking of my old teacher. I needed him more urgently than Leo, but I wouldn't dream of summoning Yankel's luminous soul out of the upper Heaven. I would rather die for good first.

"It doesn't matter anyway, the formal name. You're Leo, a very handsome and useful fellow."

I knew how to humor him. He drew up taller and saluted me, absurd since I stood in the moonlight in my silk robe. "I await your orders, General Magda!"

I tried not to laugh, because I could tell he really meant it. And most of the times I had called him before, I was in fact about to enter into a terrible battle.

But I needed Leo's help for a much more delicate mission now.

"Leo, I don't think you've ever met my little sister Gisele."

His eyes grew wistful. "Sister. I only have brothers, uncountable brothers causing trouble in the afterworld. I would like to have a sister, someday . . . maybe. . . ."

"Yes. Sisters can be very different. My sister's name is Gisele, and she is currently staying with the great Winston Churchill in England."

"England? What is that? Some great fortress?"

I couldn't help at least a smile now. "In a certain sense, yes. It is an island far to the west, safe for now from Hitler's mad dogs."

"Ah, that bad man, Hitler." Leo's face screwed up into a fury I easily recognized as a spark of my own.

"Hold on, my friend. No fighting this time. The favor I ask of you is very difficult."

"I was made for difficult!"

"Of course, Leo, of course. I need you to go to Gisele, without attracting notice from Churchill or anybody else, and tell her I sent you. Introduce yourself, and tell her that she needn't be afraid. I got her letter, and please to write to me again."

"That's it?" Leo tilted his head and considered me as if he'd never seen me before. "You can blow up armies and throw witchfire around like the wrath of God. Can't you make some spell, fly on a broomstick or something, and see to her yourself?"

My eyes welled up with tears again, and I had to restrain myself from cursing. "It's not so simple. My magic is to summon. Calling you, easy, right? Summoning souls of any kind. My spellcraft runs to summoning, too. It is very hard for me to send. I'm learning, Leo, but I haven't gotten the trick of it yet. And my poor Gisele is a terrible worrier."

Leo tilted his head and squinted at me. "Have you ever heard of a thing called the telephone? It is a marvelous contraption. . . ."

This time I could not help laughing, though Leopold was terribly serious, and only trying to help. "Yes, and that is an excellent suggestion. However, I am afraid our conversation cannot be private, that dangerous people will listen in on the line and discover where Gisele is hiding. Besides, these days calling across countries at war, and across the Channel besides, is not such an easy thing to do."

"So I will be your courier."

"Yes, and your message for her is so important. Gisele is very brave, but I can sense she is near despair."

"Despair? Can you die of it?"

"It can feel like dying." I sighed. "It is a special affliction of human beings trapped in bad circumstances. I need Gisele to be brave until I can come to her, and I don't know an imp anywhere braver than you, Leo."

He puffed his chest out at that. "I will go prove it now. Are there dragons in England?"

"I'm not sure. My guess is that there aren't any more there now, though there used to be."

"Too bad. I would have slayed them to save your sister, but I'll just keep her away from that despair instead."

I was suddenly weary, sleepy beyond words. It was the wound in my back, but also the burden of knowing Gisele was far away and all alone. "Despair isn't a monster, but something inside a person. Your message will help her. Go to her now, Leo, wake her up if you have to. Look sharp, and warn me quick if you see any demons hanging around."

He scratched at his ears, then stuck out a hip and put a hand on it, as the mists rose up around him. "I don't get it, Mama. But it doesn't matter anyway. Just think of all the good deeds I've done! I have moved way up in the world, thanks to your assignments."

He saluted me and with no further ado Leopold shot into the sky and away before I could wish him godspeed or farewell.

"Good-bye, Leopold," I whispered after him.

I was afraid to go to sleep, despite my exhaustion. I was afraid to dream. My efforts to find Gisele had led me to the realm of her dark visions, and terrible scenes of cruelty and murder awaited me as soon as I closed my eyes.

I curled up around the sleeping Raziel, listened to the sound of his beating heart. I took solace in his untroubled dreams, his solid strength, and his undisturbed serenity. He had not been spared in Poland—horrible things had happened to him. But Raziel had survived, and he was with me in this moment, so very alive.

As I stared into the darkness, I earnestly prayed that Raziel at least would stay that way.

✳ 8 ✳

"Completely unacceptable," Raziel said in Hungarian.

I fully agreed, but didn't think it made sense yet to share our sentiment with our guide to the East, Mr. Ziyad Juhuri.

He had met us after all in the lobby of the hotel for breakfast, and for that fact I was grateful. However, with him came two bodyguards, one slim, one stocky, both with black mustaches, tattoos across the knuckles, and the darting eyes of assassins.

From the look in Ziyad's eye when I glared at him, it seemed we were going to be their prisoners.

Ziyad only repeated his plan, louder and faster than he had the day before, as if the problem was lack of comprehension and not the plan itself. "The slave trade is very busy in Baku, even now. The Soviet has done what it could to outlaw it, but still the pipeline runs. Slaves one way, the oil the other. I will stay here, and will help you get out of Azerbaijan again when the time comes. These men will take you into Baku on the slave route. And I will remain in Istanbul."

I didn't have the appetite to even butter my roll, let alone eat it. "What do you think that Bathory would say about this plan of yours?"

Ziyad shrugged and looked away, but not before I saw that his eyes had gotten a bit bloodshot. "Bathory would surely commend me."

"And how do you know these men won't in fact simply sell us for slaves?"

He looked at me then, a tic working under his left eye. "They wouldn't dare. They don't know who you are exactly, but they know who I am. They know what I am trying to do. And they are being well paid."

I translated his words to Raziel. With great gentleness, he rose from his chair, picked up his hat from the empty seat next to him and put it on his head, and offered me his hand.

I got up, too, and we prepared to leave.

"No!" Ziyad cried. "You must do this plan."

"Sir," I said, my voice cracking a bit, "we have been shot at. We have been tortured by the Gestapo. And yet we still walk this earth today. Our path is danger. But I do not willingly go into the fire, with men I do not trust. It may be these men are as good as their word. But I cannot speak with them. They do not speak German, I do not speak Russian or Azeri. I cannot entrust my life to them."

Ziyad scrubbed at his face with both hands, then launched into a rapid-fire tirade with the men in Azeri. They looked daggers at me and I smiled back in response. The three of them conferred furiously with one another, a debate that rivaled the Hungarian Parliament.

They almost came to blows a couple of times, but decorum prevailed. Finally Ziyad returned his attention to Raziel and me.

"The men agree with you."

"They do?" I asked before I could stop myself.

"Yes. I did not tell them about you, but they have heard. They think you are the fire goddess, the goddess of death. They do not wish to anger you."

His reply bewildered me. "Goddess?"

"They are fire worshipers. Believe me, they have reason to worship fire, in the mountains beyond the Five Fingers of God. Perhaps they are right about you, in their own fashion."

"So what will we do?"

Ziyad swallowed, and his eyes became wet with tears. "Because you will not go, they now refuse to take you. I must go with you. It will mean my death. But at least I will see my sister once more. So."

My wariness immediately metamorphosed into sympathy. Ziyad did not shed tears for us to convince us of his sincerity. Instead he wept for the life he expected to soon leave behind.

Raziel did not speak German and could not understand Ziyad's words without my translation, but he could easily discern the import of what he said. He took a half step forward, and murmured a short phrase in Hebrew that I myself did not understand—but my heart quickened at his words, and Ziyad himself wiped his face, nodded, and even ventured a small smile of resignation.

"What was that, my love?" I asked.

"A verse from the Book of Daniel. Ziyad knows it well: 'The angel came into the lion's den and shut the lion's jaws.'"

Azerbaijan was no primordial garden, with fruits of knowledge and rare delight. We knowingly walked into the lion's very jaws. This time, the angel walked with us, shorn of his wings. He was in as much danger as the rest of us. And yet the assassins, in the end, insisted on coming with us despite the dangers. Perhaps they, too, wanted to walk with angels.

6

To my surprise, we traveled by automobile. I half expected camels as transportation, but that was just my naïve ignorance. So far I hadn't seen a single camel.

Ziyad drove, with his chief assassin in the passenger's seat beside him. The shorter, fatter assassin sat next to Raziel in the backseat, with me tucked away on Raziel's other side. He tried one time to speak to Raziel, but after it became clear they had no language in common the stranger contented himself with a tip of his bowler hat and leaned back for a nap as we sped east from Istanbul toward the eastern border, to Armenia.

Long we traveled, and far, before we had a place to stop for more than gasoline or a meal. We sped through Armenia and Georgia as if the gates of Hell had opened up just behind us. We stopped each night, for furtive meals served in houses Ziyad had arranged for our travels. The food was sumptuous, fantastic, but we did nothing but eat, wash our faces, lie down, and arise again in the morning for another day of banging along terrible roads from village to village.

The Armenians and Azerbaijanis had for centuries loathed each other, so much so that it was dangerous to be traveling east. Well it was that we traveled with Ziyad, who could reassure the western Azeris that we meant no harm.

I expected the passage from Turkey to Armenia, the first of Stalin's lands, to be a grim one. But instead of barbed-wire fences and bayonets, we found a guardhouse along the side of the road, with a sleepy guard who looked all of fourteen years old. Ziyad and the boy conversed for a long time in Russian, then Ziyad got out of the car and hugged him like a long-lost son. They kissed on both cheeks, shook hands, and that was it. We entered the domain of the great Soviet Union.

"Not such monsters as you dreamed of," Ziyad said, and then he laughed bitterly.

✳ 9 ✳

We finally arrived in Baku in the middle of a pelting rain-storm on a bone-chilling November afternoon. "It is more beautiful than it looks today," Ziyad said miserably from the driver's seat.

The city looked forlorn and waterlogged, the Caspian Sea churning just outside the city, the great Bulvar running all along the sea. A few women, wrapped up in black fabric, walked, bent over, along the broad Bulvar, burdened by huge bundles of washing. Otherwise, the streets were virtually deserted.

"Look," Raziel said to me under his breath.

I shot a quick look at our minder in the backseat, then craned my neck to the left to squint through the needle-sharp raindrops slicing through the air.

And gasped with recognition.

Shimmering through the rain I saw oranges and brilliant purples, barefoot male figures walking together along the Bulvar. One of the men turned and caught me staring, laughed, and shot into the air like a bird. His brothers followed him, and they disappeared into the storm clouds over the Caspian Sea.

I turned to Raziel, and I couldn't find my words. Finally I sputtered, "Did you see that?"

He laughed and leaned back on the dusty seat. "Yes. It has been a long, long time since I've seen such a thing. I didn't know that mortal eyes could see them, too."

"What were they?"

Raziel smiled and shrugged.

"Raziel!"

He laughed again, tried to stretch his long legs in the cramped backseat. "These are creatures of fire, what the Arabians call Djinn. Some angels who fall are of the fire, too, you know. In this land, the Zoroastrians call the fire angels Yazata. In the West, we call them seraphim."

I looked out the window again to see them, but already they were well and truly gone. "They must hate the rain even more than I do. Are they dangerous?"

"Of course." Raziel's smile faded. "Everything is dangerous here, Magduska. Don't let down your guard."

I reached for his hand and squeezed, hard. He squeezed back, his touch reassuring me more than any words ever could, and I considered our current circumstances.

Azerbaijan made Turkey look like Switzerland. In Turkey evidence of the West was as plentiful as that of the East; it is the crossroads after all; the history of Turkey was to serve as the place where they met.

Now in Baku I watched fire spirits fly, and knew that again I was out of my depth. I had faith in my magic, knew that I could draw upon it anywhere I traveled—Hebrew is a wanderer's language. But how would I find allies, communicate my intentions here, without our guides to intercede?

We arrived at an enormous caravanserai, where the Silk Road caravans stopped before they journeyed onward to Istanbul.

"Here we are," Ziyad said, his voice growing a bit less despondent for the first time since we had left Istanbul. "A good place to get some food and rest."

He parked the automobile just past the entrance, and we got out, legs stiff. The rain had dwindled to a misty drizzle. "Now you will see camels," he said, teasing me. I had asked about camels enough times for it to become a running joke with our strange little band of travelers.

The courtyard was filled with cross-legged travelers, weary in their multicolored silks and long cloaks, as they sat under brightly hued canvas awnings to ward away the rain. And for the first time, yes, camels, folded up in the courtyard sitting next to their masters.

A *mugam* band played odd-looking stringed instruments, plucking and bowing, while a half-naked woman sang a keening wail of a song in accompaniment.

But the music had stopped once we walked into the courtyard. I soon realized that the people in the courtyard were staring at me, everyone, even the half-naked lady singing the traditional *mugam* lament. A quick look around solved the mystery of why—I was the only woman traveler in the place.

Raziel edged closer to me, and the two assassins swept to either side of us, like two hired guns in a gangster movie.

Ziyad held his palms out to the man standing alone by the fountain that served as a watering trough for the camels. He spoke in rapid Azeri, soft backward-sounding vowels. The man nodded, then laughed and pointed at me. Ziyad said something sharp, and the man's amusement vanished as rapidly as it had come.

He stepped forward, and bowed low in front of me. "Greetings, madame *táltos*," he said, in halting Hungarian.

I was impressed. "Hello, sir," I said slowly as he spoke. "Thank you."

He nodded, not quite following my words. I nodded back, and he clapped his hands together, seemingly satisfied about me. He waved for us to follow, and Ziyad nodded to me that it was all right to go ahead.

As we walked across the courtyard, the back of my neck prickled. Danger! I sent my witch's sight along the perimeter of the courtyard, saw shimmering lights flickering but nothing more frightening than that. A wave of nausea rose, then receded. I chalked that up to simple tension.

The stranger ushered us to an alcove in the corner, a low table set against the floor with piled rugs as seats all around. He bowed and waited for us to sit before he turned and walked away.

"Now you will have a feast," Ziyad said. He smiled at us, but his eyes looked more desolate than I had ever seen them.

Why did Ziyad despair? Was it simply fear, or something more dangerous than that?

"Who was that man?"

"Enos, the man who runs this place," Ziyad said. "His family has maintained this caravanserai for centuries. It is the most famous one in all of Baku."

I looked out from my corner and saw alcoves like the one where we sat, rising four levels up like balconies of an apartment building, all around the courtyard. In the four corners, shops sold tea, knives, rugs of course, and bolts of silk. "Why would traders need silk?" I asked.

"They often pay in silk," Ziyad replied. "And there are other items in the back that the traders will always need." He shot me a quick glance and pressed his lips tightly together.

I didn't need my witch's arts to tell he knew something important he didn't want to tell me. So be it. I would dine, and enjoy the outlandish hospitality of the Azeris.

He didn't have to tell me to stay on my guard. The many pairs of eyes watching every move I made were sufficient reminder.

"We need to travel north," I said.

Ziyad nodded, not surprised. "You want to visit my people."

I was going to demur, but held myself back. I wanted to visit the place that physically corresponded to where the Garden of Eden had once stood at the beginning of things. As far as Raziel and I could both tell, that was somewhere in the northern Caucasus, not all that far from where Noah's Ark had, much later, come to rest.

Life has a way of bringing possibilities to the surface, just when they might make all the difference. It was a huge coincidence that Ziyad's people came from the mountains north of Baku. Too huge to be random.

"We want to visit your people," I repeated to him, with my own small, private smile. "I hear your country is very beautiful."

"Yes," he replied, his smile becoming genuine. "It is beautiful, and full of secrets."

After a sumptuous meal, our host, Enos, cleared away first the plates, then the tables. Time to sleep.

Raziel and the other men dragged out the piles of rugs and arranged them into sleeping pallets. We climbed into the alcove and went to sleep. The courtyard of the caravanserai grew amazingly quiet considering the number of men, and camels, massed inside.

The men from the Institute attacked that night.

The first sign of trouble was the smell of cigarettes. My guardian angel, Viktor, had not been in Heaven long. When I knew him as a man in Kraków, Poland, he smoked incessantly, preferring cigarettes to food in times of trouble. As a result, he was as lean as a hound and you could often smell him, smoking away, before he appeared in the flesh.

It was the same now. Viktor's place was in Heaven, not on earth. He could not manifest, not without a great deal of dif-

ficulty (he was a new angel, after all) or unless I expended a lot
of concentration and energy on a spell of seeing. I could see
him with my witch's sight if I truly looked long and hard, but
he could not easily communicate with me even then.

He spoke to me the way guardian angels generally do with
mortals, with glimmers of encouragement, with whispers of
hope in the night. And he bent the rules of angels, a bit—
Viktor always tried to warn me when trouble was imminent.

So when I suddenly smelled the smoke of unfiltered cigarettes I sat up sharply and strained to see in the near-total
darkness enveloping us. I touched Raziel's shoulder and he
was up in an instant, and Ziyad a moment after that.

Viktor robbed our enemies of the element of surprise. That
did not make them any less dangerous. A band of a half-
dozen men dressed in black and armed with truncheons were
swinging them down with a savage intensity. The men couldn't
see any better than I could, and I dodged the first intended
blow by flinching away from the sound and the whoosh of the
truncheon coming down.

One of Ziyad's assassins wasn't so lucky—he grunted in
pain when one of the other men's blows connected with him,
an arm or leg I would guess, since it wasn't completely inca-
pacitating.

Raziel's knife sliced through the air with a whiffing sound,
and he connected with his attacker. The man's hoarse screams
unleashed an unholy commotion throughout the caravanserai. In retrospect, I assume such attacks were not unheard of
there; after all, these traders carried rare spices, silks, and other
treasures and the temptation to steal their wares must have
proven overwhelming to the more desperate denizens of Baku.

But at the time, the melee seemed completely insane. The silence of the night was shattered by reverberating screams, the braying of camels, and curses in many different languages I couldn't identify.

Someone—Raziel or maybe even Viktor—grabbed me and pulled me to the rear of the alcove.

"We're trapped," I gasped. "We have to get away."

"Follow the candlelight," Raziel said at my elbow, and in an instant I saw what he meant.

A secret trapdoor had opened at the back of the alcove, and a spark of flame disappeared down the stairs.

"Let's go!" I said, and together we rushed for the stairs. I could just see Ziyad's head as he disappeared into the darkness, holding the candle high above his head.

We ran down, and the assassins closed ranks behind us. The short, round one, the one caught by the bludgeon, groaned as he ran. The other one slammed the trapdoor closed behind us.

Down we clattered, smelling a fetid stink that rose up from below. We ran too headlong for me to ask where we were going, but I could guess: special guests of the caravanserai had a secret escape built into their accommodations.

Ziyad made a sharp left and I skidded in the filth under our feet and almost fell. Raziel caught me under the elbow and together we pelted after him.

"Up!" Ziyad cried. He launched himself up a sudden staircase that rose from the tunnel where we ran.

The stairs were stone, slippery, and worn almost completely away. We came back to the surface in a stinking alleyway behind a trash can crawling with rats—I could hear them scrabbling and fighting inside. I didn't stop to find out what they were tussling over, instead I followed Ziyad out onto the street, where his auto waited for us. I now understood why Ziyad had pulled up down the street before parking for the night..-

A great cry echoed from the entrance to the caravanserai. I could not translate, but the meaning was as clear as day: "There they are!"

We hurled ourselves into the car even as Ziyad pulled away from the curb. I slammed the door shut as the Mercedes caromed wildly down the street, all but running down the men streaming out of the entranceway.

"Hold on," Ziyad said, his breath coming out in little heaves. None of us was in much better shape.

He stepped on the accelerator, and we rattled over the uneven cobblestones. And so, unceremoniously, we fled the city of Baku in the night. We were lucky to get away.

No other automobiles chased us as we ran. After ten minutes of bone rattling, Ziyad eased off the accelerator for a bit, and pulled into the hills northwest of the city.

Such a near thing, our escape. "What was that?" I asked in shaky German.

"That was the Institute," Ziyad replied, his voice so slurred I could hardly understand him.

"The Institute? This was the place you spoke of in Istanbul? I imagined it as some kind of university," I said, a shaky laugh in my voice. "If these are the professors in your country, I am afraid to meet the Cheka."

He looked at me in the rearview mirror through the shadows, eyes wild. "No, the Institute is worse. It is the Institute that brought down the magic of the czar, in the Revolution.

They know my people, the ones who weave the carpets of magic. And now the Institute knows that I have returned."

The way that Asmodel had known my trail would lead to Budapest, sooner or later. Did the ancient demon also know I searched for the gem here, in Baku?

Ziyad leaned forward and hunched over the wheel to peer through the windshield. Downtown Baku had been granted the marvel of streetlights, but the streets outside Baku were dark, and only white paint applied in rings to the trees lining the streets illuminated our path out of the city.

He didn't have to explain any further; the thugs from the Institute supplied all the information we needed. Ziyad had many enemies in Baku, and as far as I could tell he, not me or Raziel, was the object of Stalin's intentions.

I don't mean to say that Josef Stalin himself set this desperate band of men and spirits upon us. From the outside, Stalin's empire was superficially much like Adolf Hitler's.

But Hitler's Reich used their own Teutonic magic to enforce their iron rule over the ordinary people. They claimed magic for the state, and the magic in Hitler's world was malign, corrosive, and part of his apparatus of social control.

Stalin, however, repudiated magic, saw it as the chief enemy to his aspirations to world domination. As a materialist, he sought to stamp out magic as the one thing he could not control. So in his world, magic was a subversive force, something his people were working to eradicate.

In Azerbaijan, one of the captive countries of the Soviet Union, the magic was indigenous, something Stalin did not know how to control. It was not officially treason to consort with magicals or, as a mortal, to resort to the use of magic;

magic was far too thick on the ground in Azerbaijan to attempt such wholesale suppression.

Stalin himself was no stranger to the magic of the Caucasus, and the royal magic wielded by the Russian czars. The Communists fought the royal magic bitterly until it was destroyed. Stalin and his fellow Bolsheviks hated magic, believed it a tool of oppression and nothing more. And so they founded the Institute for Brain Research in Leningrad, to study and measure magic, to make a science of it.

They believed that once they understood and quantified the magic they could then control it, and ultimately destroy it.

Given these articles of Communist faith, magicals occupied a precarious place in materialist Soviet society. They could not rip the magic out of themselves, so they were inherently a threat to the system Stalin, and Lenin before him, had imposed over the vast lands previously controlled by the Russian czars.

Where did that leave a foreign witch and her outlawed Azeri guide? In a very dangerous place, indeed.

"Where are we going now?" I asked.

"The temple of fire," Ziyad replied. "We must. The priestess there will offer us sanctuary."

He said something to the man in the passenger seat next to him, and the other bent over, muttering low in Azeri, his voice harsh and hoarse. I realized with a start that the tough old assassin was weeping.

"We're going somewhere very bad," I told Raziel in Hungarian.

He shrugged and leaned forward, squinting into the night, trying his best to identify the dangers looming ahead of us.

In the gloom I saw trains running like shadows to our left, boxcars sliding along the tracks, *thunk thunk* in the night. "Do you know of the temple of fire?" I asked Raziel. As a man, he was raw and still mostly untested; as an angel, he had seen wonders and terrors I could never have imagined.

"This is a Zoroastrian temple. Do not be afraid," he said, and grabbed my hand, as if he'd forgotten he was no longer an angel. "No matter what you see."

Somehow I did not find his words reassuring.

✳ *10* ✳

We reached the temple of fire at dawn. The assassin in the front seat wept anew at the sight of the sun. I looked at the back of Ziyad's head and decided not to trouble him again for an explanation. Sometimes words fail.

We sped through a sleepy village to a fortress ringed by a thick stone wall. Ziyad pulled into the entrance, and a metal grating clanked down behind us.

It was clear: there would be no leaving here without the permission of the fortress holders. Ziyad cut the engine, and we sat, wordless, in the hot, sweaty dawn.

The engine ticked over, then fell silent. All that could be heard now was birdsong. Finally, Ziyad sighed and pulled a handkerchief from his front pant pocket. He mopped at his face and rested his forehead on the wheel.

The temple of fire. I smelled cigarette smoke again. But I didn't need Viktor's warning to know this was a place of danger.

We got out of the car. It was stifling hot, unnaturally so for November, like the air had been siphoned outside the temple walls.

Ziyad shuffled to the far side of the entrance arch, and we followed him. Sweat stuck his shirt to his back. He rapped on the wooden door with his bony knuckles, and after a few moments slowly the door drew backward.

I expected some kind of terrifying ghoul to greet us, but instead a very young woman, with glossy black hair parted in the middle, met us with a bow. Her face looked strangely familiar. The young woman said something in Azeri and we followed Ziyad and his men inside the walls, into another courtyard.

At first it looked like a castle court, nothing too far out of the ordinary. A covered well stood in the middle of the courtyard, with a tower above it.

But something seemed terribly off about the place, wrong in a fundamental way that I couldn't consciously identify. It was far too hot for so early on a day in November. The courtyard hung lopsided, the walls not square but bulging outward like they had melted even as they were being built.

Wooden doors built into the walls surrounding us crouched too low, built for an army of children or imps. The fortress looked like it had sunk a good meter into the ground sometime after its building.

Dreadfully hot. Hot and dark, the flames burning but not illuminating. And the colors were hideously wrong. The grass under our feet grew yellow, not dried and dead, but alive and yellow. The stone of the fortress was a dull red with flecks of bone gray. And the tower over the closed-up well was painted a garish orange. It seemed to glow in that unnatural heat.

My skin began to crawl, and a moment later my conscious mind caught up with my senses. That was no covered well.

It was some kind of furnace.

"She wants to know if you worship the fire," Ziyad was saying to me. I looked at him and he crossed his arms, as if he had been repeating himself and I'd only just heard him this last time.

I looked at her, really looked, and she smiled back, in her place of power. It belatedly occurred to me this girl was a witch.

Not a witch of spells, like I am. Not a witch of lore. But a servant of the fire.

"Tell her I am her sister. But I do not know the fire."

As Ziyad translated my missive, the girl and I smiled at each other from across the great gulf of our language, our disparate lives. She recognized my power as I recognized hers.

She said something in her quiet voice, and Ziyad said on the heels of her words, "She welcomes you to her temple."

"Who are these fire worshipers, Ziyad? And do they serve your cause?"

In answer he leaned toward the girl, and they spoke together in the soft, sibilant language of Azerbaijan. "She says to speak magic and you will have your answer," Ziyad finally said.

His voice was calm, but he stepped backward as he spoke. I glanced at Raziel, who scratched at his jaw and shrugged.

"Sh'ma . . . ," I sang, softly. Not a prayer I used to work spells, but one to focus my intention, bring my power to rise.

My words turned to fire in the air, as if I had lit a parchment with the words and held it while it burned. The flames licked at the air and disappeared.

"You speak in fire," the girl said, and Ziyad translated.

I smiled at her, shy now. I knew better than to work a spell in this girl's holy place. "Thank you for your sanctuary."

The assassins had stayed in the car, muttering to each other and glaring darkly through the windshield at us. "Why are they so afraid of this place?" I asked Raziel.

"I fear it, too," he said.

"But why?"

"This is the native magic of this country," Raziel said. "It is hungry, the fire. When the fire worshipers die, they put their bodies to the flame. Some say . . ." He glanced at the girl with us, still smiling, not understanding his Hungarian. "There are rumors that the fire devours living souls in this land as well."

I studied the girl with us. "No, this girl does not sacrifice unwilling victims to the fire. I can assure you of that, my love."

He licked his lips, and his face didn't relax. "This girl does not, this temple does not. But in the hills. At the Mountain of Fire. There they practice the old ways."

I whispered the Ninety-first Psalm into the air, watched in wonder as the letters sparked into the sky and faded away. "I need to find the gem in those mountains. As long as the fire worshipers do not try to stop me, I have no quarrel with them or their ways."

"They have their own interest in what you seek," Raziel said, his voice reflective. He took a tentative step toward the furnace set into the ground, held his hand out to sense the heat radiating from the earth. "Gem sorcery is of the earth, but jewels are tempered with fire, Magduska. There is a reason that the sapphire has remained hidden so long."

His voice sounded melancholy, but his face remained serene. "It was bad enough I hunted *The Book of Raziel*," I said. "Do you think the gem will cause even more trouble?"

He sighed. "Given the fact that Hitler has the Book now, and it has been empowered by the Soviet anti-magic, I don't think we have a choice but to bring the Heaven Sapphire into the war."

The girl motioned for me to step closer. She actually grabbed my wrist as she leaned forward, and she stared into my eyes with a terrible intensity as she spoke.

"We are persecuted for worshiping death," she whispered. Ziyad translated for us in a trembling voice, one that tripped over the difficult words. "The professors of the Institute for Brain Research. They hate death, seek to vanquish it as the only enemy, the strongest one."

"But death is not the enemy," I said. I hated to admit it, but I knew it to be so, at least for me. "In the end, much as we fear death, it is part of life."

"No. You are my sister, you know it to be truth. To have the light, we must have the dark. The fire must prevail, and the fire consumes as well as shines.

"Do not fear the fire. For it will consume only that which can be burned away."

We stared at each other in the sudden silence.

Her fingers tightened around my wrist. "You seek a dangerous object in this land."

"Yes," I said, unable as well as unwilling to hide the truth.

"You will be tempted by many lesser treasures, including that of your life. But hold fast to your quest, and do not relinquish it when you have found it, not until it is time."

"I won't." I leaned forward and kissed her on the cheeks in thanks, Russian-style, three times with a hug at the end. Like Gisele, this girl possessed the gift for far-seeing, but as far as I could tell she did not suffer the visions the way Gisele did.

With my kiss the spirit of second sight left her. The girl took a deep breath and stepped backward, letting my wrist out of her failing grasp.

Her eyes fluttered, and she swayed on her feet. But then she regained her footing, her eyes opened, her lips again stretched into a polite smile.

"Welcome to the temple of fire." She had forgotten her own prophecy. "Please enter and seek sanctuary here."

However fearsome the local sect, the fire worshipers had evidently cast their lot with Ziyad's folk in the mountains. They quickly arranged for transportation to the north—Ziyad's auto was too modern for the northern provinces and would be noticed immediately.

But when our transport arrived the following morning, I almost refused to ride. Something terrible had happened in the night. Ziyad and his comrades the fire worshipers had secured for us a hearse.

I had never seen a vehicle like it. It was modern in that it had an engine, not a horse or mule, powering it. But it was painted pink and white, a birthday cake of a contraption, and its windows were festooned with gold and pink curtains all around—even the windshield was framed in shimmering gold curtains, tied off with sashes to the sides.

I did not realize this contraption was a hearse until Ziyad made his appearance. He looked absolutely ghastly—as if his soul had disappeared into the fire overnight. I checked him for signs of demonic possession or malignant curse, but no. It wasn't magic that assailed Ziyad Juhuri. But death.

"You may ride in the back," Ziyad said, his voice so hoarse I could scarcely understand him. "And there is a place to hide quickly in case of trouble. Though for the sake of all that is holy I hope that matters do not come to that."

The back cabin was hot and airless, a rolling tomb. And planted in the middle, cushioned on a small mountain of rugs, was a coffin, painted white and gold, with a beautifully intricate portrait on the face.

A woman's face, with the same visage as the woman captured in the threads of Ziyad Juhuri's finest carpet hanging on the wall of his showroom in Istanbul. It was also the same visage, I realized now with a shudder, of the girl who had welcomed us to the temple of fire the day before.

I stared at that face for a long time, casting about with my magic for a name to match. I looked up at Ziyad, considered asking him for the woman's identity, her fate, but decided against it.

The poor man misread me. "I am sorry, Miss Lazarus, but none of this can be helped. It is a burden you must bear." Sobs choked his voice, but his eyes stayed dry.

I considered asking him whether the coffin was empty and, if not, why the priestess didn't go into the fire, but I decided for once not to try to satisfy my curiosity.

Instead, I just said, "Oh no. I understand. I've ridden in hay wagons, in the back of a Nazi Black Maria. We travel now in luxury, compared to that. And with any luck, nobody will think to question you, in a hearse. I only wish I could have bidden the priestess farewell."

"Do not fear, the fair maiden has not been fed to the fire," Ziyad said, his eyes now sparkling with tears.

I glanced at the coffin again. Perhaps our hostess had only stayed away from us, and not died in the night?

"I wanted to thank her for her help," I said gently.

Ziyad's expression grew hooded and fierce. "You can thank her by finding and capturing the gem."

So we left the environs of Baku, without even a single bystander to wave good-bye—probably better for the bystanders' sakes.

Just outside the temple walls, I saw a hulk of battered metal standing guard. It looked like an enormous safe, or an icebox, but consumed by a terrible conflagration, melted to the ground beneath it. I watched it from the rear window as we drove away from the temple of fire. And I could not shake the sudden conviction that the hunk of metal was responsible for the young priestess's disappearance.

Ziyad's assassins rode in the front of the car with him as we left Baku. Their names were Boris and Ilyam, and though Ziyad did not bother translating what they said in our travels, I had begun to get the sense of them as men. I was glad they fought on our side.

It was not their physique or their demeanor that revealed their prowess. No, they let slip their abilities in odd little ways. The shorter and rounder one, Ilyam, played with his knife when he was bored, balancing it by the tip on his fingers, tossing it in the air and catching it one-handed behind his back. His tall, skinny brother in assassination, Boris, used to balance on anything he could find, sidewalk curbs, car bumpers, chips of rocks extending from outcroppings. They couldn't help what they were, and they honed their talents without thinking.

As we pulled away from the village outside the temple of fire, assassins and Ziyad in the passenger area, Raziel and I hidden in the back with the coffin, my thoughts strayed again to Gisele, alone in London.

I rested my body over the top of the coffin, my fingers trailing along the back of Raziel's neck. The curtains divided us from the passengers up front, so we had a bit of privacy as Ziyad sped along the roads leading north from Baku. But I could think of only one thing.

"Will we find it?" I said under my breath.

Raziel turned his head to look up at me. "We have to," he replied. "Asmodel himself will be chasing us into the Caucasus before we know it."

✳ *II* ✳

Before we had left Budapest, no less a personage than Winston Churchill had warned us of Hitler's aspirations to seize the Soviet oil fields in the Caucasus. Hitler wanted the oil; his resident demon, Asmodel, wanted the gem. In the short term, an attack on the east would quell the rebellion stirring inside the Reich since Hitler's near-fatal "accident" at Wolf's Lair. In the long term, acquiring both oil and gem would mean the Reich would win the war—and subjugate all the world.

I shuddered at the thought of it. Bumping along in the back of the pink hearse, I visualized the gem: azure blue, a star trapped inside of it, small but terribly heavy in my hands. I called to it, but unlike the written *Book of Raziel,* the gemstone did not answer.

My magic resided in words, not gems. And I could not summon a soulless gem out of its hiding place.

"I will never find it," I whispered, half in a panic. "The gem has been lost for over two thousand years."

"It has been waiting for you." Raziel sat up and leaned against the coffin so he could kiss me.

Our lips touched, but a terrific rattle shook us apart. The hearse lurched and bumped, and the brakes squealed.

Raziel peeked through the curtains on his side. "The paved road is gone."

I looked through on the other side and gasped. The hearse now ran along a rutted track, looking more like a forest path than a proper road. We rattled over the sliding, broken stones in the track, and skidded dangerously close to the edge. Beyond the tires, wildflowers, then . . . nothingness. We traveled at the very edge of a mountain pass.

After four hours of this lurching and jolting, the hearse rolled to a slow stop. The front door opened, then slammed, and I heard footfalls crunching through gravel.

It was Ziyad. He opened the rear door, and made as if he were adjusting the coffin from its sliding around on the rough road.

"Hungry? Thirsty?" he asked.

"Yes," Raziel replied before I could reply—apparently hunger transcended all language barriers.

Ziyad nodded, slammed the door closed, and disappeared with his companions. All I could hear was the engine ticking as it cooled.

I furtively raised the curtains and dared another peek

outside. A herd of cows surrounded us like a meaty river. One of the cows lifted her head to stare wide-eyed through the window at me, and I dropped the curtain and retreated back into the semidarkness.

"We're in the middle of nowhere," I said.

"That's good," Raziel said. "One rarely finds untouched treasures in the city."

I watched Ziyad wander through the herd, to a ramshackle building at the edge of the roadside. Suddenly I was seized with a terrible foreboding.

"Ziyad isn't acting like much of a fugitive, is he? I have been hunted. So have you."

A crease folded between Raziel's eyebrows as he leaned back against the coffin. The cabin smelled of pine and wool. "He is among his own people."

I couldn't hold back a snort at that observation. "In my experience, the greatest danger is hiding among your own people. Bathory is in the most danger from his fellow vampires, is he not?"

My mouth had gone dry, dry as cotton, dry as a shroud. And yet I could not have forced down a glass of the finest champagne in Paris.

"If something happens to him, or if he betrays us, we don't know another living soul here who will help."

Raziel shrugged. "It's better than Poland. Far better."

"But it's not just Ziyad." I leaned my head against the curved cover of the coffin and sighed. "It's like we're trapped inside a story by Scheherazade. A maze inside of a maze."

Raziel's fingers trailed along the back of my neck, and I closed my eyes and relaxed under his touch. "You are not

alone, never alone," he said. "We travel together on this foreign road."

"I'm terrible at waiting," I said by way of apology. "At not
knowing what to expect."

Raziel laughed. "I know."

"Well, I still don't trust Ziyad, not entirely. He does not have
the eyes of a traitor, yes? But something terrible weighs on
him, Raziel. You don't need any magic to see it." I glanced at
the portrait on the coffin and sighed.

"For now, we have no choice but to travel with him to the
mountains."

I didn't like Raziel's answer, but he was right, of course.

Ziyad emerged from the shack flanked by his bodyguards,
carrying a paper sack. He waded through the placid river of
cows to the back of the hearse.

He hauled the back door open. "Even the dead get hungry
in my country."

The hairs prickled along the back of my neck. "In my country,
the dead refuse to stay dead," I replied with a smile for armor.

He blinked hard, but said nothing in reply.

"Food?" Raziel asked, breaking into the silence.

"Kofta," Ziyad said, and he bowed slightly as he presented
the sack to us. "The meat here is good."

I nodded my thanks and peeked inside. Bread, freshly
baked and still warm, stuffed with meat off a skewer, and herbs
piled on top.

Raziel and I devoured our meal and watched the herd of cows
drift off the road toward a mountain peak rising in the distance.
The cowherd, a furious-looking man with ice blue eyes, glared
at us as if we had come to murder him. Tripping at his heels was

a young boy dressed in rags, who did the hard work of running after stragglers and scaring them back into the herd.

Ziyad caught me staring and he nodded. He pointed at the peaks, half-hidden in a hazy mist. "The Five Fingers of God, Miss Lazarus. We must ascend them before we have finished our travels home."

The peaks reached into the sky, pure rock barren, lacking any sign of life. They looked as remote and unreachable as stars.

The wind picked up and drove the dust from the road into our eyes.

"Eat and rest. We must go," Ziyad said. And he slammed the rear door of the hearse closed once again.

Despite the hard jolting on the unpaved road, I soon fell asleep and dozed where I lay beside the coffin.

And like a whisper I rose out of my body and hovered above it, a dragonfly above the shimmering pool of my dream.

Raziel dozed, too, his hat tilted over his eyes. I considered calling his soul to travel with mine, then had second thoughts. He did not have a native magic to protect him, on this or any plane. And spirits called to spirits—we were unlikely to remain alone in our naked, vulnerable state.

I let Raziel sleep, returned my attention to the coffin—

—and was shocked to find another spirit hovering, too. I had not realized a body rested inside, and had not cast for spirits or anything else before getting in the trunk.

On this plane, spirits spoke a universal language, the language of angels. What a relief, to simply understand.

"Hello," the spirit said. She was beautiful and, I realized with a start, the same woman represented on the face of the coffin and on the glorious carpet hanging on the wall of Ziyad's warehouse in Istanbul.

I blinked hard, jolted by a sudden and unwelcome realization. "My God, you are the girl who guards the temple of fire," I said, floating closer. Unlike my soul, still tethered to my body by a silken strand of silvery light, the woman's spirit hovered free, unconnected to her dead body inside the coffin.

"Are you lost?" I asked.

"Oh no, just waiting until I return to my people. They will bury me, and I will ascend after saying my good-byes."

"Are they going to . . . burn you?"

She laughed at that, a rueful, sweet sound. "I would have much preferred it! But poor Ziyad could not bear to feed me to the fire. Instead, I go to the mountains now, where my parents' bones lie."

"I am sorry you have passed," I said.

"Why? It was my time."

I tried hard not to argue. This lovely young woman surely deserved to live, even if she had resigned herself to her fate. "What happened to you?"

Her face grew sad. "The Institute challenged the authority of the temple itself! The enforcers grow bold. They brought one of their anti-magic machines to the very gate of my sanctuary, and expected to breach the ancient walls."

I remembered the burned-out hulk of metal by the temple

gates. She sighed and continued. "The fire consumed their hateful machine, but not before I had paid for the defense of the temple with my life. And the defense of you, dear stranger. Yes, you, too."

Numbness spread through me like poison. This girl had saved my life, Raziel's life, and paid the ultimate price. "Thank you," I whispered, so grateful for her sacrifice, but abashed and saddened by it, too.

"It doesn't really matter anyway," she went on. "I have no children, no husband, nothing to hold on to here. Only my brother grieves for me now."

Suddenly I understood. "Ah. Ziyad is your brother." His furtive, absent manner and lack of caution suddenly made sense. All attributable to his sharp, sudden grief. But why had he not told us?

"A blessing you have come to me, witch of Budapest. Please, when you awake, tell my brother that I am all right?"

"We grieve for you, too, priestess. Of course I will seek to comfort your brother," I hastened to agree. "May I please ask your name?"

"I am Leyla," she replied. "And please tell Ziyad I am at peace. It will be a comfort to him."

I suspected poor Ziyad would find little comfort anywhere now that she was dead. "We appear, you die. It will be hard for Ziyad to accept that."

It was Leyla's turn to sigh and turn away. "You did not kill me, Ziyad did not kill me. It was the magic killers, the Institute scientists who bear the stain of my murder. Life is different in the mountain country. You will see. The Institute must fight harder in the mountains to contain us, and we are difficult to crush. No army wants to march over unpaved roads for days only to arrive in a poor land with no oil, little timber, and a hostile people. It's just not worth it. And we fight to the death, not a traitor among us."

It occurred to me that she must have overheard my conversation with Raziel. "I didn't mean to suspect your brother without cause."

"I did not hear," she said a little too quickly, suggesting to me she was being more polite than honest. "But you must know that Ziyad is true. The poor man walks a tangled, dangerous road, where friend and foe wear the same face. But he is a true friend to you. Please believe me."

"I will tell him what you told me. That you are at peace. But your brother and I may not travel the same road for long. . . ." I trailed off, unwilling to spell out the details of what I meant.

"No apologies are necessary. I understand all."

"Will you stay here until after the funeral?"

"Yes. I cannot bear to leave Ziyad so soon, with so many cares. I wait for at least a proper good-bye."

I sighed. Nobody hated good-byes more than I did. So I could sympathize with Leyla.

"And tell him to look in Xinaliq, where my betrothed comes from," she said, looking away from me and looking thoroughly demure at the mention of a man. "And tell Ziyad I love him, and that I never suffered. And tell him . . ."

I reached to her and squeezed her shoulders, she looked like she was going to faint. "Yes, go ahead."

"Tell him to sell the carpets. All of them."

Before I could ask her why, the hearse went over an enormous hole in the road, *bang—BANG.*

And I was jolted back into my awakening body.

Such bliss, not to return in mortal agony! Just to awaken. I stretched and smiled, glanced at the coffin, of course saw nothing amiss with my ordinary sight.

When I looked again, with my witch's sight, there she was, an indistinct ball of energy, like an overexposure on a photograph. I waved to her and she shimmered in reply.

Raziel cleared his throat and sat up as we lurched along the rutted track of the road to Quba. "Ach, my back," he muttered. "Banged my head, too, but what's the tragedy in that?"

I tsked him even as the sight of his lopsided smile warmed me. I leaned over the coffin to smack him on the shoulder, and as I did so for the first time I caught the faint, unmistakable scent hidden inside the tang of pine and the strong, dusty smell of the woolen rugs.

Leyla was with us, discarded body and soul.

I explained to Raziel my encounter and his smile faded. "Poor girl," he said, touching the coffin even more gently than usual. "She mustn't linger too long or she will get lost."

"No," I replied. "Now that I have the trick of traveling in my dreams, I'll make sure she's okay."

He nodded, his eyes serious. "Magda, compared to your trick of cheating death by return, this flying in your dreams looks simple, I know. But, my darling, remember, you can get lost, too."

"I'll be careful," I said, an edge of impatience creeping into my voice.

"Don't *yes* me like you did your mother," Raziel said, his

voice uncharacteristically sharp. "That cord you see, it is more fragile than you think. I've seen babies asleep in their cots snap that cord without meaning it. And slipping away, back to Heaven . . ."

"All right," I said, striving to ignore his solicitude. "I'll try to remember. But you mustn't worry too much, because if that silver cord does come loose, I'll come back anyway. I've done it before, as you know."

His face brightened at that, but I still had the nagging sense that I was missing something in Raziel's well-meant warning.

By now the sun was near to setting, and the shadows grew long as the sunlight snuck past the gilt curtains. We had been lucky. The weather north of Baku was clear. Even a short rain would have melted the track into impassable rivers of mud.

In the sunset, a row of trees on either side of the road stretched along our way, where horse-drawn carts pushed ahead of us. Swaddled bundles hung from nooses, every half a dozen trees or so, alternating on either side of the road.

At first, I feared we saw children, strung up inside of bags, sacrifices to the fire gods. Sickened, I squinted to see better so that I could understand, and was relieved to see they were only lambs, slaughtered and dressed, hanging from the trees like executed convicts.

Ziyad was across the hearse in the driver's seat, too far away to hear my questions, but before I could call to him the car rumbled to a stop next to one of the swinging carcasses.

Ziyad got out, slammed the door behind him, and began talking to the man squatting in the road beside the tree with the hanging lamb. After a few moments of unhurried conversation, money changed hands, and the stranger took out an immense blade, swung it over his head, and hacked down the carcass from the tree.

He wrapped the dressed lamb in a white sheet and carried it to the car. Ziyad opened the back door, and the stranger deposited the lamb on the backseat, next to Boris.

"Supper," Raziel remarked.

I had never felt so far away from the Café Istanbul.

✳ 12 ✳

We stopped outside Quba proper, after rattling through a ghostly forest of white birches, looming in the darkness, shadowed by the shades of thousands of ghosts. The road, paved once again, snaked through this forest, high above a river running sluggishly below.

I don't scare easily, but my teeth all but chattered as we moved silently through the wood. Raziel, bless him, maintained his customary aplomb. Whereas the malevolence inside of my own soul called these dark creatures to me, on the plane of the living and beyond.

We stopped in front of a low, whitewashed building with a façade of white arches that led to a hidden courtyard behind.

Ziyad bowed as he opened the back of the hearse to let us

out. I jumped, landed on rubbery legs, and wobbled around until I got feeling into them once again.

"Ziyad, your sister . . . ," I said without preamble.

He paled and shook his head. "Say nothing," he said. "No, do not speak her name. Do not speak of her."

"But she . . ."

"No!" He walked away from us into the courtyard, his back stiffened, offended. I traded a long look with Raziel and we followed him, the bodyguards carrying the dressed lamb between them, looking crestfallen as they followed Ziyad.

A dozen enormous jars of pickles sat along a long, low ledge, the glass reflecting the dim moonlight. Behind, all in a row, stood a dozen or more doors, all closed tightly against the night. They looked like human-size stable doors.

"This is a rest home for soldiers," Ziyad said. "We had a civil war in Azerbaijan from 1919 to 1922. These men fought on both sides, and live together now. First we are Azeri."

Ah, that explained the ghosts. Casualties of the war, still at war as far as they knew. But unlike the forest choked with spirits, this place, somnolent and silent, seemed abandoned. I reached out with my inner sight to the souls here, and recoiled with a barely suppressed gasp. The men here, some dozens of them, all maimed, waited behind those closed doors to finally die.

These rooms were not prison cells. The rooms of the rest home provided the solitude of monks, or of tombs. Many of these souls suffered pain, but all bore their lot without complaint.

Raziel and I followed Ziyad and the bodyguards through the

courtyard to the kitchen, a separate building across from the men's rooms.

"We will have lamb," Ziyad said, his voice faint and far away. When I looked at him, his eyes had hardened and looked like obsidian stones.

What had I done to so infuriate him? And how did his fury manage to overwhelm his despair?

We ate in the enormous kitchen, and the meal was exquisite. Discomfited as I was by our eerie surroundings and Ziyad's rage, I could not help but appreciate the good food.

Raziel hardly ate. Instead he kept a watchful eye on me, as if I was the one most likely to explode in a homicidal rampage, not Ziyad.

After the splendor of the main course, dessert was a subdued affair, with walnut jellies, apples, and strong tea. The assassins sat together outside the kitchen window and watched the stars rise, and drank cup after cup of steaming hot tea out of the samovar set up in the courtyard.

"Okay, the gem," I said at last, breaking the silence that had stretched over the entire meal.

Raziel could not speak German, but he sensed the hidden menace in my voice, sat up straighter, and cracked his knuckles.

Ziyad looked at me for the first time since supper had been served. "Yes, the gem," he said, his voice laced with grief. "The superweapon. We must hurry. Our enemies are at our heels."

"For fugitives, we have eaten like princes. I am grateful for your hospitality."

Ziyad caught the edge in my voice. "I am in my own country now," he said by way of explanation. "My enemies will discover me eventually. So will yours, I am sure. But these mountains are high, stony, and remote. And they are mine."

Lord, I loathed speaking in German. The words cut my mouth like shards of glass. "Your sister Leyla is at peace. She wishes you peace as well."

There. I had kept my promise.

Ziyad's eyes flashed with tears, and with anger, too. "I forbid you to speak of her."

I bristled at his words, but held my peace and pressed ahead. "But her spirit speaks of you, with love. With reverence and the deepest gratitude."

His lips trembled and Ziyad pushed away from us. "Leyla is dead because of me. And you."

"She says no. She fought the Institute to protect her temple as well as us, we who had sought her protection. And she tells me that she is close, and she is here to say a proper good-bye."

"My people no longer make witches," Ziyad said, his voice clotted deep in his throat.

"No?"

"No. Because they call the fire down, and the fire devours them. Whether they are buried in the ground or not. My sister was too much a witch."

Ziyad was speaking in riddles. "If your own sister was such a witch, what need did you have for me?"

Ziyad paced back and forth.

"Besides," I continued, keeping my voice deliberately unconcerned, "any medium could speak to your sister's spirit. You don't need a witch at all."

Ziyad broke. Instead of attacking me with his fists, tears began streaming down his face.

"She was only eighteen. Never married. A dove."

"I know. She was brave as a general, and so beautiful. I am sorry."

"She should have had ten children, a house."

"But she is going to a better place."

"She should have lived first!"

I pressed my lips together and waited for the storm to subside—being with Raziel had taught me patience by proxy. After a time, Ziyad composed himself, slammed back a cup of tea like it was steaming-hot vodka.

"Forgive me, witch." The fire in him had guttered out, and once again I could sense the depth of Ziyad's despair.

"There is nothing to forgive."

He shrugged and half laughed, half sobbed, the sound even more unbearable than his barely mastered fury. "The Institute will get us in the end, even here. You will not be so proud and gracious by the end of our journey."

"When you say things like that, you frighten me, Ziyad, no matter how earnestly your sister's spirit speaks for you. You fear me as a witch and blame me for Leyla's death. And I cannot fault you for any of it."

"Leyla did not know war. You do."

"Yes. And if you betray me, Ziyad . . ." My voice trailed off, and I was unwilling to speak my secret fear aloud, that the only reason we had managed to elude the Institute was because they wanted us to find the gem before they closed in and grabbed us all. And that to save his people Ziyad would in desperation surrender Raziel and me to his enemies.

Ziyad understood. "This is my land," he said. "You are under my protection. I will not betray you—I would choose first to die."

I believed him, but still I could not let down my guard. I shrugged and looked away, carefully balanced a teaspoon on the ends of my fingers. "I never ate walnut jelly before, sir. However do you make it so that the shells are so soft? Do you boil them?"

He heard the danger in my voice. "They are young, tender walnuts. And we eat them whole."

His eyes bored into mine. "Remember, nothing will protect you should Stalin's people get you in the end. No matter how old or tough you think you are. It is not my doing that you came to my land, you chose it, you sought me out in Istanbul. You insisted."

"Yes. And you helped me every step of the way. I will never forget that, Ziyad."

He ran his fingers through his hair, and Raziel rose to his feet. "Magda, his sister is breaking his heart. Stop baiting him."

I tasted another spoon of the walnut jelly. "He does it to himself, my love. He fears I will meet his sister's fate."

After this digestion-wrecking meal, we left the entombed veterans to their still-living slumber and drove for the heart of Quba.

We slipped through the Muslim side of the town, where the buildings were low and simple, with crescents and stars cut as stenciled decorations into the tall blue window shutters. Even at this late hour, children and skinny dogs roamed the streets.

It looked ordinary, sleepy. But I sat at the edge of the last rug in the back of the hearse, my senses pricked keen, on the highest alert. For Quba at night, like the birch forest we had left behind, was thick with spirits.

✳ 13 ✳

To my surprise, Ziyad did not take us to one of these silent dark buildings to meet his people in Quba. Instead, he kept driving through the town until he had passed right through it, to the edge of the river.

A white tent pitched in an open field loomed in front of us, glowing like a fallen moon. The tent had no walls, only a sagging roof.

Inside, men sat on rugs, smoking hookahs and drinking tea from samovars. Horses waited patiently, tethered in a row at the edge of the woods.

The only light came from the glowing coals of the samovars, the bowls of hookahs, and the occasional cigarette, flickering like fireflies. "Are these Arabs?" I asked Ziyad, terribly confused. "They look nomadic. Nobody could survive living in an open tent here in the mountains, could they?"

Ziyad laughed bitterly at my question. "No, not Arabs. These are my relatives, my brothers from the mountains. This is a funeral tent, erected to mourn my sister. They are waiting for me . . . and for you as well. Women are not allowed to enter, but these are special circumstances. Let me talk to them. . . ."

He parked the hearse a careful distance from the horses, so that the engine would not startle them—I got the distinct impression that these horses were not used to automobiles. Ziyad silently motioned for us to wait, and he walked alone to the tent where his countrymen huddled.

A great wailing broke out when the men sighted him. Even though I had only a passing acquaintance with Leyla's spirit, the sound brought tears into my eyes. But Raziel's face remained serene.

"You are stronger than I am, my darling," I managed to say through the tears that choked me. "When I hear the men in the tent crying, it breaks my heart. And I don't know why."

"You wish to believe you've mastered death, but nobody does, my love," Raziel replied. "Their tears remind you of the truth."

Ziyad hurried back to the car, flicking the tears out of his eyes with his fingers. "Quickly, now," he said. "Come, meet the elders."

Then he hesitated, and I realized with a sudden weariness that this was no simple condolence call. "I cannot make them accept you," Ziyad said, his voice trembling. "They have only agreed to try. If the answer is no, you can try to fight your way out. That is the most I can give you. They are in a grim way, because of my sister's death. They think that you are responsible."

I sighed. "Maybe they are right. It was the scientists who attacked the walls of the temple and tried to kill us and the magic inside. But I suspect the Institute is acting on orders from Moscow. I'm afraid that my enemies have joined forces with yours."

He shrugged. "I believe it. But these men fear your magic, as much as they fear the Institute."

He looked away, and with a great effort composed his features. "Speak with a silver tongue, Lazarus witch. And realize that some of these men worship the fire. I pray that you do not find out what that means, this night."

I emerged from the car, feeling sick and knowing I was out of my depth, formidable as my magic had proven in the West. Raziel followed, silent and watchful, his hat in his hands.

"I have the advantage of being willing to die," Raziel said. "Poor Magduska, you refuse. So it must be."

This was true. I was hell-bent on finding the gem before my enemies did. I did not know how Asmodel, or Stalin for that matter, planned to find it. I worried they planned to use me as a sort of magical bloodhound. But I had to hunt my treasure regardless.

The three of us walked together across the uneven, rocky field to the funeral tent. Heat emanated from the tent like a banked coal—there was no way that the samovars and cigarettes could be the sole source of all that heat.

Magic was afoot. Magic I could not comprehend, much less control.

The men inside remained seated as we approached, huddled in small circles of about a dozen men each, ten such groups scattered underneath the enormous tent. The floor was made of prayer rugs, spread thickly beneath their feet.

Ziyad took off his shoes, and without any prompting Raziel and I did the same. I exchanged a glance with my husband, took a deep breath for courage, and entered the funeral tent behind the others.

Ziyad led us to the back of the tent and squatted next to a group of men swathed in blankets against the chill of the mountain air. The air around them vibrated with the heat.

I looked at their faces and could not suppress a gasp. These men were not men. Their faces glowed with light. They were men made of fire; fire spirits, come to earth. And they looked like youths, too young to be the elders Ziyad wanted me to meet. Only a few of them had the mustaches you saw everywhere on men in the Caucasus.

"Hello, Raziel," the youngest-looking of them said.

Raziel crouched next to the young man and held out a hand to shake. He spoke, to my amazement, in Hebrew. By now I could follow a bit of it. "Uzziel, a long time. It is a great pleasure, my brother, to see you here."

When I looked to Ziyad his eyes were all but popping out of his head.

"This is my wife," Raziel continued. My God. Raziel, the keeper of secrets, had revealed the cosmic secret of our marriage as casually as he had greeted Uzziel. I knew better than to say a single word. I sat down on the rug and tucked my ankles under me in what I hoped was a ladylike way.

"She is beautiful, my brother," the man next to Uzziel said. "But you bring her into danger."

"Thus is war. Hiding her would only condemn her. Like the girl who has passed."

The men spoke among themselves in quiet voices, shooting appraising glances my way every so often. They spoke in Azeri, and then—with a leap of recognition, I heard it.

The angelic speech.

The young-looking one, the one Raziel had called Uzziel, leaned forward and looked into my eyes. I held absolutely still, afraid to whisper even a single word.

"She is a witch," he said in the angelic speech. "And dangerous to our kind. Why did you bring her, Raziel? And why do you lie with her?"

I blinked then—Uzziel saw right through me, and there was nothing I could say to change his opinion. If I was going to keep out of a fight, Raziel was going to have to do the talking.

"I love her," Raziel replied. "And is she not beautiful? She is true. Fierce. And she uses her magic only for the good."

Uzziel snorted at Raziel's little speech. "Her intentions may be good. But great evil is committed in the name of goodness."

Raziel's laugh was easy, unafraid. "So your enemies have accused you. Take her on her own merit, as I take you. And we will fight in this war, for you."

"Give it a rest, Uz," the oldest-looking of the men said, his voice weary. "You always are too quick to judge." He leaned forward and searched Raziel's face with his gray, tired-looking eyes. "Do you remember me, brother? It has been so long."

Raziel looked intently at the man, and tears sparkled, unshed, in his eyes. "I remember you. Of course I remember you. Do you still have your sword, Ivriel?"

"No." Ivriel closed his eyes and sighed. "I never thought I'd see you without your wings, Raziel. Somehow it hurts more to see you that way."

Raziel shrugged, cracked his knuckles. "I found my wings did me no good down here."

"You finally saw the truth. But is it not bitter?"

The men, and Raziel, were silent after that. This was my husband's family, one I had not realized still existed. I hoped they would accept me, but in the way of in-laws I also realized I could never measure up to their expectations.

"The girl, who died," Raziel finally said. "I am sorry she is gone."

Uzziel said something under his breath in Azeri, a curse or a prayer I could not tell. Then: "She was a pure soul. And she was promised to me."

I was glad I was already sitting down, because the news jolted me hard. This fire creature, who I guessed had fallen from Heaven many centuries ago, still loved mortal women as in ancient times, before the great Flood. I thought such beings had gone from the Earth since the time of Noah.

I was wrong. And again I was reminded how little I really knew about this world, and about its mysteries. The sapphire of Raziel was the least of it. Sometimes the world seemed like a strange dream, one with its own internal logic that I could never discover.

I did not dare to interrupt. I was raised in a household of women, where my congenial father enjoyed our voices and our thoughts. Here in the Caucasus, men preferred their women hidden away, subservient and silent. And the fallen . . .

"She is brazen," the second one, Ivriel, said. I realized he spoke of me.

"She is mine," Raziel said. He spoke easily, without anger, but the other former angels looked at one another and said nothing.

I held my breath and willed myself not to move a muscle. We stood at a standoff, a moment away from violence. And I could not understand why.

✳ 14 ✳

After a long moment, the threat of violence slowly receded. Uzziel nodded, then stood. "Come with me, my brother," he said to Raziel. "And we will speak of many things."

His voice banished the tension coursing through the group still sitting on the ground. Raziel stood up, too, and the two fallen angels loomed high over the rest of our heads. "I am here," Raziel replied. "But I will bring my bride with me. This is no place for her to stay alone."

Uzziel hesitated, then nodded. "She may come."

At the entrance to the tent, I turned back to look for Ziyad. He sat with Raziel's brothers, far away in the corner, and he nodded silently and waved good-bye.

And that is the last I ever saw of Ziyad Juhuri. It breaks my heart, to think of him.

I followed behind the two former angels, one of them my husband, and I reminded myself that my temper was a flaw, not my strength. I drew my power to me with my rage, but often I forgot that the rage was not my power, it merely summoned it forth.

I managed not to ask where Uzziel was taking us. Heedless of the darkness, he walked into the woods, and I trailed behind the two men like an unruly shadow. I made a terrible racket, stumbling around in the darkness, as the men moved easily, talking in a low murmur. I barked my shin on a dead silver birch glowing dully in the moonlight and bit back a low curse. I am not known for my patience, my even temper, or my humility. This walk poked me in all these vulnerable places.

Finally we came upon a clearing, and a prim little house rose out of the darkness. In a flash I remembered my teacher's hut in the woods outside of Kraków, and my eyes flooded with rebellious tears. I dashed them away with more intemperate language growled under my breath, then hurried to follow Raziel and Uzziel as they passed over the threshold.

Once Uzziel closed the door firmly behind us, his manner completely changed. Gone was the fierce, condescending Caucasian, and in his place stood a man with features as gentle and worn as Raziel's.

Raziel laughed and I turned to face him. "It takes a lot to amaze you, my love. But Uzziel has managed it."

"I had thought you were one of a kind," I replied, too serious as usual.

My husband laughed louder, and I imagined Raziel's golden wings that he had lost, stretching behind his shoulders once again. "No, not really. These are the Yazata I told you about in

Baku—seraphim who fell to earth for love of women. They are fallen, but not demons. They live as men, untouched by hunger for power, free of the evil that the ancient demons possess. I asked to fall, and the Almighty gave me permission. But Uzziel and I walk the same road."

Uzziel motioned for us to follow him across the room, which was empty except for rugs piled over the floor, in layers so deep that we sank into little hills of rugs as we walked forward.

"Are you hungry? Thirsty?" he asked, his palms open.

"Thank you, no. Azerbaijan, so welcoming to strangers. But such a terrifying place nonetheless," I blurted out.

He met my eyes—his own were black as obsidian, enormous, and filled with a sadness I did not understand. "Your fear is born of wisdom, Lazarus."

I gulped and shivered at his words—was it that obvious to the fallen ones that I was a Lazarus witch? Was I that exposed to their scrutiny, and did my weaknesses shine out as obviously? "I am afraid," I admitted. "Maybe you can tell me why."

"We're not stomach hungry," Raziel said. "The people all along the way have fed and watered us whether we needed it or not. But we are hungry for knowledge."

Uzziel sank into silence at Raziel's words. He closed his eyes and sighed. "I know, I knew it the moment I saw you once again. The great Raziel does not walk the earth for trifles. For you, my brother, for you . . . I have no secrets from you. The secrets that you keep I know you keep on behalf of the Maker. And so it must be."

"Your secrets are safe," Raziel said, and though his voice stayed soft, I startled at the sound of it. "I don't care why you first fell from Heaven. Does it matter, really? What matters now is that Stalin and Hitler have made a pact to destroy the world. And Magda and I want the gem of Raziel."

Uzziel sighed and looked away, even as he began tapping at the carpets on the floor with his foot. "The sapphire. You know better than anybody why that gem is hidden away."

"Of course. But I am telling you, the gem will come back into the world of men now, with our allies or in the hands of Hitler." Raziel winced, as if his words hurt him physically. "And you know who is the parasite of Hitler."

"No, my friend." Uzziel's voice contained a wary note. "Hitler is bad enough by himself, no?"

Raziel closed his eyes and took a deep breath. "Asmodel."

The silence that descended over us, thick and heavy, almost took my breath away. I looked from one former angel to another, trying to figure it out without asking. "Do you know him?" I finally asked in a whisper.

Uzziel snapped his attention to me, and I saw the fury in him, the tears standing unshed in his eyes. "He is my brother. I followed him to Earth, when the world was young. I lived to regret it, regret him. And I have sworn to kill him the next time I see him."

I gulped. Asmodel and I had our share of bad encounters, always ending in bitterness and bloodshed. What had it been like for Uzziel to live alongside him, follow him down and down until he refused to follow him farther?

"No man can vanquish that demon," I whispered, trembling now but refusing to back down. "And now you are not an angel, but a man."

"I am not a man," Uzziel all but growled. I sneaked a peek

with my witch's sight and saw sparks of fury showering out from his head in a fiery nimbus. "I am an angel fallen, one who left Heaven in order to walk this earth. Your Raziel is a man. I am not a man."

I blinked hard in the face of his fury and shifted my attention to Raziel. "I am sorry, but I don't understand. Forgive me for being so stupid."

Raziel shook his head wearily at my words. "You are not stupid, just a mortal who does not know the ways of angels. I asked permission to return, Uzziel chose to fall of his own accord. I returned as a man, Uzziel remains an angel, one lost from Heaven. He has embraced the fire. Asmodel started like Uzziel, but fell further and further down, became more and more a slave to his own will. But we all started the same. Uzziel, Asmodel, me—brothers. Brothers who have traveled far away from each other, far from home."

Once again I regretted the fact that Raziel had descended for my sake. Much as I adored him, I would have spared him our current misery. But Raziel had made his own choices, the way his brothers had done, the way I had done, and I would not deprive Raziel of his choices, not even if I had been able to.

The carpets undulated under our feet, little wavelets that responded to the angry words spoken above them. "Peace," Uzziel said, sounding so much like Raziel that I couldn't help smile. The carpets settled, but the patterns moved around, faster and faster, as if they could only contain themselves by shifting.

"What is the magic of these carpets?" I asked. I felt like a child here, so ignorant of the ways of the Caucasus, the magic that rose up strangely from every tree and rock, that seemed to permeate the air.

"The people who weave them," Uzziel replied. "They are my children, and their magic comes from me, not their mothers. They weave holy sparks into the silk."

He watched the carpets and their beautiful, ever-changing patterns under our feet as if, like me, he were seeing them for the first time. "I don't think the gem should be released. Not after seeing what happened the last time it was known to the world."

"You are wrong, my brother," Raziel said. "The gem is coming back to the world, no matter how much you and I might seek to keep it hidden. Asmodel will make sure of it."

"Asmodel isn't stupid," Uzziel replied. "He knows how dangerous it is. He already wields so much power—why does he seek to risk losing all of it?"

"He is seduced by the power of the gem," Raziel said, his voice genuinely sad. "The lust for it is driving Asmodel crazy, just like he in turn has driven Hitler to take stupid risks, driven by lust and ambition."

"Hitler could banish him with a single word," Uzziel said.

"Of course, but he wants Asmodel's power to augment his own, the same way the ancient one wants the gem. To rule the world."

Uzziel laughed again, and the carpets pressed flat against the floor. "Asmodel's an idiot, then."

"No, just terrified of losing."

Together we watched the carpets' hypnotizing patterns in silence. "We are hunting the gem, whether you help us or not," Raziel said.

"We can stop you any time," Uzziel replied.

"Yes. We are strangers here, in your country."

Uzziel crossed his arms and sighed.

"None of us want war, not after what happened here during the Civil War and after, when the Soviets came. We have enough trouble resisting the anti-magic of the Institute."

"I know. But war is here, no matter what any of us want."

"I cannot make this decision for everyone. Come, let us talk to my daughters. They will tell me what to do. They are the ones who will pay the price for unleashing the gem. Let them decide it."

I marveled at the mention of daughters, the children of angels, my cousins, really. What price would these magic weavers have to pay? Before I could ask, Uzziel rose to his full height, much taller than I had first thought. He rose up like a Greek god, swung his arms as if he were getting ready to throw a discus. I looked again with my second sight and his light all but blinded me.

I turned away, let my true sight pull back. Sometimes illusions make the truth easier to take.

I expected us to climb into the mountains overnight, fighting Azerbaijani monsters, demons, and bears the entire way. But instead Uzziel took us on foot through the forest to the town of Quba once again. The stars sparkled overhead, like chips of broken glass against black velvet.

We walked through silent, deserted streets. Even the dogs had gone to sleep, or they were smart enough to stay out of

Uzziel's way. We came to a stop in front of a small wooden building exactly like the other ones on the block.

The lights shone from inside. I was afraid to cast my sight into that light, of what I would find. "Is this some kind of temple?" I asked, my voice small.

"No," Uzziel said, a laugh hidden in his voice. "Carpet factory. But the carpets they make . . . perhaps this is a temple, of sorts. I never thought about it that way before."

The door was unlocked and the threshold unwarded. Uzziel opened the door, and we three stepped out of the dark, damp night into a warm room that smelled of lemons. A samovar stood in the corner, polished to a high shine.

Before Uzziel could say anything else, a woman appeared in the back of the room. She was dressed all in black, like a witch or a widow. Her salt-and-pepper hair, pulled back into a bun, revealed a high forehead and a widow's peak. Her eyes, still fine, took in the sight of us with a single, sharp glance.

"Hello, Helena," Uzziel said. "I have brought you two strangers from the West."

Helena took a sudden sharp intake of breath, then she forced herself to exhale slowly and she smiled at us, a tight, tentative smile. "Welcome," she said in Azeri—Uzziel translated from the local tongue into the angelic one, which all of us could understand.

Raziel said nothing, and Uzziel looked at me, so I stepped forward and made an awkward little bow. "Thank you," I said in Hungarian, a catch in my voice. Uzziel, who understood me as the angels did, translated into Azeri for Helena. "We come from very far away."

"I know," she replied, her manner formal but polite. "Many

come to see this place, because there is nothing like it in the world. I take it you have come to see the carpets?"

I glanced at Uzziel, unsure how to reply. "She has come to meet you," Uzziel said, in angelic so that I, too, could understand. "This is Magdalena Lazarus, and Raziel, my brother. They have come in a desperate cause."

"Very well," she said, as if Uzziel had confirmed we only wanted to see the carpets. "Please step this way. I will show you the factory floor. Keep your voices low . . . the girls work very hard, and must maintain their concentration."

As we walked, Helena kept glancing over at me, and blinking hard. I wasn't sure if she knew what I was, or if any visitor would have caused such disquiet. I wanted to apologize for our unannounced midnight visit, but decided not to try.

We followed her through a maze of tight hallways, as if we walked a labyrinth. My heart started pounding, although no magic of any kind threatened us here.

The hallway opened up into a large room, one that looked larger than the entire building did from the outside. Over fifty girls hunched over clacking looms, filled with carpets of all sizes, from tiny doormats to enormous tapestries that stretched from floor to ceiling.

I could not suppress a gasp. Helena smiled, a fleeting smile filled with tension. "A sight, isn't it."

The only sound in the room came from the shuttlecocks sliding back and forth, knocking against the wooden frames as they shot underneath the silken threads. And the creak of the wood as they shifted the warp and woof to weave again.

A group of smaller girls, who looked no older than twelve, were gathered in a corner, holding frames in their laps. "These are the trainees," Helena said. "They are hooking rugs. When they are ready, we train them on the looms."

I looked at those half a dozen girls, and my blood ran cold. They could have been me or Gisele or Eva at that age. They sparkled, not with magic but with their innocence and youth. All of them were very serious, more serious than Eva for certain, pulling at woolen bits of carpet with hooks, trimming the finished rugs with scissors to thicken the pile.

"My God," I whispered. "They are so young."

"Yes," Helena said. "We teach them young. Before they forget."

These girls, innocent and tender, wove carpets of fire under their willing, nimble fingertips. I saw the fire rising up from the carpets they wove, saw the patterns dancing even trapped on the warp and woof of the carpet frames rising over our heads.

My heart pounded harder. They reminded me too much of Gisele, and the thought of her at twelve, the day my father died, suddenly rose up huge in my mind, blocking out everything I saw.

"Are they magicals?" I whispered.

"No, not the way you mean," Helena said. I tore my gaze away to look at the older woman, who looked more like a witch than did the famed witch of Amsterdam, Lucretia de Merode.

And yet, this Helena was not a witch, either. Before I could ask, Helena answered my questions. "You are a witch, yes? You work the spells, you change the fabric of the world with your words. We are carpet weavers, we bring together the threads. And the threads speak to one another. We make no spells here. We cannot."

Every word Helena spoke was true, and yet I could not reconcile what she said with the reality of what transpired in the factory.

And the hooked rugs. They all had faces on them, faces that moved, eyes that looked at us more openly than did the eyes of the girls who had woven them. The carpets, somehow, lived.

"Tikkun olam," I said.

Raziel drew closer and put his arm around me. "They do not repair the greater world, but weave little worlds out of wool and silk. You threw sparks in the second Heaven, these girls weave sparks into the thread."

Their collective magic was greater than mine. But they did not use it to fight armies, or to master primordial gems with infernal powers. Instead they wove worlds, quietly and without a fuss. And then they went home, swept up for their mamas, washed the laundry, and baked the bread.

A room full of Giseles. I couldn't say a word, but wished with all my heart I could have been more like them. And I knew my presence put their worlds in danger. The Institute, or the Gestapo for that matter, would tear apart their carpets for any reason or none.

"This factory is over four hundred years old," Uzziel said. "And the women run it for themselves, they take the girls who never marry and give them homes, and have dowries for the girls who do marry."

"Is this an orphanage?"

"Sometimes, when it needs to be."

I watched the weaving continue, and grew faint. Raziel held me tighter.

"The poor lady needs tea," Helena said, though her eyes looked knowingly at me. "Come, to the front room. Let us sit, I will bring some refreshment."

I sighed—the last thing I could conceive of doing was drinking more tea and having more walnut jam. But I had to let this room go . . . something about the sight of these girls, weaving their lives into the carpets, broke my heart.

Back we went through the labyrinth of hallways to the front room. The carpets here looked tame compared to the living works still being born in the back.

We sat down. The tea was brought, I made polite noises and drank it, though I didn't even taste it as I swallowed. Raziel did all the talking, I nodded at the appropriate moments, and together we negotiated for the Heaven Sapphire.

A terrible mistake, I wanted to say. But by now it was an inevitable mistake. The mistakes I had made all my life had brought me to this place. The only thing I could do now was make all of the mistakes come out right, somehow. Some way.

Perhaps I didn't have the magic to do that. I suspected that none of us did.

✳ 15 ✳

By the time we had finished our conference, the sun had risen high into the sky. Helena offered us breakfast, and I begged her no. Uzziel used the telephone in the corner, a sign of Helena's status and her connections in this town high in the mountains, and we left for a summit of angels at the Empress Café, on the Jewish side of town.

"What do you call the Jewish side of the town?" I asked Uzziel as we set off on foot through Quba to the bridge that spanned the river separating the two.

"They call it Red Town now," Uzziel said, his face growing dangerously dark and angry. "When the Soviets came, they murdered many people. Rabbis, village elders from the mountains, Tats, Urdeks, and Mountain Jews alike. They wanted to show us who was boss, that none of our many different deities could protect us from them. The river ran red in 1937."

I gasped, and the pictures I had once seen playing out in Ziyad's mind now projected themselves over my sight once again. So that was what had sent Ziyad abroad, in search of a superweapon that could stop the Soviets. The One Above wasn't enough.

"Why didn't you use the gem then?" I asked him.

Uzziel stared through me, and the morning sunlight made the dark highlights in his hair gleam copper. "You assume," he said.

I had to laugh—Raziel had said something almost the same to me, the day I'd met him. "I do," I replied. "And I'm wrong most of the time. But it's better than giving up."

"You never did give up, did you?"

I thought he was joking at first, but then I saw the tension in his face. "I have the choice to give up, I suppose. But I am young, and foolish, and I have my youth and my health to spur me forward. And I have my little sister, too. Even if I wanted to just give up and die for good, I couldn't just leave her to fend for herself."

Uzziel smiled again, but it was a reflex, and something much darker lurked in it. "In a way, giving you access to the gem is a form of giving up. Once the gem is unleashed, the world we knew is ended. A world we knew since time out of mind."

"But you heard Raziel. We don't really have a choice, not any longer. The war is coming here, faster than we can stop it."

Uzziel looked at Raziel. Raziel said, "She's right. You were able to hide the thing from Stalin, from the Institute even, but now Asmodel himself is coming. You won't be able to hide it from him. More's the pity."

Uzziel sighed with resignation. "My brothers are gathered at the Empress Café, next to the Kabalists Temple. You will convince them we have lost the secret, I am sure. You've managed to convince me, no matter how much I want to believe otherwise. You'll have the gem, witch. But you won't have it long."

The small crowd waiting for us at the Empress reminded me of the Hashomer in Kraków—ready to fight despite the knowledge they almost certainly fought in vain. The tea and cookies were piled high in the middle of the table, but none of us touched the feast. Helena prowled around the perimeter, pouncing on a teacup every so often.

Uzziel had explained to me that these men were the village elders of Quba. Men from the eleven synagogues on the Jewish side of town, but also elders from among the Muslim majority, the Mountain Tats, the animists, and the Zoroastrians. Djinn, Yazata. These were the people who had suffered the most when Stalinist rule had reached the Caucacus, the people who lived close to magic. And the people who would pay the price if we succeeded in our quest and found the gem. They had met to debate and discuss our presence in their town. And they wanted us to present our case.

Some of them were Jews, wearing Western suits and looking secular, others wearing Eastern caftans. Some of them were Yazata, with features of fire. Some of them were fierce mountain men of the Tats and the Urdeks, local tribes that worshiped the fire.

They were harder to convince than Uzziel, for they still clung to the illusion they somehow could beat their enemies without the gem. They wanted their secret to remain hidden in their mountains, where they had kept it quiescent and safe for centuries.

But secrets sometimes fester, hidden in the darkness. And the only cure for the sickness remains exposing the secret to the light. Nobody wanted to see the secret of the gem, revealed at last in plain sight. Raziel and I didn't, either. But we convinced them that everything else we'd tried—Book, spell, partisan bombs—had failed.

So the men gave in to us. But it was no victory that Raziel and I celebrated when we prevailed. Instead, we sat together in silence around the table, our hearts heavy.

Uzziel broke the silence by standing up. "I will take them. And if they survive it, they will come back to us. And we will at least fight together."

"You don't have to fight," I said. "Take care of your own. We will join the armies of the West and do what we can, far away from here."

"It doesn't work that way with us," Uzziel said, his voice as gentle as when we had spoken in private. "Once we make alliance, we fight together. Here, everywhere. To the death, and beyond in the afterworld. It has to be that way."

"Why?"

"Because, here in the Caucasus, your family is who you have. Betrayals everywhere—before the Soviets, it was the czar, and the czar's secret police, and the Turks, too. People lie, they lie. Out of fear. Raziel is my brother. That matters more than anything."

He motioned for Raziel and me to follow him out of the café. We thanked the men gathered around the table, then followed Uzziel down the long, curving staircase to the street. He looked both ways, then motioned for us to follow him into the temple next door.

Morning services had ended, but a collection of slippers, work boots, and dress shoes still waited by the front door for their owners. The floor was covered in carpets, the magical kind, swirling and shimmering under our feet.

"Wait here," Uzziel said. "I want to tell the rabbi. We are going to Xinaliq."

At the word, a chill went through me like an arrow. I didn't know what Xinaliq was, but the word filled me with a strange longing and foreboding, all mixed together. Like it was a place out of my dreams. Or my nightmares.

Uzziel returned a minute later. "We don't have time for you to meet the rabbi now, and besides, it isn't safe for him to know you. He's not family, you see. But he sends you with his blessings."

It was only then that I noticed the carpet, tightly rolled up and tucked under Uzziel's left arm. Raziel stepped forward to help him with it, an awkward and heavy burden to carry.

"Helena wove this one herself," Uzziel said, and headed out the front door to the dusty street outside the synagogue. He unrolled the enormous carpet and set it down, right on the cobblestones.

"Have a seat," he said. "And hold on."

✳ 16 ✳

The carpet swooped up from the street into the sky, over the Red Town and past the birch forest. After a first panicky glance, I decided not to look down, instead to stare at the carpet itself and hold on as hard as I could. The wind whistled in my ears, and after I realized I wasn't about to fall to my doom I stole a peek beyond the thick white fringes woven like a mane into the edges of my flying steed.

The rocky hillsides rose up all around us, the sheep below roaming the crags, looking like tufts of dirty cotton. Uzziel and Raziel spoke together too quietly for me to hear, their heads together. And I wondered at our ability to fly like angels with the help of a strange, wondrous magic.

We landed soft as thistledown on a craggy mountainside,

in the middle of a tiny village. The clouds gathered menacingly below our feet.

"Welcome to Xinaliq," Uzziel said, a little out of breath.
"This is where the Mountain Jews live. You will find silver
chalices from the Temple, bits of breastplates . . ." He trailed
off with a sigh.

I looked around. A dozen stone huts clustered on the edge
of a mountain pass. They looked like they had grown up from
the rock, instead of having been constructed by human hands.
A goat wandered aimlessly among the huts, nosing at the dust,
looking for something to eat.

The hut at the farthest edge of the cluster looked the most
deserted. It was the only hut with a red door. Uzziel said
something, but I didn't hear him. I stared at that door, stared
and stared.

Uzziel laughed and touched my shoulder, and I came back
to myself with a hard snap. "You don't need my help," he said.
"Good luck. I'm going back down to the Red Town. If you
manage to survive the next few minutes, I will be in the valley
with my brothers. And if not . . . it is better if I stay far away
from here, for any number of reasons."

Raziel and Uzziel looked at each other for a long moment,
the only sound the wind whistling through the sparse trees
below us that clung to the mountainside. Raziel opened his
arms, and the two men embraced.

I looked back to the front door of the hut at the edge of the
village. There was a spot on the red door. It hummed with
magic, throbbed with it.

I tore my gaze away to return to my companions. Uzziel

was gone; he had flown without saying good-bye, and taken our only carpet away. "You were studying the door," Raziel said with a slow smile.

"We're crazy for doing this, aren't we? And how are we getting out of this place, if we do manage to find the gem up here?"

He only shrugged, and that sad, sweet smile only grew wider.

I sighed and walked down the stony little path that wound among the stone huts, toward the hut with the red door. A couple of chickens ran crazily in my path, underfoot then away with a cacophony of furious cackles.

I paused to look around the village. Woodsmoke lazily curled up from the largest hut, nearest the entrance to the town of Xinaliq. Otherwise, except for the insane chickens I could detect no signs of life, the goat having wandered off a while ago.

"Where is everybody?" I asked.

"To be honest, I think they are hiding. Despite the properties of those carpets, I don't think people fly around on them as a matter of course. Just like in Budapest, most of these folk are regular mortals who only fear magic, of any kind."

"That's why there is an amulet on that door." I pointed at the red door, and only realized how badly I was trembling when I saw my fingers.

"It's not an amulet, not exactly."

By now we had reached the lonely hut at the edge of the village. We stood in front of the red door, red like a gaping maw, red like raw meat.

A hand hung upside down in the middle of the door, at my eye level. At first I thought it was a real human hand, but after

I blinked hard I saw that it was bejeweled, with mother-of-pearl fingernails and red jasper for palm lines.

"The five fingers of God," I whispered.

"Yes, the *hamsa*. A mark of the Lord's protection, for both the Jews and the Muslims here. It is ancient, my love . . . this looks very like a Temple *hamsa*. But I imagine it has been put here only recently."

"We cannot pass."

I stood before the door, holding Raziel's hand now, and I wanted nothing more than to curl up in the dirt of the road and hide from that mark of the Lord. Those five fingers struck down Pharaoh, they smote the Amalekites. They smote the Hebrews, too, when they got too far out of line.

"You can pass."

"Not for what I intend to do."

Raziel's hand squeezed mine. "Trust me. You can pass."

But I didn't know the words. I didn't have the spells, the magic trick, the Hebrew words. I just stood in the dust before the threshold, humbled and, I will admit it, ashamed.

I bowed my head and racked my brain. How could I force my way in, trick my way in? I could hurl witchfire at the door, but I knew just by looking that it would hold. And that hand would hurl the fire right back at me.

I almost considered walking away, giving up. But we had come so far. This terrifying gemstone was our last hope. Gisele waited for me in London, Eva risked her life in Budapest, and Churchill marshaled his human armies. But if Hitler reached the oil fields, and this gem, none of their sacrifices would matter.

I took a single step forward, slipped my fingers out of Raziel's grasp.

"I am Magdalena Lazarus. May we please enter?"

The *hamsa* never spoke. No cosmic flashes emanated from its palm. But silently, on well-oiled hinges, the big red door swung open.

And Raziel and I stepped over the threshold, into the darkness inside.

✳ 17 ✳

As soon as we passed by the *hamsa* guarding the front door, I knew for sure.

The gem was hidden here. Lord only knew why the ancient jewel of Raziel lay dormant in a stone hut instead of in the center of a king's diadem.

It was not in the world. It was here.

The hut was nearly dark; rugs covered the floors and the walls, and hung over the windows like flaps. The sunlight streamed in from behind Raziel and me in the doorway, illuminating the path into the room, a walkway of golden light.

The carpets in the stone hut had magic; I saw the figures woven into them, moving, swaying, dancing as I stepped forward. I cringed as my footfalls passed over those woven faces, but they did not seem to mind.

But the gem . . .

I sensed its presence in the room immediately. And it sensed mine. The gem knew as well as I did when I arrived.

It did not call to me the way *The Book of Raziel* had in a burnt-down warehouse in Amsterdam. But it watched me, it took my measure.

How did I know this? Have you ever met someone you knew was going to change your life, the first moment you met them? You know such a thing in the pit of your stomach, at the base of your throat, in the secret recesses of your madly beating heart. And you know it in an instant.

I knew in an instant.

A little girl sat on a lumpy-looking bed shoved into the corner. She stared at me with wide, unblinking amber eyes. It took me a moment to realize that she was blind.

Raziel moved past me to kneel by the bed. He murmured in Hebrew for a few moments, words that I could not understand but that contained gentle warmth.

He was comforting that girl, the way he had consoled me, countless times throughout my life, whether I could hear him or not.

But I went into trance now, captured by the power of Raziel's gem. The Gem of Raziel had instantly, almost casually, overpowered me, a little fly paralyzed by the spider's venom.

I sank to my knees in the far corner of the drafty stone hut. A wooden cigar box rested on the floor. The carpet under it was bleached white.

I watched my fingers stretch toward the box, watched as they pulled up the hinged top.

Leyla's face stared up at me, painted on the inside of the lid, as expressive and lovely as her ghost had been, the paint shot through with sparks of gold.

And below it, inside the box wrapped in a bleached bit of cheesecloth, rested the primordial Gem of Raziel. The Heaven Sapphire. The *tzofar,* bearer of the light of creation.

I gasped when my fingers touched the thing, unwrapped it. Chills, hot and cold, shot through my body like an electrical shock. I could not stop shaking.

"No," I whispered, but my word of power meant nothing here, in the presence of this thing.

It regarded me like a disembodied, star-shaped eye. It took my measure, it decided to make use of me.

In a mere instant, in time out of time . . .

Raziel slipped his fingers over mine—when had he come to my side? "Easy, Magduska," he said, his voice as gentle as when he'd spoken to the blind child on the bed.

"Close your eyes, before it's too late," he murmured in my ear, as soft as a guardian angel whispering blessings from beyond.

It was supposed to be too late for me to obey him. The stone had already taken possession of me. But somehow I managed to heed Raziel—only he, in all the world, could have interrupted the gem's spell.

My eyes fluttered closed, as if I had fallen asleep. And a tidal wave of images roared through my mind: golden columns, crashing flames, men in jeweled breastplates, wailing women.

The visions reminded me of Gisele, and like that she arose in my mind's eye, clear as life. I saw her awakening in an airy bower, the light streaming in through the high-paned windows.

She was still at Chartwell, sleepy and safe. My beloved little mouse . . .

Raziel smoothed away the tears streaming down my cheeks. "Never look into the gem again," he said, his voice low and calm. "You will never return from a second look, Magduska."

His words brought me back to my senses, and I gulped for air, my eyes still squeezed closed. Suddenly I sensed the cold drafts in the room, the scratchy wool rug under my knees, Raziel's strong arms wrapped around my shoulders.

"This was your great gift? My craft and creed, Raziel, the thing is death."

"I know."

That startled my eyes open, and I turned to look at him, my beloved. Raziel I could look at forever.

"How could death be any kind of gift, any consolation to man for losing his way?"

He smiled then, his eyes wise and sad. "The world is a consolation for the gem, rather than the other way around."

I sort of understood what he meant—the gem was a hole in the world. Daily life, even with its terrors and disappointments, is a welcome alternative to an eternal gaze into the gem.

"It is a microcosm of the Lord's plan," Raziel continued. "The ordinary world does not much survive encounters with the gem."

"But how could I possibly ever use such a thing? It knows what it knows, it wants what it wants. It is an eye, a staring eye. . . ."

I trailed off, caressed the smooth, cool edges of the brilliant blue gem with my fingertips.

"You sense its power," Raziel said. "The Lazarus witches kept it safe. Their power lay in resisting the gem. Do you yet understand?"

My mind flashed on the word "no," the engine that powered the manifestation of my magic, from the time it had first come forth at the age of nine. "You mean, the Lazarus power is based in restraint?"

"Ultimately, yes. You have been given certain gifts, you and your sisters—to summon, to see. But do you understand how your power is subordinate to this gem?"

"No," I replied, honestly more confused than I had ever been before in my short, confusing life.

"Your 'no,' Magda, your ability to withstand the power of the gem—that is the bedrock of the Lazarus magic. Over generations, your mothers have taken the task of guarding the world from this gem."

"You mean, all of my power is meant for nothing more than keeping this ancient stone hidden away?"

Raziel could hear how little I liked that idea. He sat back and tried not to smile. "All my power was meant to do the same. Once, the Gem of Raziel served as a focus for the world, a fulcrum upon which the world balanced. But the world can no longer contain this gem. Too many seek the power of it for themselves, and the world itself could shatter."

My head hurt, trying to make sense of all this. "But sweetheart . . . you came all the way here, with me, to seek your gem. This dangerous, world-destroying, useless thing."

He sighed. "It hasn't been my gem for thousands of years."

"Well, yes. But I came to make use of this gem, to stop the war and save Gisele's life."

"I know. But the best use of it is no use. It was going to be uncovered shortly one way or another, by Hitler or by Stalin. I preferred it come to you instead."

My mind reeled with the news. "But how can I fight my enemies with this thing? If I even look at it I am lost!"

Raziel said nothing, just smiled. And allowed me to absorb the implications of what he didn't say.

"So if Asmodel looks into this gem it's all over?"

Raziel shrugged again.

I stole a glance at the girl in the corner, still looking into the middle distance, listening to our voices. "She looked into it, didn't she?"

Raziel sighed. "Yes. She was just a baby. Her mother was too careless. But now she sees . . . other things."

I thought of the high priests I had seen in my visions, my Gisele, and I said nothing of them.

Instead I blundered ahead, knowing it was stupid to keep insisting on answers when neither Raziel nor anybody else had any to give me. But stubbornness was all I had, and it had kept me and my girls alive this far. "It is madness for me to think I could control this gem in any way. Or even keep it hidden."

"It is," Raziel agreed. "Forget mastering the *tzofar*. All you need to do is not look upon it. Use your 'no.' You are strong enough to withstand the rest."

I covered the smooth gorgeousness of the Heaven Sapphire with the cheesecloth. Closed the cigar case with a soft, final-sounding snap.

After so much effort, so many battles, so much blood and death, I had finally succeeded in my quest. I had found and claimed the fabled Heaven Sapphire.

It was the worst thing that had ever happened to me. There wasn't a thing I could do to use it. Any attempt would prove fatal—or worse.

I had never felt more grateful for my fallen husband, who had left Heaven behind to help me somehow bear the burden of this gem. Raziel was the only one standing between me and the road to Hell through the eye of the sapphire.

"Does it speak?" I asked.

Raziel shrugged yet again, not even a whisper of a smile on his face this time. "Raziel" means "Secrets of God," and well is my soul mate named. Raziel, too, had his 'no,' and he, too, wielded his silence like a profound magic. There was more magic in what he didn't say than there was in all the Caucasus surrounding us.

And in that moment I finally understood why my beloved husband faithfully kept those holy secrets. Because once they got loose, the truths hidden in Raziel's silence would tear the world apart.

The girl in the corner sang into the silence, wordless little nonsense that set my skin to crawling. The chills attacked me again with a vengeance.

I closed my eyes again, this time to shut out the sound of the little girl as best I could. "Ugh, terrible. That song is poisonous. Like absinthe for breakfast."

Raziel laughed then. "Don't tell me how you know that."

His voice, utterly calm and ordinary, banished my fear and set the world to rights once again. "I sometimes think you are the antidote to this magic's poison."

"There is no antidote."

This time I laughed, and struggled to my feet, the cigar box balanced in my hands. The gem was the size of a croissant. It seemed to weigh as much as a Mercedes.

"This isn't a sapphire."

"It's not only a sapphire. Here, give it to me."

I gratefully handed the thing over, and enjoyed watching the muscles in Raziel's arms bulging as he took on the weight of the gem.

"So what do we do with this thing? Throw it in the Caspian Sea?"

"No, that wouldn't work. Noah himself tried that, not all that far from here. And here it is . . . My own brother Gabriel fished it out and saved it. He was afraid of Leviathan getting it, I have my own worries."

Asmodel. Raziel didn't have to say it—for once I understood exactly what he meant.

"I thought finding the gem would prove my greatest triumph," I said under my breath. But instead of triumph or even relief, a cold gray dread sank into me like a winter's soaking rain.

The best I could do with this terrible relic of ancient history was keep it inert if I could. But the Heaven Sapphire was alive. It had a mind, and had lived in solitary obscurity for thousands of years.

It was hungry. Very, very hungry, for life.

✳ 18 ✳

"What if we just hid the gem again?" I said, knowing even as I uttered the words that the time for hidden obscurity for the Heaven Sapphire was finished, forever.

Just then I heard the screeching of tires outside. The little girl screamed.

I almost jumped out of my skin.

"No," Raziel said, his voice still calm, even as he leaped into action. He ran for the window at the back of the hut facing away from the path leading to the front door.

I heard a car door slam, the sound almost masked by the poor little girl's shrieks. Raziel perched on the window ledge, cradling the cigar box in the crook of his arm.

"Quickly, Magduska!"

We both guessed who our sudden visitors were: members

of the secret police from the dreaded Institute. It was impossible to pass through Quba unnoticed, and we hadn't even tried. But I was surprised they had traced our flight into the mountains so quickly.

Raziel slipped his legs through the window and dangled over the ledge, balancing the cigar box on the sill. I whipped the carpet/curtain in front of us to hide us, slipped over the ledge, too . . .

And found that our feet dangled over a sheer cliff that stretched far, far below us, into the mists and out of sight. The fall could be a few meters or hundreds. We could not tell by sight.

"Magda," Raziel whispered. "Climb down my body and feel for a rock shelf. We have only a few moments."

The hut's walls vibrated with the bang of the front door as somebody slammed it open. Loud voices inside yelled something in Russian, even as the girl kept screaming.

I shimmied down the back of Raziel's body, swinging and feeling frantically with my toes for any place we could hide. It was nearly sheer, going straight down.

"No ledge," I whispered back up, my cheek resting against the small of Raziel's back. I transferred my weight off of Raziel and onto the base of the stone hut instead. My feet balanced on a little spur of rock sticking out from the edge of the cliff.

Raziel climbed down one-handed, hanging on to the cigar box with his right hand. His whole body trembled with the effort of holding on to the rocky cliffside, and I was sure he was going to fall to his death.

The voices of the men, both speaking Russian, got louder and louder. The girl's screams abruptly were cut off.

Raziel and I looked into each other's eyes, willing ourselves silent, and stuck to the ledge. The stone spur beneath my feet began to crumble, and I started sliding down.

"Oh no," I whispered. It was an absurd thing to say, but nothing more brilliant came to mind.

My magic was useless here. I can bind souls, remove them from bodies, repel them. I can throw witchfire summoned up out of my life force, and I can work certain curses and spells. But a cliffside has no soul, and I could not summon my own body out of the sky.

And Raziel had no magic of his own. He started slipping, too.

A terrible vision flashed in my mind, placed there by the gem or not I do not know. Raziel and I, dead at the bottom of the ridge, the men in the stone hut taking the gem away, me wanting to return from the dead but trapped, trapped, instead hovering over my abandoned bones for the rest of time, and the battle raged on forever.

New power surged into my quivering muscles, and I held on tenaciously, refusing to fall. I whispered strength into Raziel's arms—I could do that much at least—and we clung there, shaking and grunting with the effort, as the men inside the hut slammed their way out again, back into their auto.

I saw the beetle black vehicle, a big gangster car, shoot past the stone hut and back down the side of the pass.

"Up," Raziel gasped, and with a terrible effort we pulled ourselves up, up . . . and back onto solid ground.

We lay there, lungs heaving, for too long. "We've got to chase them," Raziel said between gasps.

My mind wavered over his words. "Shouldn't we just let them go away?"

"They are going back down the mountain to Quba, and the Red Town."

In a flash I understood. "They are going back to the people in town."

"Yes. To punish the magical folk for cheating them yet again, while we got safely away."

I lurched to a sitting position. My arms still twitched and ached. "How will we ever get there in time? To warn them, at least?"

I looked at the cigar box, still balanced in Raziel's hands. And could feel the intensity of the gem's stare from inside.

Even through the opaque wood, the thing was watching me, gauging my thinking, my thoughts.

"We'll have to bring the sapphire with us."

"Yes. It's safer with you than anyone else in the world, Magda."

He was wrong. The gem was safest with Raziel, its giver. Long ago, he had mastered the gem enough to bequeath it to a mortal woman.

"I don't have magic," he said, reading my expression and responding to my fears. "Solomon had no magic, either," he continued, "and look what happened to him."

I gulped. The great king, he of the thousand wives and Holy Temple, the blessings of the Almighty Himself. Solomon had held this very stone in his hands. And even he, with the gem to command and the best of intentions, had faltered and succumbed to its power, overwhelmed by Asmodel. And the Temple had crumbled into dust.

What had I done, unearthing this thing? "We have to warn our friends in Quba about these agents from Baku, from the Institute. Maybe the gem could stop them some way."

Raziel's smile was bleak. "Maybe. But that's how a lot of trouble started, a long time ago."

✳ *19* ✳

Raziel and I stood on the pinnacle of a mountain pass, far above the valley where Quba and the Red Town straddled the river.

How could we possibly make it down the mountain in time? Could we fly somehow? Raziel and I found the answer in the same moment.

"Magic carpets," Raziel said. "The only way."

Madness. Uzziel had taken Helena's flying carpet back to Quba. We were carpetless. I would not have known the way on foot, did not know how to drive a carpet in any case. And what if its magic flagged for even an instant? We would be dumped into the cliffs far below.

We had only a moment to decide. Raziel nodded at me— he was ready to take the risk, and only waited for me.

"But aren't flying carpets different from your ordinary magic carpet?" I asked.

Raziel shrugged. "I don't know. But I'll bet that you can figure it out." Perhaps, but we had no time to lose.

I wondered how fast an auto could make it down the pass. And then I forced my mind away from the thought, and instead turned my thoughts to the task of mastering a strange new magic.

Raziel and I looked around inside the hut, then dragged a nice, big carpet outside to the street. I paused to consider the blind girl, now sleeping peacefully in her bed.

"She's much safer here alone than with us," Raziel said.

I swallowed hard. He was right. If our plan succeeded, we were heading straight into mortal danger.

I looked at the dusty old thing lying inert on the path and I sighed. "I cannot move inanimate objects with my magic," I said, tamping down my rising frustration as best I could.

"Uzziel has no spellcraft. Think, Magda. Quickly!"

I racked my brain for some spell, some trick that would liberate us from the ground. I sat in the center of the carpet, cross-legged, hoping that the physical contact could give me purchase for a spell.

"How did your brother do it?"

Raziel sat down next to me. "I don't have any idea." He cradled the cigar box in his hands.

I replayed our journey up the mountain in my mind. Uzziel worked no spell, I was sure of it.

A tail feather from the lone rooster we'd seen before fluttered past in the unceasing mountain breeze. I snatched it and held it furled in my left fist. And had my inspiration.

"Helena, home, the women's factory of Quba," I sang.

The carpet knew its origin. It knew its true home. And, like in a dream, it gravitated to its beginning.

The carpet shot into the air, almost tossing me off right away. "Raziel . . . ," I said, sounding for once like the scared girl I actually was, not the fell witch of Budapest.

"Never mind. Hold on!"

And I could no longer say a word, we flew so fast and hard, the hills and twiggy trees whipping quickly past us.

I crouched over the carpet, entangled my fingers in the thick fringe woven along the front. The wool carpet under me whipped like a flag in gale.

There was no way I was going to manage to hold on. . . .

No sooner had I had that thought than the carpet banked sharply to the right and shot through a mountain pass. I couldn't hold back a little shriek, a gobbled-up scream that never quite made it out of my throat.

The carpet righted itself again, and I lowered my head to shield my face from the wind, and to take a gulp of air.

When I looked up again at Raziel, I could not believe my eyes.

He was laughing. Not at me, not at the way I awkwardly clung to the carpet edges for dear life, but for joy. For the first time since Raziel had surrendered his wings, he was totally free.

The thought stung. My love wasn't enough to give my beloved such untrammeled, uncomplicated joy. Because the shadow of fear hung over both of us, trapped in the ordeal of the war.

I realized that Raziel would die happy if he lost his seating and plunged to his death on the rocks below us.

He glanced at me then, and if anything his fierce joy flared up even higher. "I love you!" he yelled, his face glowing as brightly as on the day I first met him, when he was a celestial agent of vengeance, unfurling his wings on a train platform in Vienna.

I could not even whisper in reply, I could not bear to break the spell of his joy and freedom. All I could manage was a smile. Death stalked us, close as our own shadows. Yet Raziel, heedless of death itself, made every moment so immeasurably precious.

The hills and spindly trees soon gave way to the valley, town, and river below. The carpet glided to the street and landed at the front door of the women's carpet factory, on an utterly ordinary street in the shabby part of Quba.

I rose to my feet and standing on the carpet, trembling, I looked again at Raziel. He stood at his full height, and again flashed me that fearless, defiant smile.

And right in the street, in the midst of our danger, I, too, for a moment was free of our pursuers, had eyes only for my husband.

His brothers, the Yazata, only saw Raziel's missing wings when they looked at him. But when I looked at him, tousled and exhilarated from our wild ride down the mountain, I saw what he had gained, becoming a man.

Courage, will, action.

Passion.

His very mortality was a gift to Raziel, gave him something

dangerous, precious. He could die. Would die. And he was ready to die, in service to something greater.

"Told you we'd make it," he said.

"Right again," I whispered. "But how do we know the men from the Institute aren't already inside, with the girls in this factory?"

Raziel didn't answer that, and with a start I understood why. Those solemn, silent, humble girls in that factory would never betray us, no matter what was happening inside. They were the ones betrayed.

Those weavers invested their strength in silence. None of them were inclined to talk, most of them didn't speak Russian at all, and the secret police wouldn't bother with these "insignificant" girls.

My heart turned to stone when I finally realized where my thoughts led. "We've come to the wrong place," I whispered. "Don't you see? The girls aren't in any immediate danger. We don't need to warn them. It's the men, the fellows at the café, the ones who trusted us—they are the ones of interest to the Institute."

Raziel whirled around, but the dusty street was deserted. When he looked back at me, his eyes were wild, and the freedom in them was gone. "Too late, then."

"Not too late to try."

My sense of geography wasn't all that good, so I closed my eyes to cast. When I cast, I looked for souls, with my witch's sight.

And I found them, quickly, too—the men who spent their afternoons drinking apple tea at the Empress Café.

Now outnumbered by the thugs from the Institute.

With my eyes still closed, I pointed in their direction like a compass needle. When I opened my eyes to look, I saw that I was pointing over the bridge to the Jewish side of town.

"Café this way," I said. And I broke into a run.

Raziel overtook me, even with the unnaturally heavy gem inside the cigar box, still tucked inside his left elbow like a parcel. I chased him, my thoughts moving faster than my feet.

What did those agents want? Raziel and I for certain, but they wanted the gem more. Worlds more.

I stopped running. "Raziel," I said, my shoulders knotting with the tension. "You've got to get away. This whole thing's a trap. Take the gem to Churchill."

Raziel stopped, too, out of breath. He looked again to make sure we stood alone on the street. The river moved sluggishly under our feet—we stood together in the middle of the footbridge.

"You go, Magda. Take the gem—you have the magic, can guard it. You were made for it."

I smiled at him. The world around us seemed to stop, too, poised on this moment. "No, there's got to be more of a point to me than that. You are strong, and better yet, nobody is looking for you. I am the witch of Budapest. That's Somebody. You will make it to England, maybe with your brothers' help, and Churchill will remember you well."

He chewed on the inside of his cheek, considering my words. And then he nodded, making up his mind just like that. "If you were as wicked and weak as you think, I would never leave you behind, Magduska. But you are stronger than me. Go, stop the secret police if you can. Distract them. And I will get away to England."

He nodded once more, lifted his hat to me as if we were mere acquaintances meeting by chance, and then he sauntered away, cigar box tucked under his arm like an actual box of cigars and not the doomsday weapon and fabled gem the Heaven Sapphire.

I watched him go, but only for a minute. When I was sure Raziel was safely away, I turned to face the Jewish side of the city, cast again to see the men we knew surrounded, and broke into a run.

I would stop the Institute. I believed my magic itself would be enough.

But I didn't know about the horrifying weapons they wielded. Had no way to know. Against them, alas, my magic was about to meet its match.

I ran up the stairs to the Empress as quietly as I could, on my toes so my heels wouldn't bang against the metal steps.

I drew close to the half-open door that led to the terrace, and held my breath.

The men who had met us so recently now stood with their hands up, a small stack of knives on the big, round table where Helena had served us tea and cookies.

The Soviet agents from the Institute pointed guns at their faces. But the men were calm.

Poor Helena, however, clutched at her temples and screamed.

A small, toadlike man with round spectacles pushed her against a huge, greasy-looking metal contraption set up against the far wall.

I looked again at the metal thing, shaped rather like an enormous samovar, but studded with gears and oil-stained fabric belts. This was another hunk of metal, like the one I had seen melted by the gates to the temple of fire. Eva had told me once about these contraptions, but I had never seen a functional one up close. It was hideous.

My stomach turned with absolute revulsion. From what Eva had told me, from what Leyla had died to stop, I surmised that this thing was a soul-sucking machine. Not too elegant or precise a way to describe its function, but that was in fact its purpose.

It was designed to grind up and kill magic.

I rolled a ball of witchfire in my hands, until it was an electric blue ball of energy, and I hurled it.

And, oh, the shock to my throwing arm. As if the contraption was electrified and it electrocuted me from across the room.

Nausea overwhelmed me and I lost my balance, I staggered out of the stairwell, and shook my head to get the buzzing out of my ears.

Even lifting my arms cost me a terrible effort. I tried to recite the Bane of Concubines, but the invocation died in my throat.

It occurred to me through a haze of pain that Helena was screaming because she, too, was in terrible suffering. Not only witches felt the agony of this infernal machine.

And suddenly, too late, I understood.

This was the Soviet technology the Nazis had used to enslave *The Book of Raziel*. Anti-magic, my mother's ghost had called it.

I didn't know how this machine was able to generate the anti-magic. But I did know it acted against anything, anyone, magical within its range of power—about ten meters or so, I guessed. A machine like this could control only a large room. But how many such machines did the Soviets possess?

Helena fainted, her screams mercifully ceased. The bespectacled little man who had pinned her to the thing let her body drop to the floor with a thunk.

He turned to face me, and began to laugh. It was a sound as horrible and skin crawling as the Nazi wizard Staff's laugh, long ago on a train platform in Vienna.

"Ah, the famed witch Magdalena Lazarus," he said in very bad German. "Welcome to the jurisdiction of the Soviet Union. Where magic is strictly against the law."

I slashed my witchfire against him, and blood spurted in a straight line on his cheek, like from a dueling wound. But that was the most I could do.

The man spat Russian curses and slapped a filthy-looking gray handkerchief to his face to stanch the bleeding.

The room turned brown and gray, as if I had been banished to the flat world of newspapers and newsreels. I fell to my knees, then onto my hands. From very, very far away I heard voices.

And that was the last I heard. I had run headlong into a trap. As I fell forward and slipped away, my last thought was of Raziel.

"Away," I tried to whisper.

But I was already gone. Not to the astral plane, not to the second Heaven, not even to Gehenna.

But to nothing.

✳ 20 ✳

I awoke, to my surprise, in a bed. It was a metal cot, and it was locked inside a metal cage, but it was the honeymoon suite at the Gellért Hotel in Budapest compared to the cell where I recently had been imprisoned by the Nazi regime in Poland.

I guessed that I was inside the Institute itself, in its Baku Division at the polytechnic. Prisoner, test subject, I did not know. But I suspected that these distinctions would prove un-important in the end.

I lay there, stretched out over the gray wool blanket, not able to do much more than breathe and worry.

Breathe: I was grateful to be alive after the terrible scene at the Empress. It had been a long time since my magic had proven so utterly insufficient to the task of fighting my enemies. The

man with the spectacles could have chopped off my head and I
could not have lifted a finger to stop him.

Worry: My last-minute idea to send Raziel away had, in
retrospect, turned out to be a brilliant one. But though Raziel
had no spellcasting magic, and as far as I knew was impervious to the anti-magic contraptions of the USSR, I feared that
alone, without sure allies, he would not be able to get out of
the country and to the West. A great deal of hostile territory
stood between us and Albion, both angel and nation.

But I could do nothing about these worries. And the worrying itself exhausted me beyond all measure. So I surrendered, and breathed. And considered.

Ziyad sought the superweapon, ostensibly to free his people.
Or so he had told Bathory on that long-ago evening at the
Café Istanbul on a Tuesday in July 1939.

But I had made a bad mistake, assuming the truth of what
Ziyad had said. At the time he had come in supplication to
Bathory, I could tell he told the truth. But a gigantic war had
erupted since then, and now the Soviets had allied themselves
with the hated Nazis, had carved up Poland between them.
Hitler and Stalin had made a pact of alliance, both of them
buying time until one would inevitably betray the other.

And with this alliance in place, Asmodel could seek the
Gem of Raziel with full Soviet cooperation. Both Asmodel
and the Institute worked to destroy any magical resistance.

And that meant Ziyad and his people, those solemn girls in
the carpet factory, were doomed. My magic was useless in this
prison, and if Asmodel managed to get his hands on the gem
now . . .

I could not bear to think of it. My thoughts turned from Ziyad and the innocent girls in the factory to my captors. What would the Soviets want out of me? They had neutralized my magic without much fanfare. I wasn't sure if the "super-weapon" Ziyad sought—the Heaven Sapphire itself—was a priority for the regime. Their plan was to neutralize magic, not to exploit it. . . .

But then I understood, and a chill flash-froze my blood. Of course. The Soviets were known for their fetish for science bent to ideological ends. They wanted magic reduced to only another kind of science so they could control it, destroy it. They first founded the Institute for Brain Research in Lenin-grad to dissect and crush the magic native to Mother Russia. Dissidents and magicals disappeared into the Institute, only to re-emerge, if ever, as imbeciles, their brains robbed of function. I had heard whispered tales among the vampires, even back in Budapest before the war.

Someone like me, born with magic of the blood, was no threat to the Soviet state, not with the anti-magic. But I was a worthy subject for study. And the Baku branch of the Institute clearly sought to outdo the central agency in Leningrad.

My heart thudded painfully as I imagined the kind of experiments they must have conducted in order to invent such a cruel machine as I had encountered at the Empress. How many witches, adepts, and magical creatures had been imprisoned and murdered by the Institute in the name of research, to provide the scientific development for that foul contraption?

I was an unusual case, I knew. I was born with my magic the same as any magical creature. And like the adepts I could hone my magic with lore, creed, and spell. I was the living embodiment of both kinds of magic, a rare specimen indeed.

The scientists here would dissect me, digging through my flesh and brain to expose the secret of my magic.

Unlike the Nazis in Kraków, these captors didn't seek the hidden knowledge I possessed, knowledge that could affect the progress of the war. No, these Soviets were scientists. What these men were after was the secret of me.

The door to my cage swung open, but I could not even so much as open my eyes to look at my jailer. That is how powerful the anti-magic of the Institute had proven.

Light, probing fingers slid up and down my body, and I could not shrug away, demand they stop, scream, nothing. I was paralyzed.

The two hands paused over my breasts. I was disgusted, and my anger was as good as a shot of whiskey for steadying my nerves.

After what seemed like an eternity, the fingers slid off me. I heard the snap of a cigarette lighter, then smelled the thick, rich smoke of a cigarillo or pipe.

A man said something in Russian, and a contralto female voice translated into the German:

"Welcome to the Institute for Brain Research, Baku Division, Azerbaijan Industrial Institute."

I said nothing. I could not have, even had I wanted to.

"My name is Professor Pyotr Raskonikoff."

The woman rolled and hocked the German like she had a small creature stuck in her chest. Apparently this professor was quite the distinguished fellow, given the embellishments the translator made upon his name.

"You will provide a gigantic contribution to the progression of the Soviet peoples," he continued, waiting for the female translator to finish before he spoke again.

"First you must sleep, and the device's frequency will be turned down. Especially for your benefit, Miss Lazarus! And then we will have a little talk."

The tobacco smoke tickled my nose, but I could not even sneeze. I heard footsteps, then the squeaky door to the cage closing and locking once more.

"First you will sleep. We will assist you."

A terrible screeching sound arose inside my brain, then . . . Nothing.

Once again, they had shut me down. And the world.

The next time I awoke more gradually, with less pain. I guessed that they turned down the power level of the machine and I had slipped into an exhausted but near-normal sleep.

This time I could move. I sat up, and straightaway threw up into a trash can conveniently left next to my cot. After heaving for a while (my stomach was painfully empty even before getting sick) I managed to sit up on the cot and take stock of my surroundings.

Grim. Everything gray—gray blanket, gray bars, gray metal desk, gray telephone on the desk. And the small man with the spectacles sitting behind the desk: he, too, was gray.

"Professor," I said, my voice rusty with disuse. My throat hurt.

His eyes narrowed, he pursed his lips, but the professor said nothing.

"You will make my fame," he finally said, in halting German.

"How lovely for you," I replied in Hungarian, the Budapest sarcasm dripping from my words.

He frowned at that, as if he had somehow deciphered the words, and picked up the telephone receiver at his elbow. He dialed the telephone, and after a short discussion in Russian a door at the far end of the room swung open and a woman appeared.

I assumed it was the translator from before. Plump and matronly, she looked more like a nursemaid than a Soviet secret police translator.

I didn't dare try my witch's sight, not after that disaster at the Empress. Instead, I studied the two of them, considered how to get out of this place alive if possible, dead if necessary.

Another chill shook me, and I almost started up with the heaves again. I wasn't sure that I could die and return, not in this place. It was worse than warded, it was sterile of magic. Even the air, the metal, and the wool of my prison had been stripped of any spare energy I could use for divination, spell, or escape.

I could only leave here on my own two feet, and by human ingenuity. My native magic was banished.

I felt gray, too, gray and lifeless and bereft of myself. But then I looked at the professor's stubby fingers, fumbling with his file folders, and I imagined those fingertips groping my breasts in front of the lady translator. Testing his strength by humiliating me, knowing that I could not fight back.

My fury conducted no magic in this terrible, gray place. I still had my fury, though, and I held it close, stoked it like my private little furnace.

My fury had uses other than magic.

"I have tried my best to remove the disease of magic from my subjects," the learned little professor began, his translator stumbling to keep up with his words.

I stared at the barely congealed slash on his cheek, and I considered the methods by which he had tried to cut the living magic out of souls in this place.

"Physical surgery was the first and obvious option," he continued. "But fire creatures, wood hobs, even vampires—they do not have a physical locus for their magic. My brain surgeries only killed them."

I was shaking now. My courage stayed with me, warmed by my anger, but my body was exhausted.

"But you are an interesting case, fräulein."

My heart leaped at the word. He didn't know I was married. Had Ziyad or somebody else been tortured into informing this man about Raziel, the specifics that would expose him to capture? I could not dare to hope, but I couldn't help but wonder.

I forced myself to listen to the man's mad ravings instead, cloaked in the brain-numbing jargon of academia.

"You are a special case, yes indeed, Fräulein Lazarus. You have magic inherent from the moment of your birth, *nein*? You need not confirm or deny—we have a full dossier elucidating your kind and creed."

He pushed his spectacles higher up on his round little nose and squinted to read the paperwork overflowing out of the manila folder he balanced between his palms like a holy book. "'Lazarus creed . . . witches of the blood . . . Eldest daughter type, soul summoner.'"

It occurred to me that he probably knew more about the Lazarus creed than I did, and that the lost information was gathered up between the professor's hands. Lost to me, like my mother was gone, to the next world. He looked over the tops of his spectacles at me, pursing his lips. "Don't attempt a summoning now, please. I do not want you to cause damage to yourself."

My stomach lurched again as I remembered the pain at the Empress, but I swallowed hard and steadied my nerves.

"In your case, I believe the frontal lobe is the locus of your abilities. We will test the hypothesis, measure the breadth and scope of your magical deformities. Test you also for subversive thinking, for your capacity to bear pain. And then . . ."

For the first time, the little professor's lips twitched into a smile. "Then we will see how well I can remove the ability while leaving brain activity intact otherwise. Shall we succeed, Miss Lazarus? I am determined that we do. For I will receive the Lenin Star of Science for this finding.

"It will be a model for the populations of the Soviet nations," he said awkwardly himself in the German, as if he had memorized the phrase. The translator sighed.

"Why are you telling me all of this?" I finally asked.

"So that you understand what a gift you are being given," he replied, sounding genuinely surprised. "Your sacrifice will save many other magicals, who instead of destruction will enjoy re-engineering by the Soviet state. You will help to save your kind."

He waved a vague hand at his translator. "Olga, you have been rude. Bring the subject some coffee and bread."

Absurdly, she translated his command, and clomped away on her high heels through the door, leaving the professor and me alone.

I did not even try to struggle. The anti-magic hummed in my brain like a weird electricity, and I knew any attempt at magic would lead to terrible pain. Maybe even permanent damage.

So instead I studied my captor. Not so very long before this, the Gestapo chief in the Polish city of Kraków had taken me into custody, but there the comparisons ended.

The professor had no interest or intention of breaking my will or my spirit. He was indifferent to my spirit altogether, unlike Gestapo Chief Krueger, who was determined to understand my motives before destroying me.

This little professor didn't seem to realize I was human. I was a subject, not an enemy. My only utility was as an interesting data point in his award-winning research.

This man had no inner life that I could discern. His mind was subsumed within the larger machine of the Soviet state. All he wanted was to burnish his prestige, earn a higher status, garner acclaim and reward.

He never looked up from his reports as we waited for Olga to return, and did not seem at all discomfited by the silence. Instead, he shuffled his papers like playing cards and made a few notations on a clipboard with a black pencil.

He looked up after this, and I caught his eye. He smiled, but not at me. Something contained in those papers had made this bureaucrat-scientist happy.

The door behind him swung open and Olga returned, balancing a tray with coffee in an urn, and some pasty white sweet rolls on a plate.

She served the professor first, laying the coffee and rolls before him, brisk and impersonal. He said something in Russian, and then Olga brought the tray to the edge of my cage.

"Thank you," I whispered in German.

Olga looked at me then. I did not need the gift of second sight to see how terrified she was. Not of me, of course, but of her employer, the gray, quiet little man behind her, now slurping his coffee.

"Eat in good health," she choked out in reply, and she slid the tray along the floor until I could reach it from behind the bars.

I briefly considered the food in front of me, wondered if they had drugged it. But Olga had served her boss from the same plate, and besides, at this point I was too hungry to second-guess the food at hand.

So I ate. The coffee was bitter and weak. The rolls undercooked and chewy. But I was grateful for every bite.

"It is time for the examination," the professor said suddenly, almost as an afterthought. "Miss Lazarus, remove your clothes."

I startled, then realized I had no choice but to obey. With a sigh I rose to my feet; the meal had strengthened me more than I would have guessed by looking at it.

I didn't bother pleading or bargaining with this man. Better to choose my battles. I unbuttoned my blouse, pulled the tail of my shirt loose from the top of my skirt. Carefully, I folded up my shirt so it would not wrinkle worse than it already had.

Unlike Krueger, this professor was not animated by urgency. He had all the time in the world to test his hypotheses, refine them, test them again. I was caught in this man's hell of perfection.

When I looked over at them, Olga was trembling. The big-boned matron's eyes were brimming with tears.

My spirits sank. I'd been hoping this exam, while humiliating already, wouldn't be painful. But judging from the matron's reaction, a world of pain was about to be born in this room, delivered by the professor's hands.

I worked off my skirt, trembling now myself with fear as well as embarrassment. It had been a long time since I could not defend myself at all, using my magic or at least my wits.

The professor's clinical gaze swept over me, and my skin pebbled into gooseflesh. I abruptly felt smaller, weaker, as if his very glance was an anti-magic, canceling me out.

"No brassiere or panties, either, Miss Lazarus. All of it, off." Olga translated for the professor, blushing furiously, obviously feeling all of the decent shame the man should have felt.

He stepped away into the hallway, and for a fleeting moment I thought the man had seen me as a human being. But he returned a moment later with a rolling metal tray. The top shelf was piled with shiny metal instruments, some kind of gauge with a dial of measurement of some kind, like a speedometer on an automobile.

No, he felt no shame. The professor was eager to begin his groundbreaking research and earn his Lenin Star.

✳ 21 ✳

By the time he was done with me, I was exhausted and weeping, in too much pain to even be ashamed of what he had done.

The pain was one thing. The tests he conducted were very painful. But worse than that, so much worse, was the enervation, and the sense I no longer belonged to myself. No, he did not torture me. Torture was not what he was after. But by the time he was done for the day I had almost forgotten who I was, and my magic seemed like an absurd figment of my imagination, indeed a sickness and a delusion that the professor was kindly going to excise.

He hadn't done it yet, though. My magic still lived inside of me, a pulse that radiated painfully from my core. A source of weakness in this place, not strength. Olga took all my clothes away, and gave me an ugly, shapeless hospital gown to wear instead.

"Say your prayers, girl," she said, a sob trapped in her throat. "Maybe you will be the professor's first test subject to survive."

And then she said something in Russian under her breath to herself, not to me, hiccuped, and turned and walked out after the professor. I was again, mercifully, alone.

I slept. And I dreamed. Not even the dreadful anti-magic machines of the Soviet empire could reach inside my dreams and kill them. Not yet.

I stood in a patchwork of tilled fields. Frost glazed the empty earth. All around me, mists rose from the ground, wraiths of water.

I was cold, alone.

A crow circled my head, cawing his fool head off. I watched him as he flew around and around like a feathered bat.

"Caw!" he cried. "Caw! Caw!"

He was trying to warn me. And the bird looked familiar. But I couldn't understand him, no matter how frantically he buzzed at my head.

The crow landed in front of me and tilted his head to look up into my eyes.

I knew that expression, that face. "Leo," I whispered. My faithful little imp—I'd asked him to find Gisele and somehow he'd found me again, hidden away as I was.

"Call! Call!" the crow said.

Trapped inside my dream, I could not decipher Leo's message. Call? How could I call anyone? I was asleep, locked up inside a mental and physical prison. Based on my past experience, the only thing I could do now was endure. And look for my chance to break free when it came.

"I don't understand, crow," I said, still inside my dream. The crow started hopping up and down, beating his wings at the air in frustration.

"Tell Raziel," I began, and the crow calmed. "Whatever it is that you need to tell me, find Raziel. He will help you. And tell him I am locked away in this prison. He must get me out soon or I will be dead."

The mists thickened around us. The shadow of Asmodel's face rose over the fields. A strange buzzing filled the air like a siren blaring over the deserted landscape. Birds flew into the air, flocks of terrified quail and mourning doves.

Hunters' guns thundered in the air. I heard screaming cries, the crow flew away over the cold dirt—

And I awoke on the cot, my heart pounding. The night was black as ink; my captors had kindly turned off the lights. The cries I heard were real. They sounded far away, unreachable and full of anguish.

I had to get the hell out of this place or I was finished.

Morning came as it always does, no matter what happens in this enormous, cruel world.

I strained to hear the sounds of birds outside, the sounds of screams, but could hear nothing. I did have a single window, but it was outside my cage, across from the professor's metal desk. I craned my neck to look up into the sky. It was raining.

Presumably the doctor's initial tests were done. The professor had taken his sweet time the day before. The surgery was already scheduled, no doubt. I did not have high hopes for a successful outcome, not even from the professor's point of view.

I expected to die on the table. And then would come the great gamble: could I return to my body even in this sterile place? Technically I could work my spells in the afterworld, far away from Baku, in the second Heaven, but I would have to manifest here, return to my body here using my magic. Or not.

I wished with all my heart that I could send a message to Gisele, to wish her good-bye. And I still worried about Eva, trapped in a maze of illusion, pretending to evil she didn't possess in order to fight the Nazi regime from within.

They had their battles to fight as I did. Thinking of them, I was no longer alone. I clung to my love for Gisele and Eva, like a protective amulet. And I saw Raziel in my mind's eye, flying free on Helena's magic carpet, and I swore to him silently that I would endure this place.

Until I found a way to escape.

✳ 22 ✳

I never found a way out.

I had believed, with the passionate intensity of a naïf, that the professor did not really know how to kill magic in a soul. I thought he was softening me up, weakening me in order to learn the secret of me.

But alas, it was much worse than I had imagined. He had perfected his butchery in a line of research tracing back to the Russian Revolution of 1917. For the entire length of my life, this colorless little man had devoted his every moment to studying and dissecting the mystery of magic. I had no secrets to keep from him.

The professor did not return the next morning with Olga. No, he came with two enormous, burly men wearing the uniforms of hospital orderlies. They took me out of my cage and frog-marched me down the long, antiseptic-smelling hallway to another floor.

I could not read the Cyrillic lettering over the doorway we reached. But I didn't need a translator. The bright lights and metal table in the room I entered told me everything I needed to know.

I tried to wrench free of their grip, but I was no match for the orderlies. I even tried a flash of witchfire, but it burned within me, like an electrical fire trapped under my skin.

By the time I had gotten strapped down to the cold metal operating table, my heart was pounding against the cage of my ribs like a prisoner trying to escape. The two goons left, and I was alone with my torturer.

"Why do you struggle?" he asked in broken German under his breath. I knew he wasn't talking to me—he was too much of a narcissist to even notice whether I heard him or not. "Why do you all struggle? Once I succeed, the sufferings of your people will end."

His voice sounded far, far away. . . . The pounding of my heart inside my ears was much louder and more insistent. My back twisted with fear and I considered whether I could possibly commit a kind of astral suicide, pull my soul out of my body altogether, before he killed me with his terrible science.

But no. I had no magic here, it was suppressed by the Soviet anti-magic field.

A door swung open at the far side of the operating suite. My head was fixed in place by a steel band so I could not turn to see.

"Ah, Skorvald, come. The patient is in need of sedation." He said this in Russian, but such was my panic that I strained to imagine the meaning of his words. I was that desperate to find

some minuscule measure of control here. At least the illusion
of it, if I could not have it.

I saw the surgically gloved hands out of the corner of my
eye. The hands tested an enormous syringe filled with a clear
fluid—some kind of anesthetic, I figured.

I tried to cry out, but my voice died in my throat. In the
midst of my fright I could not remember German anymore,
could not speak Russian at all.

"No," was all I whispered, in Hungarian. But that single
word held no power here. My captors didn't even understand
what the word meant.

The needle went into the muscle of my right leg. It hurt—
my muscles were cinched tight with fear and the man with the
syringe made no effort to warn me in advance.

The numbness spread, from my leg to my heart, then through
my whole body. I could no longer talk, no longer move . . .

No longer breathe. . .

A clear mask went over my face as I sank down, down, and
away from the hell of this place.

From what the professor had deigned to tell me before, and
from the hint of Olga's tearstained farewell, I realized as I fell
into the darkness that if I survived this operation it would be
a true miracle.

Because not one of the professor's other magical patients
had survived his tender ministrations.

Again I dreamed. But a dream like I had never had before. It
was more vivid than my waking life. Every moment glittered

like a jewel, with emotion and meaning. The feelings I had locked away for after the war had come to this hidden place to wait for me to release them.

I knew it was only a dream, even as I dreamed it, that in fact a sadistic scientist dissected my body in the world of the living. But this dream meant more to me than life itself.

I was back in my kitchen in Budapest, all the while knowing it was lost to me forever, that I would never visit it again in my life, if by chance I happened to survive my ordeal. Gisele stirred a pot of something, her back to me, and under her breath in her low, scratchy voice she sang her psalms, all out of key.

I was home: the warm, dusty kitchen, Gisele's voice, humming as she stirred. The smell of bread and chicken paprikash, and the sound of traffic rising from Dohány Street.

All of it, gone forever.

Gone forever, but here forever, too.

"Gisele?" I said, my voice tiny and uncertain. I wasn't sure that this scene wouldn't melt into a nightmare—after all, once we had imprisoned the primordial demon, Asmodel, in this same cozy, homey place.

She turned at the sound of my voice, and I gulped. It was really her, and she hadn't turned evil or horrifying. But the sight of her frightened me all the same.

She smiled at me, that sweet lopsided smile of hers, and all the feelings I never let out flooded through me.

"It's you," I said, tears streaming down my face. "I thought we'd never meet again, my darling. How I love you!"

"Hello, Magduska. I've been waiting for you, oh so long it seems. Now I understand why poor Mama always got so impatient. Come, sit."

I wanted to run to her and hug her, but something in her words warned me away. Instead, feeling vaguely unsettled, I sat at the rickety kitchen table, rested my hands on the fresh, unburned lace tablecloth.

Gisele put the food onto a big, chipped plate. *Turos teszta*—a humble dish, the kind of thing you make for little Hungarian children. Flat egg noodles, with sour cream, cottage cheese, and lots of sugar on top. Steam rose from the plate and I cleared my throat, pretending that the huge lump in there didn't exist.

"Come on, eat. You'll feel so much better," Gisele said.

I tried to smile, gave up, and instead attacked the dream noodles with a long, pointy fork. It was the most incredible thing I have ever eaten, anywhere. It tasted of home and family and love. Each bite spoke volumes of love. With every swallow, I took in Gisi's love for me, pouring through my body like a miraculous warming medicine.

I paused and glanced over at her—while I ate, Gisi perched on the wobbly chair next to mine, the one we had just recently tried to repair with twine.

"Where are we?" I asked.

"A safe place," Gisele replied, a little too quickly. Her little hand reached for mine, and she squeezed my fingers reassuringly.

I wasn't used to being the comforted one in the family, but I was long past being too fierce to accept her kindness. "I miss you terribly, mouse," I said. "I am all alone, in a bad place. I don't think I am going to survive. This might really be goodbye this time."

"I know. That's why I came."

I studied her face, her peaceful, untormented expression,

and a terrible foreboding crept through me. "How did you get here? Isn't making a place like this a rare magic?"

"Oh no, my darling, you, of all people, should know better. Love is the greatest magic there is—you taught me that, silly. And it is very simple, love is. I don't need magic to conjure up home. Just love."

I poked the fork at the noodles. "I didn't know love was such a good cook. Thank you, my darling."

"You are welcome. I wanted to ease your pain. And help you! You've always helped me in my darkest hours, protected me when I couldn't protect myself. And you've gone haring all around the world, got in trouble in the first place, all because I begged you."

She slipped her fingers out of my grasp and dabbed at the corners of her eyes.

I braced for the waterworks. "I believe your visions," I replied. "And I swore I'd keep you safe. It was really that simple."

"You did keep me safe, Magduska! Look at me—the terrible visions are gone, gone! Look at me!"

I looked her full in the face, saw how peaceful and carefree Gisele was. And I couldn't stop my own tears from falling. "I'm so glad," I finally managed to say.

"I'm not suffering anymore. Whatever you've done, out in the wide world, you stopped my visions for good. Thank you, my darling, thank you!"

"But it may not have made any real difference in the end, my little mouse. Because who cares if the world has changed, if you . . ." I could not bear to finish the thought. Miracle of miracles, she was the clear-eyed one and I the weepy basket case.

Gisele leaned forward and I saw the weary wisdom in her eyes, so like Raziel's. "I know what you're thinking. That I'm dead, that this here is Heaven, and that we've lost everything."

I was too miserable by now even to nod.

"Don't be fooled. Don't get confused—it's easy to get confused. You didn't seek our Book in order to save me, even if you think you did. Saving me was not the point, wasn't even possible. You went to stop the visions. And you did. I am at peace, so happy now. You made those visions fade away to nothing. And so I came here to say thank you."

"And to say good-bye," I whispered.

I took a long look around at the dusty little room with the hideous yellow flowered curtains. I would have given anything to go back there, live the life I had before.

But this was the last time.

"What happened to you?"

"Never mind, Magduska."

"Never mind? Never mind! You've left this world and tell me to never mind . . . you know me better than that, mouse."

She sighed, and a shadow of her old cares flashed across her features. "If you must know . . . Asmodel sent a demoness to murder me. She told me she couldn't kill you, so I was the next best. She snuffed me out like a little candle."

I listened to her calm recitation with growing horror. So Obizuth's warnings had come to disaster. Waves of longing, of loss, washed over me, and the scene wavered through my sudden tears.

Gisele smiled. "What does it matter in the end, Magduska? Our time here in the kitchen is short. And I have something very important to tell you."

"Nothing is more important than you, Gisi! I would have died to save you, again and again. I failed you."

"But that's the thing, my darling. You didn't fail. You did save me, that is what I am trying to tell you."

My mind insisted that I had failed, failed completely, because my Gisele was dead. My heart just grieved, and worried and picked at the details.

"Well, if you're dead, I must be done, too. No point in trying to survive that madman's maiming me."

"No!" Gisele said it low and loud, a true Lazarus witch at last. "No. Stop for a minute and listen to me! My goodness, you're a stubborn thing."

I shrugged and glared at the noodles getting cold on the plate. "I can't help it."

"Listen to me. You have a choice. I didn't."

I looked up sharply, the ancient fury rising up in me like a personal demon. "A crappy choice."

"Well, I guess it really is. But it's yours to make."

I sighed, gave up. "Go ahead, Gisi, tell me what you came to tell me. But don't be surprised if I don't do like you want."

She didn't bother wrangling with me. Instead she crossed her arms and rested her elbows on the table, in a most unladylike way. "That horrible man is digging in your brain right now. He is in fact killing your magic, killing you. You are dead on the table right this minute."

In a flash, the dull wooden floorboards shimmered into nothingness and I looked down beneath my feet to my body, lying on the metal operating table, strapped down, the top of my head a gory mess.

Fear turned me numb. I tore my gaze away from my scalp and looked at my sister. "It's all over, then," I said.

"Not quite. You can go back and finish what you started for good and all. But your magic as you know it is over."

"Forget it," I said, though both of us knew I still wavered. "Without my magic, without you, what is the point of living?"

"You need to answer that question for yourself."

I sighed and gulped. "I'm in a terrible fix down there."

"Yes, you are. So are Raziel and Eva."

For a moment I could see Raziel's face, so clearly it was as if he had joined us here in this heavenly projection of our Dohány Street kitchen. Raziel had left his wings behind to stand with me. Could I survive without my magic for him?

And Eva . . . her face flashed before me, too, all the artifice gone, pure terror covering her face like a shroud. My poor Eva. What had happened to her? How could I abandon my fight as long as she was still fighting hers?

I crossed my arms, too, and rested my forehead on them like a pillow. "What can I possibly do to help them? I'm nothing without my magic."

I could not conceive of myself now, without my magic manifest. But losing Gisele was worse.

"What if I stay here with you?" I continued. "What happens next?"

"You rest. And your sins fall away . . . eventually."

"But what about—"

"Raziel? Oh, that man, that king of the rebel angels, he'll keep fighting no matter what. And Eva will make it through somehow. But I can't tell you when or how. That, nobody knows."

I lifted my head and stood up from the table, trying and

failing to banish the terrible fear that sank into me like the fangs of a wolf. "Here, the fight is over."

"For you, yes. If you stay."

"Could I . . . watch? Or help from here?"

"Well, it's pretty much against the rules. You have places to go, you know. But I suppose a glimpse or a prayer would be permitted. After all, they gave me permission to come here and cook your *turos teszta* for you."

A mere glimpse was not nearly enough. "But I can't live without you," I said.

"Yes, you can," she said. For the first time I caught the flash of tears in her eyes. "Listen to me. This home is gone, yes. But you'll have new homes, a new love who is living for you. If you are finished with it all, okay. I understand, you've been through enough, for sure."

She paused then, and I could see this scene was straining even Gisele's patience. My mother would have pulled my hair by now in her frustration. "All I am telling you is that you have a chance to go back. And I don't."

There it was. The confirmation that Gisele was in fact dead. And that no magic in the world, not even the Gem of Raziel itself, could undo her death.

I couldn't withstand this confirmation with heroic stoicism. Even I'm not that cold. Instead I grabbed her into my arms and hugged her tight, as if I could keep her with me forever if I just hugged her hard enough.

"If you're gone . . . ," I whispered, unable to finish the thought with words.

"You know the right thing to do," she whispered back into my ear. "My job is done, but yours . . ."

She disentangled herself from my arms and swiped at the stray tears that had escaped from her eyes. "I never found a soul mate, just had my sister. You have yours, you know your soul mate. But Raziel will understand if you go."

"But how will he love me without . . ." My voice trailed off, stumbled over the words.

"Without your magic? *Pfft*, he loves you true. And don't you love him, wings or not?"

She shrugged and sighed. "You think of me as sweet and kind. But I'm the one who forced you to hunt the Book, to fight Hitler's demon. To die, again and again and again, to kill. And now I'm sending you back, even again. I'm not the angel you thought I was, Magduska. I never was."

Her words made me gulp. "Churchill told me the same about you, once. I'm finally starting to understand."

She shrugged, and laughed even as the tears rolled down her round cheeks. "Time's up, my dear. Bless you for doing everything you could to save me. Remember—you did. You did save me. Those visions would have haunted me into for-ever. And now they are gone."

Her words made me pause to think of the bigger picture. She was made of sterner stuff than I had thought, but she thought too much of me. Gisele reminded me to think beyond my own skin. She always had.

"If your visions are gone, does that mean the war is over?"

She sighed. "You know the answer to that. The particular nightmare I have is over, but that doesn't mean a new night-mare isn't brewing."

I sighed deeply. Gisele no longer had her visions. The prophecy of the Witch of Ein Dor was turned aside. But if I ran away from the fight to come, I could never rest easy in the afterworld.

Never.

"But how can I do anything without my magic?" I persisted.

Gisele made an exasperated little noise, even as an enormous smile broke over her face like sunshine. I basked in that warmth, knowing it was the last time I was going to feel it in this world. "Easy," she said.

"Not so easy," I replied with a growl, and she laughed and laughed, the old belly laugh she had lost in the last year of her life.

"I adore you, Magduska Lazarus," she finally said. "Remember me, and know I am ever so much happier now. The fear is gone. I am happy. And Papa is waiting for me! Don't worry, Mama and Papa will watch over me, now."

I couldn't speak anymore, not after that. I just nodded and smiled and cried.

"You can use your magic now, here, away from that Soviet beast. Go back, and your will alone will be enough to keep you in your life. I won't lie, it is going to hurt, going to be a hellacious fight. But you're stubborn enough to do it."

So stubbornness, not magic, would carry the day. So be it— much of my magic had been in fact simply my stubbornness, augmented with a healthy dose of the impossible.

"Good-bye, little mouse," I managed to say. "Watch over me if you can."

She smiled at me then. "You already have Viktor for that."

Both of us knew she was right—she was no angel, I finally understood it. She had her own destiny to pursue in the afterworld, and no more time to fuss over me. I had already way-laid her for too long.

"So fine, I'll go back," I said. "But you're the one who is leaving me."

"It's the way of things," she said with a shrug. "Better for you, too. You have greater things to live for than babysitting me. I'm no baby anymore."

I started whispering the family spell of return, the one I had forced our mother to teach me. I knew I invoked the spell of return for the last time in this life.

As I wavered and shimmered, I waved good-bye to Gisele. And she blew me kisses, her smile more carefree than I had ever seen in life.

How I hated good-byes. But for Gisele and me, this was the last one.

✳ 23 ✳

I shot into my body with a horrible velocity. I groaned, and a great cacophony of Russian rose all around me.

The top of my head felt like it had been blasted off. I vaguely registered the fact that they had shaved off all my hair, and my scalp and all the rest of me was cold, horribly exposed and cold.

But the worst was the fog of my thinking. The learned professor had assured me that he would barely be touching me in physical terms—merely an incision over the pineal gland, the scientifically located origin of the mystical third eye.

But the pain was not minor, no. This was no minor operation I had endured.

"Gisele . . . ," I whispered through dry, cracked lips. The cacophony rose higher around me, a symphony of concern.

A cool, moistened swab passed over my lips, a blanket slid over my shaking limbs, and I began flying through the air, dizzying, slowly at first, then faster and faster, faster than flying carpets. . . .

I drifted away again.

⌀

This time, no dreams. No visitations of angels, no stubborn little imps to warn me. Just nothing. The Soviet version of paradise.

⌀

I awoke in a hospital bed, surrounded by flowers, in January.

The professor himself sat at the foot of my bed, and when he saw that my eyes had fluttered open he jumped to his feet and pushed a button on the wall.

He spoke to me in Russian, in a voice that I think was intended to soothe and reassure.

I could see dreams of the Lenin Star reflected in his eyes when he looked at me.

Other than the professor and the garish, stinky hothouse flowers, everything in the room looked gray and drab and dead.

The professor pressed the button again, then muttered something unsoothing under his breath before rushing out of the room.

Alone. Blessed solitude, a prisoner's gold when there are no other friendly prisoners, only jailers. Alone, with my thoughts and my wounds, but blessedly free of that horrible little man.

Now that I was alive again, I considered doubting my dream of Gisele. Maybe it was only a terrible, wonderful dream. And my girl somehow was still safe, under Churchill's protection . . .

But then I reached for my magic, where it had been hidden safe within me. And for the first time in my life that magic was missing. I called upon it in my mind, summoned to it. But it did not answer.

It was dead. The famous-to-be professor had ripped the magic out of me. And Gisele had made it clear that if I chose to come back, to live, this would be the last chance. I could never return from the dead again. I had, finally and irrevocably, run out of lives.

My magic, all of it, like Gisele, was gone.

I dozed, too exhausted to do anything more than simply exist. A hand closed over mine, and I felt the gentle pressure of the fingertips.

I sighed, could do no more than that.

"Magduska," Raziel said.

My eyes flew open.

I blinked hard once, then blinked again. Raziel stood over my bed, and I swear he looked as celestially glorious as he did the day I first met him in Vienna.

"I must be dead," I said. "Or this is a dream."

"No, it's really me," Raziel said, with a smile so sweet and sad that tears came to my eyes. Where was my famous control, my renowned sangfroid?

"But are you a prisoner? How did you get here?"

He squeezed my hand a little tighter. "Everything has changed since you were taken into the Institute. Everything."

"I never thought . . ." I sighed and closed my eyes again, already exhausted.

"That you would see me again?"

"Yes."

"I promised you, from the beginning. I will never leave you, not in this world or the next. I left Heaven so I could be closer to you, so you could know it."

I sighed again, feeling the pain trapped in my heart. Remembering my dream of Gisele. My head pounded with every heartbeat.

"She's dead, isn't she?"

Raziel said nothing.

"It wasn't just a dream I had. Gisele's gone, and I couldn't save her no matter what I did." I took a deep breath, steadied myself. "I'm afraid you'll say the same about me before too long."

"Afraid?"

"Yes, that you will regret falling from Heaven like you did. Because I won't survive anyway."

"Do you regret doing everything you could to save Gisele?"

"No!" I pulled my hand away, scrunched down in the bed in my misery, like a little creature hiding from hawks overhead. "I regret not doing even more. I regret not giving my own life somehow, figuring out how to die in her place."

I started shaking all over. "But it's too late for that now. Isn't it?"

I felt Raziel's weight as he sat on the edge of the bed. His hand clasped mine again, and I opened my eyes.

I stared into his eyes, and I disappeared into the depths of them, into the dark sweep of the tale he had to tell.

"I made it to England alive. And with the gem. But all was confusion when I got there . . ."

"Tell me everything," I said with a low growl. "And don't you dare try to spare me by leaving anything out. I want the bad news, all of it."

"It isn't all bad news, Magduska. Not at all."

Perhaps not, but Gisele's death overshadowed everything else in the world. I felt the pain of her murder in my very bones. Because now I knew my dream of her was true—as Gisele had admitted to me, she had been murdered by the last demoness, Enepsigos. Asmodel had gotten his revenge on me at last.

But I needed to know everything. If I didn't want to die of grief, I had to make Gisele's murder mean something in the end. I couldn't bear the thought of her dying in vain.

✳ 24 ✳

"I fled from Quba with the cigar box tucked under my arm, and walked on foot due west, as far as I could go before night came. But I didn't make it very far before they found me.

"My brothers, the fallen seraphs of the Mountain of Fire. They knew I had escaped the clutches of the Institute somehow. And they chose to walk with me. I will be honest, they are afraid of you, even now. Especially now. But they know me. And the sight of me, walking the earth like they chose to do, decided them to join me.

"My brothers found an auto for me, and we drove together down to Baku, down those terrible, rutted roads. By the time we had returned to the capital, I had learned to drive on any kind of surface, and my brothers sent me on my journey west, with their blessings. I will tell you the rest when we have time, and rest, and peace. Let me just say that after Uzziel smuggled me out of the country, Knox did the rest once I got back to Hungary."

"You saw Bathory? And Eva?" I could not help interjecting.

Raziel looked worried, and it wasn't until he kissed my shaking fingers that I realized his concern was for me and not for my question. "They are fine," he said, his words concealing a world of questions and fears he would not let me pursue. "Eva still lives. Bathory still rules. For the moment, at least.

"But never mind," he said, his voice gaining force. "Budapest is not where my story takes shape. It is in England, at Chartwell, where I must take up the tale.

"By the time I reached Churchill's home I was alone again. The place was in a state of consternation when I got there. Gisele . . ."

His voice trailed off. And as I turned away, the stitches in my scalp pulled at my skin, mortified it. "She was dead," I said, to spare him having to break the news to me. "Murdered. Do they know . . ."

"The murderer? The English do not. But I do."

He hesitated then, and I leaned back against the pillow. The room was cold, so cold, cold and gray and devoid of life. Only Raziel's face, animated and full of pain, confirmed that I had not already died and passed on to some ammonia-smelling gray purgatory.

"How do you know?" I whispered. I could hardly bear to speak the words aloud, though I was desperate to hear his answer.

"The demonesses who killed you first," Raziel began.

My heart sank. Raziel's words confirmed my dream of

Gisele as true. I now knew what he was going to say, but I nodded for him to go on.

"There were three of them. Obizuth, Onoskelis, and Enepsigos. You killed Onoskelis in Budapest."

I shuddered, remembering our night cut short in Bathory's mansion on Rose Hill.

"Obizuth has repented, she seeks your freedom since she fears the Nazi menace more. She knows Asmodel firsthand, you know."

I knew. Obizuth had told me so herself once, long ago, in an elegant, horrible suite at the Gellert Hotel.

"But there were three of them," Raziel went on. "Enepsigos was left."

I said nothing. Enepsigos, the cruelest and the strongest, was the worst of the demonic sisters enslaved by the Staff wizard.

"She chose to become enslaved again to Asmodel. She chose to destroy Gisele, at the demon's bidding."

"But why?" I finally managed to force out. "What could Gisele do to them? What harm did she ever do?"

"It wasn't her, my love. It was you."

I closed my eyes against the sudden wave of dizziness that overtook me. They had sworn to destroy me, and the only demoness true to her oath had taken aim at the one thing that meant more to me than my life.

My sister.

I forced my eyes open, and I breathed deep until the dizziness retreated. "They can't stop me that way," I whispered.

"Don't look too deeply into the demons' motives," Raziel said. His face was still unearthly calm, but his voice contained all the anguish he would not let himself feel. Instead I felt it, I felt it infecting my body like a fatal plague.

"How could they get to her? Wasn't Chartwell properly warded?"

"Against certain kinds of magic, yes. But against possession the English are rather poorly defended. To be fair to the English, it is very hard to defend against an evil spirit determined to worm its way in."

"How do you know it was Enepsigos?" I hoped that Gisele had managed to visit Raziel, to wish him farewell, too.

But no. "Because the demoness came to me and told me. She told me everything."

We stared at each other in silence. I had heard Asmodel's rantings about the terrible slaughter he intended to wreak. I could only imagine the horrible things Enepsigos had done to poor Gisele before she killed her.

"She didn't have time to torture your sister before she died," Raziel said, a little too quickly. He knew what I was thinking. "She didn't have the time, or the magic at her disposal. I knew when she was lying to me, and when she told the truth."

"I don't believe you. She is cruel, that demon. She drinks terror like blood."

"She wanted to, Magda. She tried to convince me that she did. But . . . I saw Gisele's body. She did not suffer."

"Don't lie to me. Please."

Raziel sighed. I could see he had wanted to spare me the details, but we both knew I wouldn't let him off the hook so easily. "I am not lying. Believe me, Enepsigos wanted to do far worse to her. When she killed you, she tortured you worse."

I remembered how the demonesses had torn me apart, the

first time I died. I grudgingly accepted his words and motioned for him to go on.

"She told me she had possessed the body of one of the Chartwell maids and nobody there was the wiser, not even the girl, who liked to do love spells and the like and was not adept in magic, was unwary. Enepsigos was hiding like a parasite in the girl's mind."

I thought of Gisele's letter, of her simple gratitude for the kind girl who had brushed her hair. And I shuddered.

"She's gone back into the girl," I warned. "Enepsigos doesn't like to leave loose ends behind."

Raziel hesitated. "You're too curious, do you know that? The poor girl jumped in the river and drowned herself the next day. . . . She thought she had killed Gisele in some kind of trance."

The dizziness came back. "So two have died on my account."

"Stop it," he warned. "Do not take the demoness's actions onto your shoulders."

"I should have killed them all when I had my chance. Sacred oath be damned."

"That would have hurt you more fundamentally than even this, Magdalena. You say to yourself what Asmodel would say. Stop doing his work for him." He crossed his arms and pressed his lips together. That, and the way he said my full name, was the worst rebuke he had ever given me.

Gentle, fierce soul.

"I'm sorry," I finally forced out. "You are right, I am wrong. You know how proud I am, how much I hate to admit my errors. But I'll shut up now and let you tell me what you want to tell me. How you want to tell it."

Raziel reached forward and gathered me into his arms, and I cried. The demonesses had won. My sister was dead, and so was my magic. Everything I had fought and clawed to win I now had lost.

And my man understood my grief without my having to explain. He grieved with me, I will confess; this supremely strong man wept with me. The old ways, my old loves, and my most beloved family were all gone. Across the veil to where I could never reach them again, not without calling a séance, disturbing their souls, and disquieting them in their graves.

And I could no longer even disturb my mother, the ghosts, or the Witch of Ein Dor, either. Because my magic, too, was dead.

I cried for what seemed like an eternity. And then I became too exhausted to cry anymore. I squeezed Raziel close one last time, then collapsed against the pillow.

"Tell the rest of it, my love," I said. "And I promise I'll be a lamb."

Raziel blew his nose in his handkerchief before going on. "Churchill himself attended her funeral, Magduska. He wept, though he didn't know your sister very well. And he spoke of the evil hidden inside of goodness, the shadow at noon. He saw her off with honor, my love."

I was too worn out to protest that evil wasn't hidden inside my sister, and that even the great Churchill's eulogy must have been inadequate. My little mouse had proven so much greater than her end. But Raziel already knew all of that.

I heard the squeaky clattering of a nurse's shoes on the linoleum floor outside my hospital room, and I tensed. But the clacking continued away down the hall.

"How did you manage to get back here?"

"Churchill sent me."

My poor cut-open brain tried to wrestle with this information and failed. "Did you sneak back in at the border? Did your brothers bribe the border guards?"

"No, I arrived in a plane, with Knox and a vanguard of diplomats."

"Here?"

"Why, yes, at Baku. Knox went on to Moscow from here, though."

My mind reeled with the horror of it. "So Stalin has captured you all. Are you here to take me with you to Siberia?"

He laughed at that. "My poor sleeping beauty, the Russians have been attacked by Hitler's army. Stalin is now the great ally of Winston Churchill, and even the French."

"Attacked?" I closed my eyes and groaned . . . the intense brain wrestling I was doing gave me a terrific, stroke-level headache. "Why would Hitler do such a daft, insane thing?"

Raziel didn't bother replying to that—we both knew such insanity was that dreadful man's specialty. The fact he was willingly possessed by the horrible demon Asmodel, who unceasingly raped him from the inside, did not do wonders for the Führer's calm rationality.

"He could not wait anymore," Raziel said quietly. "He wants the oil of the Caucasus, and more to the point, he wants the Gem of Raziel. Stalin's people had told their counterparts in the Reich that we had located the gem, and the news drove Asmodel especially over the edge. After thousands of years of torment, he lost his patience in the final moment."

"But I thought Hitler would attack the West first. That his

alliance with the Soviets would hold long enough for him to crush France at least, avenge the Great War."

"No, no western front. Hitler lusted for the oil of the Caucasus, Asmodel for the gem. They could not resist an attack on the East any longer."

"But doesn't Asmodel know that you got the gem safely to England? By the Maker, he doesn't, does he?"

Raziel smiled and said nothing. But the sharpness in Raziel's eyes told me I was right.

"How could Asmodel not know something like that?" I asked.

"The demoness was focused on Gisele, not me. I hadn't even quite made it to Chartwell when she attacked."

Exhausted, I lay back against the pillow with the ammonia bleach-smell, and I closed my eyes in weariness. "So what do we do now? I am empty, Raziel, and I'm not quite sure why I ended up here, still alive after all. Tell me what to do. I promise I'll do anything you say."

What he said shocked me so much that I rued my promise only a moment after making it. "We gather an army like we did at Wolf's Lair. And we finish off Hitler for once and for all."

"But I can't do a thing," I protested.

He laughed again, more like his old laugh, this time without the sharp edge of bitterness in it. "I thought you were going to do what I said? Stubborn! You've changed less than you think you have, my love."

"But the professor. The . . . operation."

Raziel reached for my hands and stroked the backs of my knuckles. "The professor believes he has gelded your magic, ended it. I chose to let him believe that."

I couldn't bear to tell my beloved that despite his supreme trust in me, I believed it, too, believed it fervently. I based that belief on everything I sensed and knew about my own magic. The colors had drained out of the world; the energy of the world coursed along, I was sure, as it had done before the professor maimed me. But I could no longer sense the currents of energy surrounding every human soul. I could only see with my eyes, only hear with my ears.

I swallowed back my misery. I would not despair in Raziel's presence, not after all that he had been through, all he held back from me now. "But I am like a horse with a blanket wrapped around his eyes. How can I do anything at all without magic, if I can no longer see the magic in the world?"

"We don't have time for me to show you, my love."

"But how can I possibly summon an army from a hospital bed? With my magic removed?"

Raziel smiled. The bitterness had come back. "I will do the summoning this time. My brothers will come. And their brothers will come. And do not forget, my love. We still possess the gem."

I caught myself goggling at him, and with difficulty kept my mouth from hanging open in amazement. How my beloved had changed. The first time I had spoken to Raziel, he warned me against fighting my fate, against using the inheritance of my Book to change the future. Now he intended himself to use the gem that had spawned the Book to smash Hitler and his army.

But Raziel had warned me, back in the old days, for a good reason. The dangers of using the Book, much less the gem itself, were very, very real. "Are you sure?" was all I asked. Who was I to warn Raziel? I was just a maimed girl, he was an angel of the Lord, fallen or manifest or whatever he was.

But he was also my husband. I couldn't bear to lose him, not after losing everything else. But I couldn't hold him back in any way, I couldn't stop Raziel if I tried. He was a force of nature, a whirlwind, a terrible storm.

"I've already called Uzziel and my brothers," he said. "We have no time left."

✳ 25 ✳

My sister was dead; only my own grim determination could heal me. And I did it. I got away, with Raziel's determination. I am sure the professor intended to keep me for demonstration purposes—he had confided as much to me once night fell, after Raziel had gone. But I knew the very next day, once Raziel had come back for me, that I would remain the professor's pet no longer.

And within the day it was true. Raziel returned, with a phalanx of mountain angels and a blustering Russian official who had a row of medals across his chest and a murderous eye. He did not care for science but for killing the great Soviet motherland's enemies. And Raziel, not to mention the great Churchill, had convinced this man's superiors that I was somehow needed in the fight against the perfidious Nazis.

So the professor was thwarted, by the Soviet system he labored within. Somehow, Raziel and I had outflanked him in the power hierarchy. It was a great miracle.

The professor remonstrated to the official, even screamed in Russian at him, but it was no use. His experiment was cut short. And the holy vision of the Lenin Star faded from his eyes as they led me away.

I did not need the gift of prophecy to see Siberia in the professor's immediate future. It gave me great comfort, and it helped me to bear the ordeal of getting out of that hospital bed. I could barely walk, and wore only my hospital gown and shabby, worn-out slippers. Raziel grabbed me by one elbow, the Russian official grabbed me by the other. The angels surrounded us, before and after, and we left the hospital like a unit of partisans guarding a prisoner.

So I marched down the endless white hallway, knees knocking, knowing I smelled sick and stinky and not caring very much. All I cared about was that no matter what happened next, I was not going to die in this hospital, under the professor's ministrations.

The official led the way into the rear seat of a cavernous Ford automobile. I collapsed inside, Raziel slid in after me, and before he had even slammed the door the driver peeled away from the curb and into the heart of Baku. The angels followed behind, crammed into the flat bed of an open lorry.

Raziel took off his coat and spread it over me. "You're shivering," he said.

I hadn't realized until he spoke how very cold I was. It was January now, and a dusting of snow coated the streets of Baku. It made an unfamiliar place look even more strange and foreign—I had imagined Baku as a tropical, balmy place. How wrong I was, about so many things.

"What next?" It was easier than I had imagined, to surrender to Raziel's good sense.

He looked at me and blinked in surprise, then wrapped one of his arms around my shoulders. "First thing, we get you some warm clothes and a bath. And a decent meal. You're all skin and bones."

I had no appetite whatsoever . . . all I could imagine eating was Gisele's noodles with sugar and sour cream. But I was too tired to explain.

We rolled up to a grand marble palace. "What is this, some kind of hotel?" I wondered aloud.

"No, it is what it seems to be. An oil baron's great mansion. It belongs to the government now, and it has been lent to Churchill's people. They wish to impress."

I shot a nervous glance at the Soviet official next to me. Surely if they could find somebody who spoke Hungarian, they would have. The Soviets, from everything I knew, were more efficient than the Hungarian government, and wilier, too.

Raziel caught me staring at the official, as fear rolled off me like a fog. "I don't care what he overhears," Raziel said. "It doesn't matter. All that matters now is killing Hitler. The French are invading Germany even as we speak."

I could not follow Raziel, squinted at his words like a foreigner. My poor mind could not digest these many incomprehensible changes to the world. As if the professor had removed all of reality along with my magic.

"Maybe this is all just some kind of purgatorial dream," I muttered under my breath.

"You are no Catholic, my love," he replied. "And you still walk in this world. We have to strike fast now. If we can't stop Hitler from taking the oil fields, he will win the war. Everybody can see it."

I nodded, but was too tired to form the words to say anything more. My mind melted into a furious static, and I closed my eyes against it.

Raziel's fingers caressed my face. "We are almost there. I'll take you inside."

He scooped me up and carried me out of the car and into the palace, and I was so far gone I didn't even protest. I just closed my eyes and rested my head against his broad chest, and he lifted me up a grand, curving staircase to the baths upstairs.

There were ladies there, servants of some kind, protesting in Russian. But we swept past them to a bathroom tiled entirely in mosaics, even the ceiling. He drew a bath in the enormous clawed tub, even as he still cradled me in his arms.

I cracked my eyes wider open to study the mosaics, as the tub nearly overflowed with hot, sudsy water. "Even Heaven doesn't have a bathtub like this," I said.

Raziel kissed my shoulder and unwrapped me from the bloodstained gown. He popped my naked self into the water, and after the shock of the heat against my skin I instantly relaxed, so much so I almost slipped under the water, the tub was so huge.

Raziel scrubbed me clean everywhere, and I mean everywhere, even the places that only he knew. He left the top of my shorn and mangled head alone. But the rest of me was clean, and felt nearly good as new. Another miracle.

I wanted to soak and soak, but Raziel wouldn't let me. "We don't have the time," he finally insisted, and with a sigh I stood up on my own, and with shaky legs I looked around.

What had happened to the oil baron who had built all of this finery? Shot, or exiled. Or perhaps he had managed to work his own magic, become part of the regime that had destroyed his world.

"The Soviets are as bad as the Nazis," I said with no small trepidation, looking at the twinkling glass trapped in the ceiling.

"My love, the czars were no angels," Raziel replied, and before we could get lost in the maze of politics he grabbed me out of the tub and wrapped me in gigantic fluffy towels.

I sighed with sheer physical pleasure. "When I left Budapest last summer, I thought everything was crystal clear. Get the Book, stop the war. It was a hopeless quest, but a noble one."

Raziel rubbed down my limbs until they glowed, pink and clean. He reached for a cotton robe hanging from a hook on the back of the door and wrapped it around and around—it, like everything else in the room, was almost grotesquely oversized.

"But now . . ." I trailed off.

"Trust me," Raziel said. "Don't try to untangle the web. Just trust me."

With a sigh, I did. I didn't have the strength for intrigue or politics anymore. Ideology and moral clarity were for the young. And at twenty-one, I no longer felt young.

For you see, Raziel had rescued me on my birthday. He had given me the greatest gift anyone has ever given me. The gift of my life. My parents gave it to me the first time, and I had done my best to throw it away, again and again and again. But now that I had almost lost it for good, Raziel gave it back to me, one last time.

I intended not to lose it again until I reached a ripe old age. Unless someone took it away from me.

"Happy birthday, my love," Raziel said. He took me by the hand and led me to the bed. It was past ten o'clock in the morning, but the heavy brocaded curtains hid any glimmer of the sun.

"We have until three P.M." Raziel whispered. "Uzziel is coming for us then."

It wasn't a long time, but I have found that time is not a linear chain of events, nor a single thread. It is a great wood, with meadows and caves and steep cliffs where you don't expect them to be. And when you find a little clearing in that wood, it makes sense to linger there, as long as you can, perhaps forever in your heart.

Three P.M. both arrived in an instant and never came at all. Part of me is still wrapped up in that giant bed, with the man I adore, the man who pulled me out of death for good. And there I will stay with him always.

✳ 26 ✳

But three o'clock came in this world. Alas, it always does, every day, however lost in the woods of time one wishes to get.

Raziel bundled me in a ridiculous amount of warm wool clothing, covered me in an absurdly huge mink coat, put a Russian fur hat on my head, and carried me downstairs to the waiting car. I was sweating before we got over the threshold.

He gently tucked me into the back of the limousine, nodded once at the driver, and the sleek black machine darted through the broad Baku streets, down to the main Bulvar by the Caspian Sea. The smell of oil was even sharper in the cold air, down by the water.

"Where are we going?" I managed to ask. Now that we were well on our way, I understood all the bundling. Even wrapped against the weather, even though the car was warm and dry, I shivered and shivered. My strength had gotten all used up.

"We are going to meet with my brothers," Raziel replied. And though that was all he said, I shivered even harder. Because without my magic to protect me, I was afraid of what these fallen angels would do, what revenge they might wreak on me for being the sister of those who had stolen their wings away.

Now, I still believed the angels had themselves to answer to when it came to their wings. The women who had seduced them hadn't held machine guns to their heads, they could have said "no" and flown away, back into the higher emanations of the Lord.

But they didn't. They chose not to use the word "no" the way the eldest Lazarii witches did. They succumbed to the luscious, addictive word "yes" instead. Yes, yes, yes . . . once you get used to saying it, it tastes as good as chocolate and is as hard to resist. But that isn't the chocolate's fault, is it?

And it wasn't the women's fault, much less mine, that these angels had chosen to fall, to say a holy "yes" to the things of this world. So in my mind I furiously defended myself against their accusing eyes, their hardened hearts.

When I glanced at Raziel, he was smiling at me. "You are the same girl who I loved from afar, who all but drove me crazy when I found her in Vienna," he said. "You don't need to outwit these men. You don't need to frighten them. And you don't need to charm them, either. They will love you, for my sake at first. And then once they know you . . ."

His voice trailed off as we pulled up to a small house built on the edge of the beach, outside the city limits. "One of these men lives here outside Baku, and he has built this place for our kind to gather."

A fallen angel had built the place, but it had a distinctly Russian flavor to it. A circular drive was crowded with small, strange-looking Soviet cars, and a cat was sleeping on the hood of one that was still idling. A delicious smell wafted out from the kitchen window, and music from an old-fashioned player piano sounded tinny and far away.

Raziel wanted to carry me, but I insisted on walking through the door. The inside of the place couldn't look less like a Quba mountain hut . . . wood paneled, with guns and animal heads mounted on the wall. Now I saw the source of the piano music, an automatic piano playing a tune all by itself, its keys depressing the notes as if an invisible ghost sat at the bench set carefully before it.

"Alexander the Second used to have that piano," somebody said in Polish. "It came all the way from Moscow to here."

I squinted into the dark, cavernous room to find the source of that little fact. I almost died for good when I saw who it was.

My guardian angel, Viktor. Before his death, he had fought as a partisan in Kraków, and afterward, unwilling to give up the fight, he had accepted the difficult, some would say hopeless, assignment of watching over me from Heaven.

But now he stood before me, wings unfurled, still an angel but standing in the darkness, in a clump of other men. I was the only female presence for what seemed like a thousand kilometers.

"Aren't you going to get court-martialed for coming down here with me?" I asked without saying hello.

A great roar of laughter rose all around me. I bristled at their amusement; I wasn't trying to be funny. Raziel drew closer to me, and I saw a smile tickling his lips.

It was then I knew it was somehow all right. I hadn't offended, and these men weren't laughing at me or my ignorance.

"I'm sorry for being so rude," I managed to say. Humility came hard to me—much easier to be powerful and thoughtless, the fell witch of Budapest. Now I was just Magda again, not the Magda of my girlhood with latent power to unleash someday, but the scarred Magda of my adulthood, powerless and therefore more patient. Maybe even with the beginnings of wisdom starting to sprout inside of her.

"You can't be rude to an old Hashomer fellow like me," Viktor replied. "It's just the idea of serving in an army of wings. It makes me happy. Brings back the old times before the war."

"I'm glad you are happy, Viktor. You deserve nothing but happiness and peace."

He shrugged, and I could all but see the ubiquitous cigarette smoke wreathing around his shoulders as it had when he was alive. "I gave up peace when I said I'd watch out for you here in the below," Viktor said. "I'm not ready for peace, not yet. And I'll be happy when that bastard Hitler is roasting in Hell forever."

I gulped at that. Hell is not a very Jewish place, and certainly not a place contemplated at great length by witches. But even though I didn't know much about Hell, I figured Hitler was already living it, with Asmodel his own personal torturer, invited in and welcomed by Hitler himself.

"So let's make you happy, Viktor," I said. "But I don't know how much I can do about it—"

I swallowed the rest of my words in surprise. Because Raziel was none too daintily stomping on my foot to shut me up. He clearly didn't want me speaking of my lack of magic, not now.

So I didn't. I knew he didn't want me to lie; Raziel never did. But he didn't want to make a point of my weakness, either.

I could understand that. So for once I did the prudent thing, and shut my mouth. And I did my best to imitate my lovely, lively friend Eva Farkas, the one who had no magic. I just smiled at Viktor, like I was glad to see him.

And that was easy. I had grown to love my guardian angel, Mr. Viktor Mandelstam from Kraków, Poland. And it was an honor and a pleasure to see the man again, an angel entrusted by the Almighty Himself with the power and the glory of his wings.

"Thank you for being here," I said instead of pointing out my shorn scalp or my inner lack. "You, Viktor, and everybody. I never thought an angel could walk the earth among us, not until Raziel did it."

"This is why we laughed, Magda," Viktor said. "We angels do it all the time."

The thought of it stole my breath. "Of course," I said after a minute's thought. "I always thought that angels were far away, out of reach."

"No," Raziel said, his voice gentle. He took me by the elbow and led to the big, round table set up in the corner. It was covered with a checked cotton tablecloth, and held a bowl of fresh fruit and upside-down teacups. "Don't you remember the trolley car? You were nine."

I gasped with the sudden recollection of it. It was my first summer in Budapest. I was taking ballet classes across town, inside the Ring Road, and had only managed to convince my mother to let me go alone after many sulky tantrums and proclamations of my maturity. I think my poor mother finally gave in to teach me a lesson.

And a lesson I got, though maybe not the one she wanted me to learn. My mother had drummed in my head, "Look both ways, look both ways," and I had.

But I only looked for carts and automobiles. The trolley ran on a separate track, and the electric trolleys were so quiet I wasn't used to hearing them yet. I had just put the tip of my foot on the trolley track when I felt two hands pull me back roughly.

I stepped back just as the trolley whizzed past, not five centimeters from the tip of my nose. The wail of the trolley horn went off an instant after that, too late for the trolley or for me.

The hands had saved me from ending up under the trolley. I whirled around, but nobody was standing behind me. Just faraway people only now pressing into the intersection, after the trolley was already gone.

"That was you," I said to Raziel, out of breath now, the way I had been when it had happened.

"Yes, I pulled you back, and I wasn't gentle about it. You are not a woolgatherer, but you weren't paying enough attention that afternoon. Budapest itself distracted you."

I stopped to consider that afternoon so long ago in my favorite city, that little incident now forever changed by a moment's revelation. "I thought you could not intervene in human affairs. I thought such things could get you fallen."

"Human will is sacred," Viktor said, his voice soft and reflective, for once. "We cannot intervene in the process of choosing. But something like this . . ." He trailed off and looked to Raziel to finish the thought.

"My student of angelic creed is correct," Raziel said. "You weren't choosing to end your life. I cannot stop you from jumping off a bridge, only try as hard as I can to recall you to life with birdsong, the sunrise, anything I can reach out for that might reach you, too. But you weren't choosing anything that day; you were only a girl who didn't pay enough attention."

"But plenty of children, quite innocent, die in accidents. All the time! No human choice involved there, either. So how does that happen?"

All of the angels, fallen and active, looked uneasily at one another. "What?" I insisted. "Don't tell me those innocents don't have angels watching over them. Don't tell me their angels care any bit less."

"Not all angels are created the same," Uzziel said. I hadn't realized he was here until I heard his voice. "We are given the law, but the law has many interpretations. Some of us are strict, some stretch the law until it tears."

My poor, addled, operated-on mind. I could not fathom a world so haphazardly constructed. But then I considered this place where I stood, how brutal, gorgeous, and terrifying it was, and the caprice of God's creation began to make some sense.

"So the Fall, and the Garden," I said under my breath. "You

are telling me the angels themselves have quarreled since the beginning of things."

Their silence only confirmed the obvious.

"So, what is this now? I thought this was a human war we fight."

Raziel shrugged. "I think you are making too big a deal of the differences between the angels and the children of men."

I goggled then. Now, I readily admit that about many things I am a fool. But it was just dawning upon me how thoroughly I had missed the nature of the battle we fought. How deeply the dispute ran. It did not run back to Weimar Germany or to the Great War or even the war of 1870. No.

This fight was as much between Raziel and Asmodel as it was between Hitler and Stalin. More. Hitler and Stalin were mere gnats, as I had once observed to Asmodel. Raziel, Asmodel, Uzziel—they had battled one another, over deep and bloody ground, for centuries.

I stole a glance at Viktor. He had been an ordinary mortal, no adept with magic, no werewolf or vampire or hob or fairy, and yet here he was, wings tucked behind him but winged nevertheless. I took a sharp intake of breath.

"I keep thinking the angels and the people, the vampires and the werewolves . . ." My voice trailed off as the sewn-up incision on the top of my head began to throb.

"From the other side, things look very different," Viktor began. "It is understandable to me how you look at things. Look, I was a socialist, I didn't care what happened after my death. The fight for my people was all that mattered.

"But who are 'my people'?" Viktor continued. "I thought the magicals were the enemy. The angels, remote or perhaps mythical. But I was wrong, Lazarus. Terribly, tragically, wrong.

"You are made a certain way," Viktor continued. "All of us are made a certain way. But we are all the same—in that we are made."

I rubbed at my eyes, drowsy with headache. "So you're saying it's all the choices we make, our wills, that matter? Whether we have wings or fangs isn't important?"

Viktor, damn his wings, didn't answer me—angels have an annoying tendency to just smile and nod instead of telling us ignorant humans how the world really works. But his smile said volumes. His smile said, "What does it matter, Magdalena? Just choose. You are going to die after all, sooner or later but for good, one day. How you decide to live before that is up to you."

"But aren't you breaking your angelic vows by coming here?" I asked. "Didn't Raziel break his vows by coming back to Earth after Asmodel destroyed him?"

I spoke to Viktor, but my words were meant for my husband. He had assured me a thousand times he had decided to come for his own sake, not mine. That love demanded such a sacrifice, and that he gladly made it, took it as a joy and a badge of honor to lose his wings to stand with me and Gisele and the rest of us blindly fighting for our lives here in the world.

So it was Raziel who replied to me. "My love, the battle is not between the angels and the Fallen Ones. When I said I walked Asmodel's path I wasn't kidding. But we keep choosing, even after the first choice is made. We took on free will, the gift given to the children of Eve. We keep choosing. And it is the small choices that make the biggest impact in the end.

"It was my choice, to pull you out of the path of the trolley, that led to me standing here. I fell to earth that day, not the day I asked to return and was granted that gift."

I sat down, my head hurting like the blazes. I shrugged off the heavy mink coat, though the dacha was freezing. "I am too stupid now to follow you, my dear. I've been stupid ever since I said good-bye to Gisele. Not the day she was killed, either. The day I left her behind in Keleti Station and left Budapest to hunt the Book. Ever since I made that choice, I've been confused and wrong and full of bad decisions."

Viktor laughed and I could smell cigarette smoke, though I did not see a burning ember in his hand. "Welcome to the world, Magdalena Lazarus. The tragedy of humanity is not that we make so many terrible choices. It's that we don't ever learn, or even realize when the choice is made."

So Viktor still saw it as "we." Even his wings did not separate him from our mad race of fools.

"We're all confused and wandering," Uzziel said. "It is not the province of mortal man alone. All creatures who choose must do so in ignorance."

"We don't know what will happen as a result," Raziel cut in. "So. I choose to use the gem to stop Asmodel at last. Will that turn me into a creature like him? I hope not, but I don't know."

He stared levelly at me, that serene, steady expression of his, so beloved and infuriating, and I just loved him, Raziel, loved him in that moment like I never had before. Because I had never understood how much he was like me, not until that moment. Like me, but so much more patient, and stronger, and less tossed by fury and grief.

"I won't let you get like him," I said. "Stupid mortal that I am, I believe there's a chance you won't. Because unlike

Asmodel, you think and weigh, and you agree to be wrong when you are wrong. You can bear the consequences of your choice. He won't."

"So who is the biggest rebel, then?" Raziel said, a laugh hidden in his words. "Asmodel retains the angelic trait of distance from living reality. I have given all that celestial knowing away. If you're stupid, my love, I'm stupider. You have grown up in the world of mortals. I am just starting to understand why it is so deucedly difficult to make any choice at all, much less the correct one."

"This is a very interesting philosophical discussion," I said. My voice slurred, my head hurt so much. "But let's say what we really mean. You mean to take your gem, the Heaven Sapphire, and use it to destroy the elemental creature of air, Asmodel."

I had no power to craft spells any longer, none at all, but the air seemed to vibrate around my words nevertheless, as if I had spoken a secret invocation. "How can you possibly do it, my dear? Without working magic? I thought I was the only one to work the magic of the gem . . . or so you told me."

"You had the magic to withstand the gem without being seduced to use it. That is all I ever said, mind. But now the choice is we use it now, or Churchill tries to use it—he's not stupid, and Knox knows about the gem's properties. Or Stalin uses it."

"God forbid," Uzziel said, under his breath but loud enough for me to hear.

"And I don't think anyone else stands a chance of using it without becoming corrupted by it. Asmodel was corrupted, years ago, just by the prospect of using it. Why do you think I threw it into the ocean in the time of Noah? Asmodel."

"So you're going to work the magic of the gem. Why do you need an army at all then?"

"I will call the spirits the way you did at Wolf's Lair. Because I can't destroy a million souls at once in a battle. Nor would I want to, if I even could. Not with the gem. It works one soul at a time. And is much more dangerous, for that. For the wrong soul, corrupted, can do a great deal of damage. As we have seen in these terrible times."

I thought of Ziyad, looked among the men of fire who had gathered in this place. But Ziyad was gone.

"Was Ziyad corrupted?" I asked. "Is that why he is missing?"

The men looked at one another, and even Viktor avoided my gaze. "He isn't corrupted," Raziel said. "Magduska, he made a great sacrifice, in the name of the good."

Nobody was going to solve the mystery of Ziyad's disappearance for me, and I was too worn out to press the question. I thought of my own mother, who had entangled her own soul to fight my battles. And I sighed, when I thought of the trouble I had caused as well as the good, in this world and in the beyond.

"What will it cost the afterworld, to fight this battle as you say?"

Viktor laughed aloud at this. "Those bastards at the Institute may have carved you up like Frankenstein's monster, but maybe they also injected you with wisdom. You now think of the whole world, not just the bits you know. Brava, Miss Lazarus."

I smiled at that. Even my own angel still used my maiden name. But the days of my maiden name were done.

"I've kept my true name a secret, to protect Raziel from

magic worked by the hand against me," I said. "But to hell with secrets. I am defenseless, after the hospital. The truth can only protect me now."

I looked at Raziel, who only nodded. I had nothing more to hide, not from my own angel certainly, and not from the people here, once winged or not, who now fought on the same side as me.

"Raziel HaMelech. Once angel, *malach,* now my husband. The king of the rebel angels, my sister called him. My name is now Magdalena King, Lazarus no more."

I sighed and rested my head on my forearms, on the table-cloth. "Okay, I give up, and I'll do what you say. But I can't do a thing now. You all have a bite and we'll go. But I couldn't eat now if you held a gun to my head to make me."

✳ 27 ✳

Churchill himself was installed at a grand dacha in Krasnaya Polyana, near the Black Sea, and once the plans had been laid by the brothers of Raziel, Knox returned from Moscow and flew with me and Raziel to meet the great man.

I feared to see him again. He was the last person I knew to see my mouse alive, and I was afraid he knew a different girl than I grieved over now. Gisele had tried to warn me that she was changed or, more precisely, that my fond mental picture of her no longer was very accurate.

Even more, I feared to show him my own diminished self. My pride, still formidable, had taken a terrible blow in the wake of the surgery I had survived. But even worse than embarrassment, I feared Churchill's pity.

I needn't have wasted my worries on him. I fussed and fretted for a whole three days, while I waited for the now itchy-as-hell incision on my head to heal, found some decent clothes and a clever assortment of hats that hid my chopped-off hair and the nasty-looking scars from view.

We three flew together in a Tupolev ANT-14, a tourist plane that could hold three dozen people. This time I was well bundled in furs and a cunning little black hat trimmed in ermine. No more freezing on planes for me.

Knox barely said hello, only grew still and squinted at me, as if he could look into my soul and see what was now missing. I nodded my greetings, too choked up to speak. Funny how I now associated the big, mustachioed American with Gisele, since he had taken her away from me forever. Just as Gisele had once foreseen.

Raziel stroked my gloved hands as the plane rumbled down the runway and into the sky. "All of this will soon be over, for better or for worse," he said, his voice all but drowned out by the drone of the twin propellers beating the air outside our window.

I nodded, knowing what he meant, and taking some cold comfort in it. Hitler and Asmodel were on their way, striking eastward from their Prussian base, the Wolf's Lair, to the Caucasus oil fields and the ancient hiding place of the Heaven Sapphire.

If the Nazis succeeded in defeating the Soviet army and smashing through to Baku, they were effectively the victors in this conflagration, unless the gem could somehow reverse the military victory.

The best way to defend the oil fields was to attack first, using the gem, before Hitler's army arrived. And with the French and English armies now mobilized, opening up a second front on the Wehrmacht's rear could slow down the German attack enough for Raziel to reach the vanguard in time—and stop them outside the Caucasus altogether.

The problem was that nobody had yet been able to stop the Nazi juggernaut. And Raziel, brave and wise as he was, could not work the spells I once could wield. The gem was a different weapon in his hands than it would have been in mine.

Knowing I could no longer work magic to stop Hitler embittered me. But I was still too physically tired to ruminate too much upon the fact.

The Tupolev landed with a hard, skidding bump. Stalin hated to fly, so this airfield wasn't equipped for handling the arrival of a head of state. Fortunately for all of us, we weren't anybody outwardly important, just the shadowy grunts who did all of the work behind the scenes, out of the glare of the footlights.

We slipped into Krasnaya Polyana like vengeful ghosts.

A car idled outside the hangar, steam rising in an enormous plume all around it. A Russian sat in the front passenger seat, cradling an enormous machine gun in his lap.

Knox nodded his greetings to the driver, and presented some official-looking document with big Soviet seals and stamps festooned all over it.

"I am surprised we have no handlers," I said to Raziel as we straggled behind Knox. "It wasn't so long ago that we were cosmopolitan enemies of the Soviet motherland."

Raziel shrugged. "I don't know. I think they assume I have

some Azeri ties, given my brothers. And remember, Stalin himself is from Georgia. He understands the mountains of the south better than his Muscovite party machine ever will."

I smiled, to hear Raziel sound so world-weary and clear-eyed. He opened the back passenger door for me, and with a sigh I slipped inside, between him and Knox. Raziel slammed the door, and the car pulled away smoothly, following a gravel path straight into the forest.

"No snow falling," Knox said in French. "Good luck."

He smiled at me, and tears pricked at my eyes. He had never before spoken to me in so patient and kind a tone. Before, I was a threat to Knox, somebody who had previously made a hash of his careful plans through my naïve and misguided magic. Now, I couldn't do anything to anybody's well-laid magical plans. Just follow along, and maybe learn something if I paid attention and kept my mouth shut.

Raziel couldn't talk at length with Knox. Knox's Hungarian, while admirable for an American, was too faulty, so he instead leaned back against the cushions and sighed. While I considered Churchill, and how we could possibly speak this time. For I still spoke no English, and couldn't call upon Albion, as I had the first time we'd met.

And worse. I wouldn't call on Albion even if I could—for Raziel, and I, too, had brought the angels themselves into this thing. The war had invaded the very heavens. That was another reason it would have to be over soon. Such an unnatural situation could not obtain for long.

We drove deeper into the forest, ascending steep, winding roads and disappearing into the woods like lost children in a fairy tale. As we drove higher and higher into the mountains, the ground turned white with already-fallen snow.

Churchill stood at the doorway of the dacha nestled in the snow, waiting for us. This was not only an honor, but a sign of how little time we had left before the battle would be joined.

A strange lassitude overtook my limbs as I walked toward him, the English Bulldog. I had already lost the most urgent war, to save Gisele's life. I fought now so that Gisele's death would not be in vain. My grief for her almost killed me, too. Gisele would have scolded me for weeks over that.

As we drew closer to the great man I tried to smile. The few phrases in English that I knew fled from my poor brain as we approached, but it didn't matter. Churchill enveloped me in a gigantic, wholly unexpected embrace.

I stiffened for a moment, then relaxed inside his arms, felt the hidden frailty of the man inside his bulky clothes. Despite Churchill's strength, he was not a young man, and the hug revealed it.

Somehow his frailty gave me strength. We need not be a David to fight Goliath, only willing.

"My poor purple witch," Churchill said in his terrible French. Behind me, Knox groaned—he worried at the indiscretions Churchill could make in that lovely Latinate tongue that he over-trusted. "You are still very charming, dear Miss Lazarus. Charming, so!"

He patted me on the back and let me go. Without another word, he turned and crossed through the open door at his back into the dacha, and the three of us, Knox, Raziel, and I, followed close behind.

As I went inside I gave only a single glance to the Russian

fellow in the greatcoat and wool hat guarding the door with his machine gun.

A roaring fire and a low table set with English tea and scones only deepened my grief instead of setting me at my ease. My sister would have loved those buttery round treats, the sweet, milky tea . . .

Raziel caught me sighing and led me to a chair. "Magduska, rest," he commanded, and gratefully I obeyed. I suppose I should have felt guilty, surrendering to his kindness and leaning on his strength. But I knew I would have done the same for him without thinking twice.

With an audible groan Churchill settled into the chair nearest the fire. "*Sacre bleu,* arthritis," he muttered under his breath.

Knox stepped between me and the great Churchill, and said something in rapid, unintelligible English. I closed my eyes against the Babel of languages.

"We have a surprise for you, Miss Magda," Knox said.

I was no longer Miss Magda, but I was too worn out to correct him. Instead, I opened my eyes again, and almost fell off the chair in my shock.

For my former employer, Count Gabor Bathory, stood before me in all his vampiric glory. He had come to me again.

I didn't know whether to laugh or cry. I just blinked up at him, and waited for him to reject me, his maimed, useless girl assistant. Me, Magda Lazarus, the fiery, thoughtless one who had accepted my vampire's protection upon my return from Poland, and who had barely even thanked him before leaving Budapest behind, and exposing him to demonic dangers he hadn't earned.

And now I was useless to him. How Bathory detested useless, broken things.

We stared at each other for what seemed like an eternity. I waited for him to toss me away with a single comment, a flick of his aristocratic white hand.

And then Bathory kneeled, and he kissed my exposed wrist, long and gentle. The submissive vampire kiss, the one that proclaimed the receiver's superior authority.

He was deferring all of his considerable power to me. Not to Raziel. But to me.

I had never seen something so incomprehensible and unbelievable in my entire life. The terrifying Lord Vampire of Budapest, Bathory, had declared his fealty to me, with a single subservient kiss.

"Forgive me," he said. "I had once believed your power resided in your magic. What a fool I was. Forgive me, my mistress."

I goggled, and only stopped to blink when the sound of Raziel's laughter permeated my thoughts. "Magda, your mother was right—you could catch flies in your mouth, your jaw is hitting the floor so hard. Come back to earth, my love!"

I blinked hard, and finally had the presence of mind to stand up, and pull Lord Bathory to his feet. "You are beyond ridiculous, my dearest count," I finally managed to stutter out. "I have never heard such amazing nonsense."

He looked me right in the eye, then, and I remembered how terrified my mortal friend Eva was of the vampire's gaze. How I had myself warned her against staring into a vampire's eyes, that an ordinary mortal had no recourse against their thrall.

But I felt no thrall. I felt absolutely nothing.

"It is true, then," Bathory said, his voice heavy with wonder. "My dear little ex-witch, you are more of a marvel alive than dead."

I blinked again at his words. "Count Bathory, I am too muddleheaded to follow your words where they are leading. I don't know a single thing I thought that I knew. I am cut apart, and maimed, and . . . useless." My voice caught on that last, however much I tried to keep the tone calm, light even.

"I have never heard you speak this way, not even when you ran from your gifts," Bathory replied. "And yet, you clearly still don't realize."

"No. Please explain, dear sir. And while you're about it, please take back your fealty. It is absurd to offer it to a magic-less one like me."

"But that is just the thing." Bathory's voice was lit from inside with wonder. "You are truly magic-less. Completely devoid of the gifts you once possessed."

"Why, yes," I said, my voice dry as tinder now. "And I'd appreciate your not scrubbing salt into that wound over and over."

"But you looked into my eyes, far into me, as I looked into you. My dear, you not only cannot work magic. You are utterly impervious to it."

My scalp had more or less healed—some Soviet doctor had plucked the stitches out and pronounced me good enough a day or two before. But the skin tingled and itched now, as if Bathory tickled the wound with his words.

"I don't think any spell against you could stick," he continued. "None."

Knox spoke in rapid French. "No, it's true, Miss . . . errr. Mrs. . . . Miss Magda. Before I came to Baku, I had even the witch of Amsterdam, Lucretia de Merode herself, concoct a spell of binding, just to test it. And it slipped right off your shoulders. It dazzled her."

"So what?" I said, a flash of my old temper flaring. "What difference does it make, what other people can or can't do to me? I can't do a thing myself."

Bathory bared his teeth in his frustration, earning an outraged rebuke in English from Churchill. "Oh, dear, infuriating child," he murmured before turning to speak with Churchill. For Bathory, fluent in Hungarian, English, French, and even Latin, could talk to everybody present in the room.

Churchill chortled when Bathory explained the change in me. He spoke for a long time, his eyes glinting and twinkling in turns.

Finally, Bathory returned to me. "Please sit again, you are pale as marble. You are marvelous and thrilling, my dear little chicken, but you are terrifying as well. Sit, now."

I did as I was bidden, completely confused and befuddled. "Did you not hear about Gisele?" I said, not meaning to cut my former boss with my words. I honestly didn't know.

His eyes grew moist and I realized he had known, before I did. After all, Gisele was his in a way she was not even mine.

He had tasted her blood, and their spirits had entwined after that. From what I knew of vampire lore, the death of a vampire's lamb caused terrible suffering to the sponsor.

I had forgotten. I had wanted to forget.

"Please, take back your fealty," I said again. "It is too much of an honor, completely undeserved."

"My dear," Bathory said, his voice hoarse now with emotion, "the battle is joined. The Arrow Cross have overrun

Hungary now that the Nazis have attacked the Russians. Hundreds of thousands of Hungarians, the cream of our young men, are attacking Stalin's army as we speak."

"My God," I said. "What happened to Eva in all of this?"

"Ah, Eva, my poor kitty. Even a cat has only nine lives."

My blood turned to ice. "No."

My "no" no longer held any power. Bathory shook his head sadly. "I do not know her fate for certain, but I fear that Eva, too, is dead. Martin Szalasi had his throat ripped out by his own wolves in the battle for power in the streets. Budapest is in utter chaos. Martin did not have the cunning or the brutality to survive."

If a vicious dog like Martin was too tender to live, my beloved Budapest had truly become a hell. How could Eva survive such a conflagration?

My mind reeled with the thought that my girl Eva had lost her fight at last. I couldn't bear to dwell upon it, or her. It was only after a moment that I managed to move past Eva's fate to catch the import of what Bathory didn't say. Of course. Hungary fought on the side of the Nazis. Bathory refused to offer the Nazis his fealty—he wasn't averse to fooling them, but the time for subterfuge was past. We now fought our battles in the open.

Bathory's rule of the Budapest vampires was at an end. My dear count no longer had a country.

He smiled when he saw I understood, careful this time to keep his fangs well hidden away from the mortals surrounding us. "My dear, you may have no more magic. You are no longer my little chicken, she with the hidden witchery, waiting to come forth."

I nodded, miserable as hell but unwilling to give in to

despair, not in the presence of Churchill. I no longer cared what the man thought of me, but some remnant of my old pride demanded that I maintain the decencies for Raziel's sake.

"I see that you do not understand, Magda. You only see what you have lost, the gift you were given by virtue of your birth, and not what you have gained."

The old Magda, the eldest of the eldest of the Lazarii witches, would have given my old employer what for after that. But he was right—I was that powerful witch no longer.

"My head hurts," I replied. "I am sure spirits attend us here, but I cannot see them, nor sense them in any way. I did not even notice my old teacher's spell when she cast it. You are right, dear count. I do not see what I have gained in all of this. Besides my husband. Love is worth all, even losing yourself. So I won't complain. But I don't see what earthly use I have any longer."

Bathory began pacing like a caged black panther, coiled up and fighting not to strike. "You are such a bullhead, you haven't changed a bit. Stop your thinking for half a second and listen. You have no magic. Your enemies do not know that. Lucretia herself could not tell at the time she hurled her spell—she did it to test your defenses, and she was shocked, shocked to find that you have none."

I couldn't help laughing a bit at that. "Forgive me for failing to understand the benefit."

"You will, eventually," he said, evidently taking me exactly at my word. "But hush. You are the fell witch of Budapest, the most deadly and fearful creature to emerge in a generation. You are now in possession of the famed Gem of

Raziel, the gem that Solomon the Great used to build the Holy Temple."

I sat perfectly still, willing myself to listen for once, just listen, not protest or interject. To allow the words to enter my mind without judging them first.

"You will ride in the vanguard of the storm, with your band of fallen angels. This is a fight, brother against brother. The spirits of the air, the elemental demons and devils, against the angels of fire who have taken the side of mortalkind."

"And what side does the Almighty fight on?"

Bathory glared at me until I sat back and gave up on getting any kind of answer. "Asmodel does not know what happened to you. He does not know even that the Soviets didn't augment your powers instead of destroying them."

"But wait. Everybody knows how much Stalin hates magic of any kind."

"Stalin is a bloody hypocrite."

Churchill cleared his throat, and Knox hurriedly translated this entire exchange from Hungarian into English. Churchill's booming laugh filled the room, and then he lit an enormous cigar and puffed away, squinting at Bathory with great, undisguised curiosity.

"You will take the blasts directed at you. And Raziel's brothers will do the attacking."

The fact I could do nothing to protect myself from an attack didn't seem to concern him. I shrugged. "All right."

Bathory stroked his mustache, ready to make an even more impassioned argument for his battle plan, and then he paused, dumbstruck.

"No, really," I said, "that's fine."

Bathory blinked hard, cleared his throat.

I nodded at him. "If any of this is going to work, it will be Raziel and his brothers who will do it. You are basically saying I will be the decoy. I will go down while Raziel leads the battle. So be it."

I did not for the life of me understand why Bathory thought my lack of magic was such an advantage. Perhaps because our enemies would put all of their efforts into destroying me, and leave their flank open to a conventional attack.

Either way, I didn't mind. I had prepared to die, actually thought a heroic death the perfect way to depart this world. Much as I treasured life now as a gift, part of me still wanted to join Gisele in the afterworld.

I knew that Gisele would be disappointed in me if I showed up without having done my best to keep my promise to her, even now. For I had promised to do everything in my power to stop her visions from coming to pass. Just because those visions tormented Gisele no longer didn't mean that the monsters she had prophesied had vanished from Europe.

I had promised to use the Book to stop Hitler if I could. I wasn't giving up the fight yet, no matter how sharply I grieved for Gisele. I could die of grief later. But the time to fight was now.

And if I died in the fight, well . . . in many ways, if it was my fate to now die, that would serve as the perfect end of the story, the Book of Magdalena Lazarus. It sounded good to me, had the perfect ring of martyrdom to it.

"You don't have to convince me," I said to Bathory, and to everyone collected in the cozy room with the roaring fire in the hearth. "Let us fight."

I turned my gaze to Bathory, and looked him full in the eye, not afraid of him anymore. "And I accept your fealty after all, dear count. If we manage to win, you will end up King of Hungary, and I can go back to being your ex-assistant. But for now, you are the government-in-exile of the Budapest vampires."

And if Bathory had no country, then neither did I.

✳ 28 ✳

Two times before I had battled Asmodel. The first time, as a witch unsure of my power. The second, as the Lazarus, in command of my inborn gifts, fighting to claim *The Book of Raziel* as my inheritance.

I knew this was the last time. Third time for keeps, as Eva and I used to say as girls. And this time I fought the ancient demon without my magic, vulnerable to his terrible power.

Raziel's brothers joined the Soviet army southwest of Stalingrad. They went to fight the magical creatures that fought alongside the German Wehrmacht. And after a lot of insisting, Viktor, my angel, went with them, to fight once more against the Nazis.

After the angels had gone, it was just Raziel and me. I had

nowhere else to go, nowhere to run. Third time for keeps. This time, either Asmodel or I would win.

Bathory, technically a foreign national from a hostile state, stayed behind with Churchill, and mustered what vampiric allies he could, though most of his people had sided with the Reich, after Hungary had succumbed to the Arrow Cross Nazis and come into the war on the side of the Germans.

In the end, Raziel stayed with me, Raziel alone. Together we safeguarded the gem, and prepared to join Raziel's brothers at the front so that our superweapon would not go unused. But the thought of the damage it would cause troubled me. And I was afraid of the corrupting influence of the gem, even upon a soul as pure as Raziel's.

We left to follow the army. We had a tentative, shaky sort of plan: instead of running in the vanguard, the conventional army would, we hoped, shield us and the gem from Asmodel. And Raziel would make of the gem what he could.

We took our time getting to the front, in a sputtery rust brown truck, backfiring and burning oil in a sooty plume as we pressed northeast from Krasnaya Polyana. Raziel drove, I sat next to him in the front passenger seat.

"Asmodel doesn't fight in the vanguard," I said. "We won't find him on the battlefield, either."

The ancient truck jolted and jounced over the uneven terrain. We had driven hard and long, behind the Russian army, and now sped through the countryside north of the Black Sea.

"No, our fight with Asmodel will take place on a different battlefield, I am sure of it," Raziel said.

"So how are we going to find him? Isn't his host, the Führer, guarded as usual by the SS Werewolves, German army, and by spell?"

Raziel smiled then, so quickly I almost missed it. "The gem will bring us together, you'll see."

"They aren't at the Wolf's Lair any longer." I had no way to magically verify my suspicions, but I was virtually certain they followed the army, one way or another.

"No."

"So where are they?"

"They seek the Garden."

We had arrived at our destination for the evening, and Raziel brought the truck to a rolling stop. We stood now on the broken high plains, cold and frozen and dead, the depths of February. Our surroundings could not have resembled the primeval Garden of Eden any less.

The smell of burning rubber polluted the stark, frigid air, and I coughed a little and wished for earmuffs. "They may seek the Garden, but they are going after it the long way, through hell."

Raziel smiled again and sighed. "Well, yes. But they know you are coming. They are watching for you. They've sighted you by now. Asmodel will be sure to get you, himself."

Raziel and I intercepted the path of the German blitzkrieg, knowing that Asmodel had a special interest in me and what my magic could give him. We sought to tempt the ancient tempter, and while I distracted him and drew him out Raziel's brothers could deliver the coup de grâce to his army from behind, by surprise.

That was our initial plan. But even as we formulated it, I could see the flaws. For one, we all assumed Asmodel still had an interest in me, the Lazarus witch of Budapest. For another, the chance that we could surprise Asmodel with the Heaven Sapphire seemed dim indeed.

But we didn't have a better plan, just this one. And maybe in the end, a plan with so many holes, one that didn't make any provision for retreat, would prove the right one for the job after all.

Raziel and I drove toward my doom, and I knew it. And the knowledge gave me a certain serenity. We had no second plan. This was it.

"You really think that Asmodel is going to find me, and venture out of his defenses to attack?"

"From his point of view, you have attacked already, and he's just capitalizing on your overreaching."

I sighed. The wind picked up along the low steppes and crackled the iced-over grasses on the plains. "But what if he doesn't attack? What, then?"

"Well, then. Then we're finished, that's what."

"So how do we get his attention?"

"Oh, you have his attention. It's just a question of calling him out here and now."

One more night before we reached the front, before here and now could no longer be avoided. For now, we rested at a pretty little dacha in the middle of nowhere, which Knox had arranged, and the caretaker gave us wood for the fire and some sausage to eat for dinner.

We ate in silence as the darkness overtook us. One night left. And then we fought for keeps.

⚬

Now that I had lost my magic, our situation was very clear to me, and very sad. We possessed the Gem of Raziel, we had each other, and we believed in the justice of our cause. All good.

But it was not enough. None of it was enough because Hitler and his army, the greatest power in Europe, had already proven it could crush any other in its path.

We knew we had to fight. We intended to fight. But when examined with dispassion, without the soft glow of magic to mitigate the hard reality, our chances of success looked slim indeed.

The caretaker of the dacha didn't appear quite human, but I was too despondent thinking of the imminent battle to inquire into his origins. With a wink and a smile, once dinner was done and the fire in the bedroom properly stoked, the old man made sure that we had what we needed, and he shuffled off to bed.

Churchill had toasted our marriage before we left, making it clear, even without proper French, that he approved of us together. I didn't know that I did. I adored Raziel, with all of my heart and soul and body. But loving him was wrong; he was made for wings, not a wife.

I thought I had put my guilty feelings to rest when I had said "I do" in our wartime ceremony. But now that I no longer had my magic, my vows took on a different cast.

I thought all these dangerous thoughts as we prepared to go to bed, very late, at almost three in the morning. Raziel watched me, stewing under the blankets, but knew better than to poke at me. "You are exhausted, my love," he murmured into my shoulder. He kissed the back of my neck and left me to my desperate thoughts. Of all people, Raziel understood that he could not lift my black spirits by poking and prodding at them.

I had to exorcise my demons for myself.

I listened in the flickering dark until Raziel's breathing became slow and even. How that man could sleep, no matter how precarious our circumstances. For a while I believed that listening to Raziel sleeping would somehow heal the grief eating me up alive.

But no. Raziel was my husband, not a martyr or a human sacrifice. I had to solve the puzzle of why I still lived. I could no longer vanquish my enemies or even fight them. Bathory's bright ideas aside, I still didn't understand what role I could now play in battling my foes.

Maybe unearthing the sapphire stone would prove enough by itself. No small thing, capturing the Heaven Sapphire, even if I did secretly worry the stone would ultimately prove our undoing.

"Leo?" I whispered into the night. Hoping that my imp could hear my ordinary human voice, that he would come to me despite my maimed state.

I called to him again and again, out loud and by wishing for him, too. But nothing. He seemed so close to me, somehow—I couldn't see or hear Leo, but he stayed in the forefront of my thoughts. I was with Leo in my heart, but I couldn't hear him, no matter how hard I tried.

I don't know why, but losing my courageous little imp was the last straw. Something snapped inside of me, some tether to the world I had known. I wandered in a no-man's-land of grief. To be honest, I don't think I was in my right mind.

I slipped out of bed, my feet shaky under me. The cigar box was wrapped in a woolen sweater and stuffed under the bed. Not much of a protection laid on the gem, but considering it had resided in a stone hut for hundreds of years, lying around like a paperweight, we probably guarded it better this way than in some ostentatious kind of prison for the thing.

As I pulled the box from under the bed, I wondered about my "thing" assumption. What made someone a person and not a thing? The gem had emotions, it had memory, it had will. What separated it from a soul, besides the lack of a living body?

I lugged the box across the room to a wing chair set up next to the fireplace. Except for its heaviness, I could no longer decipher anything unusual about the bundle I hauled around.

I unwrapped the sweater and put it on, then opened the cigar box and released the jewel of Raziel from its white swaddling cloth. I looked at it in the flickering firelight, and it was beautiful, a king's gem no doubt. But I could no longer see into the gemstone, and I suspected it could no longer see into me.

I cradled the sapphire in my hands, and the stone grew warm under my touch. I held it to my heart, and whispered, "I'm sorry," to it.

The gem grew warmer. "Forgive me for treating you like a prisoner," I said, a tear escaping down to my chin. Part of me was embarrassed, crying over an ageless, all-seeing Eye. But most of me really did just feel sorry for the fate of the Raziel sapphire. It reminded me too much of the fate of its bearer, Raziel himself.

The warmth seeped through my fingers and into my body, so much like the warmth that Raziel himself emanated that

I stopped crying. A gigantic wave of peace and gentleness washed over me, calming me, comforting me.

I smiled through my tears with a growing wonder. Finally, after all my journeys and choices and battles, I understood. The Heaven Sapphire was not made to conquer armies. Raziel hadn't brought it into the world to terrify, or to punish, or to open the mind to visions.

He had brought the gem to Earth to comfort the daughters of Eve. That was all. That was what the gem had been created to achieve. Nothing more. It was we makers of magic who had subverted its original purpose.

I know, I am slow. Raziel had told me exactly this when I had first asked him why he had brought the gem, later translated into the Book, to Earth. To console.

Now that I desperately needed consolation, I could finally understand.

I cradled the gem to my chest, whispered "thank you" again and again and again, and the gem sparkled in the semidarkness.

Raziel turned over in his sleep and groaned. I looked up from the gem—

And Asmodel stood next to my chair, between me and my husband, a small smile playing over his spectacularly beautiful features.

When the world was young, Asmodel had looked like this, like an older, blond brother of Uzziel. And Asmodel loved a human woman, one who had once cradled this very gem to her breast.

But then his frustration set in . . . and choice by choice, he strayed from the Garden into a world of pain and evil.

"At last," Asmodel murmured. "At last, at last . . ."

The gem grew cold. My grip tightened upon it, and I turned to face my nemesis. "How did you get in here? Through all the anti-magic in this part of the world?"

He smiled and crouched next to my chair, his face level with the gem. "I have my ways, Lazarus. Or should I say . . . King?"

I gulped and set the gem in my lap. Ice-cold now.

"You married him. A shame. Your fate and his are now entwined together, tighter than Bathory and his lamb, tighter than Churchill and his England."

I had no words. I had nothing, nothing at all. In all our fevered planning for war, we had never expected that Asmodel would leave Hitler unguarded and come to us of his own volition, in the dead of night, far from the battlefield.

"I *wanted* you to find the gem," he went on. "I attacked you in Budapest, I harried you with the Soviet Institute—Stalin was most accommodating when he heard what I was after. I killed your Gisele, too. And you did exactly as I wanted."

My mind flashed on the cows milling over the foothills of the Five Fingers of God. And I realized that Asmodel had herded me more expertly than did the shepherd and his son.

I gulped. "Well, it worked. Here we are."

He smiled, and the demonic face warred with the angelic for control. "You have sacrificed your soul for the gem's power. The fact my agent could kill Gisele without revenge proves it. The German army is almost past Stalingrad now. Once we break though, we reclaim the Garden."

"Even without the gem?" I asked, my voice quiet. Asmodel spoke aloud my deepest, darkest fears. But I could not hide from them any longer—after all, my fears had all come true already. Keeping them a secret, or revealing them to the world, no longer mattered a whit.

He growled at that. "Stalin refused to give it to us. That is what made us decide to attack our worthless ally."

"You are assuming that Stalin ever had it to give to you. Stalin never had it."

He hesitated. By now, he knew me well, almost as well as did Raziel, and he expected, I'm sure, some fireworks of fury, some crackling witchfire, or at least a whispered ward thrown over my husband's shoulders.

"So where is your host?" I asked. "You know, Herr Hitler. You left him all alone to his own devices? Isn't that rather unwise?"

Based on the battle plans we had made before the angels went, I knew that the vanguard of avenging angels, together with a division of the Soviet army, had already begun the offensive out of Stalingrad. On the physical plane, the battle already raged.

"None of that matters," Asmodel said. "All that matters is the gem. Give it to me."

The sapphire grew warm against my fingertips once more. I tried my hardest to look into it, to fry my eyes and my brain for once and for all so that Asmodel could not possess me, which now he could all too easily do.

But I could no longer see into the gem. It could only comfort me now, not destroy me.

"I'm sorry," I said. "I can't give you the gem."

Raziel stirred and behind Asmodel's rounded shoulder I saw that he was awake.

"You will," Asmodel said. "And because of our long love affair, witch, I will give you a choice. One last choice before the time for choosing is gone forever. You can join me, like the creature who murdered your Gisele has joined me. Or I will finally kill you for good, too."

"You are assuming, dear demon, that those are the only two choices that I have." Just within my field of vision, I could see Raziel noiselessly sliding out of bed, reaching under his pillow.

I wished I could warn him that his Mauser would have no effect on Asmodel. I could no longer sense the wards and the immense power the ancient demon had amassed through the perverted use of *The Book of Raziel*. But after our battle in Wolf's Lair, I knew that he still wielded the power.

A bullet could not reach Asmodel.

"Give me the sapphire, witch," he said, more menacingly this time.

By now I saw that Raziel had pointed the Mauser at the demon's head. If Raziel pulled the trigger, I knew in my bones that he would die. Asmodel's wards would exact their revenge for the bullet, and they would protect the demon from any physical harm.

Because despite the fact I knew my magic was gone, Asmodel, somehow, didn't.

Before I could warn Raziel away, the air next to Asmodel shimmered and a slender, sharp figure stepped out of the darkness.

And I rose out of the chair and onto my feet, holding the gem like a rock. Because it was Enepsigos who stood in front of me now. The third demoness, she who had murdered my Gisele.

She was smiling. "Stupid girl," she purred from next to

Asmodel's shoulder. "Stupid, stupid. You threw your sister away on a fool's errand. You worked for Asmodel more faithfully than I."

"Shut up."

She laughed, and I saw the flash of her cruel, slashing teeth, her sharp fingernails. "Bind yourself to serve the evil one. You will at least get something back for all your trouble, besides pain. And death."

I shrugged. "I'm mortal, Enepsigos. Death is part of the bargain, no matter what magic I wield. Death is the master, not Asmodel."

She snarled, and I could see that my weary acceptance enraged her beyond all measure. "Stupid!"

Raziel slid past Asmodel to join my side, and inwardly I groaned with worry for him. I could no longer protect him with my magic, not ever again. "We have company," I said.

"I can see that."

Asmodel laughed when he saw the two of us together. "I have won, brother. If she gives me the gem, you have lost. If she doesn't give me the gem, you have lost. You will suffer long and hard, and I will gain the gem in the end anyway."

"Give her to me, master," Enepsigos growled. For some reason, I drove her crazy.

"No," Asmodel said, a note of surprise in his voice. "The girl is mine."

"I want to eat her heart. For daring to mock me with my pain."

I thought of Gisele's death, and my heart grew cold, not angry. I knew with a heavy certainty that defeating Enepsigos or even Asmodel wouldn't bring Gisele back.

But that wasn't why I was fighting them now.

I could no longer fight them magic to magic. I was only Magda now. And the sapphire I held in my hand no longer a superweapon for me to wield.

But in other hands ... "Here, demoness, take the gem," I said, and I tossed it to her.

She goggled in surprise and almost dropped it, but then scrabbled with it, and squatted on the floor before the fire, clutching the treasure.

Raziel grabbed my arm. When I looked at him, he stared deep into my eyes. "Magda, why?" Raziel said.

It was the closest he'd come to ever doubting me. "I can't use it. If you use it in an attempt to destroy them, my love, I'll lose you, too. And to what end? At best, you'd end up like Asmodel. I couldn't bear it."

Enepsigos looked into the gem, and howled in triumph. Her scaly fingers clawed over the gem's surface, and she pulled it up to her face, staring and staring. Her tongue probed the surface of the gem, the point of the star, and her eyes glazed with the intensity of her stare. Her howls devolved into shrieks, and still she gazed.

Asmodel looked at me. "What did you do to her?"

I shrugged. "Nothing."

"Why do you not use the stone? Why do you not destroy her with your inheritance?"

"I don't need to."

Asmodel's features melted a bit, and the golden, angelic beauty of his face went a bit askew, like a slipped mask. "Don't you want to, witch?"

I sighed. I could not fight Asmodel magic to magic, but I hadn't lied to him. My strength lay in the truth, no matter how grim. "No. I don't want to fight you. War gives me no pleasure. But you brought the fight to me. You bring it here, where I am defenseless. Your death is not on my hands."

"My death?" Asmodel chuckled then, a horrifying sound. "Death has no dominion over me. And once I have the stone in my hands, I shall have dominion over death. Like a Lazarus, a keeper of the gem."

By now, Enepsigos had stopped screaming. Asmodel strolled over and casually plucked the stone from between her palms. A thin line of drool trailed out of her mouth and over the nipple of her left breast. Her eyes stared endlessly into nothingness. The gem had gnawed her soul away.

"She looked into the stone, just like you wanted," Asmodel remarked, his smile so cruel now that I flinched. "You got your revenge on her the back way, didn't you."

I caught Raziel's movement out of the corner of my eye. "Don't try to shoot him, it won't work," I said under my breath to Raziel. He muttered a curse in Hebrew and lowered the Mauser again.

"She only sees now through the stone," Asmodel continued, as if I hadn't said anything. "She is trapped inside the star. So did King Solomon lose his power."

By now, the demonic features had overtaken the angelic ones on Asmodel's face. He dragged Enepsigos to the fireplace, grabbed her by the hair, then shoved her face-first into the roaring fire. Enepsigos, the most vicious and effective of the three demonic sisters who had first murdered me, made no move to shield herself from the flames.

I watched her twitch and burn. Smelled her flesh burning. So did Asmodel reward his faithful demoness for her service.

I listened to Asmodel's low growls.

"You, come here, to the fire," he snarled.

I looked at him and remained perfectly still.

"If you don't come here, I'll tear Raziel apart."

"You cannot. Before Wolf's Lair, I bound you by spell so you could not touch him. Or me."

He snarled again, but his eyes flashed with impotent rage.

I couldn't help smiling. "Could you have forgotten? I never will."

He looked back to Enepsigos and kicked her deeper into the flames, taking his fury out on her inert body. She twitched again as the flames licked over her scaly skin, but Enepsigos made no sound. "If you don't come here, I will take the gem and destroy the world."

I said nothing, and still moved not a muscle.

He growled, rolled the gem between his thick fingers. Hesitated.

"You failed, Lazarus."

He was right. I still said nothing.

"I stand here, owning your Book. Owning your gem. Your sister is dead—you swore to protect her, and you failed. You failed in everything that you tried. All you succeeded in doing was tempt Raziel into falling."

I sighed at that, for the Prince of Lies was right again. "Are you going to use the gem or not? You are talking and talking, but I suspect you are afraid. What will keep you from ending up dead inside the gem, like Enepsigos?"

He growled under his breath, and his fangs grew to reach below his chin. "You will use the gem. And serve me!"

"No, I won't. I can't."

Every minute I delayed him, every minute we dickered over the gem, was another minute that the Soviet army threw its weight against the German attack. And what I had been unable to stop by magic, mortal soldiers might destroy with their guns, their bayonets, and their government's anti-magic.

"You are right, Asmodel. I've lost everything, just as you have described. So what more do I have to lose? And what do I have to gain, by picking up the gem, mastering it for you, fighting for glory and for power?"

He smiled then, an awful sight. "So it's true. You have lost your magic."

I winced but said nothing. Raziel held out his hand. "Give it to me, my brother. And I will keep it safe."

Asmodel roared with laughter. "You think me a fool? Magda cannot use the stone, or she would have. You trusted her, and look how she has betrayed you."

The sapphire suddenly flashed with light from the fire. Enepsigos was nearly dead by now. Or more precisely, forced into a lower level of existence, the way I had dispatched her sister Onoskelis. It is difficult to kill a demon.

The fire blazed higher, roared out of the chimney, licking over the demoness's prone body. The fire raged out of control.

"For the last time, give it to me." Raziel took a single step toward his brother, and the gem.

Asmodel looked back and forth between his hands and the fire, the stone trapped in his talons.

And then, with a terrible roar, he fixed his gaze upon the stone. "I claim the power of the Heaven Sapphire for the Reich!" he roared.

I gaped. Unlike Enepsigos, Asmodel mastered the stone.

I could do no more to stop Asmodel from claiming the world, now that he had enslaved both Book and gem.

He roared again, grew even bigger, swaggered around the room, knocking over the chair by the fire. I sprang backward, shielding my eyes from the flames.

And only saw through my fingers as Enepsigos reached with one horribly burned hand for Asmodel's ankle. Revenge animated her body, as it had once fueled my determination to return from the dead. She and I were sisters of the air, and I remembered that my stubbornness was an inheritance I had received from the fallen angels in my lineage. Like me, she refused to die until her retribution was complete.

Enepsigos twined her burning flesh around the demon's leg. He screamed and staggered, and the flames licked up his leg, hungry for the gem.

I could not fight Asmodel for the Heaven Sapphire. I did not have to. Ziyad's superweapon detonated at long last. The flames gathered into a blue, hovering ball, wavered in front of Asmodel's face—

Then engulfed his features in blackening, searing fire. The sapphire itself had broken the demon's mastery.

He screamed and tried to throw away the gem, but it had melted to his hands. The fire invaded his body through his mouth, his eyes, burned away his visage until he stood, a smoking skeleton holding a blue-flamed gem, fit for a king's diadem.

Demoness, gem, Asmodel all fused together in flame. The inferno roared through him, then shot into a flaming line of energy running behind him and through the walls of the dacha.

"He is still connected to the Führer," Raziel said, his voice soft with awe. "The fire runs through the ethereal plane, the silver cord connecting Asmodel to the demonic host."

Blue flame shot through the wall, blasting into the night like artillery.

The entire structure caught like tinder, and we fled for our lives. Stood barefoot in the snow until the horrified caretaker found us in the frozen, dead garden behind the patio. We tried to explain that it wasn't his fault, that he would be in no trouble. But the poor old creature spoke no Hungarian, no Hebrew, and we spoke no Russian.

We stood together, and watched the little dacha burn. Blue flames kept shooting into the night from where we stood to Hitler's hiding place, where Asmodel had unknowingly made his demonic host vulnerable to destruction.

I turned to Raziel. "Now I know why your brothers in the mountains worship the fire," I whispered.

✳ 29 ✳

Once daylight came, we drove right back south, in the dodgy rusty truck, oil burning all the way. At midmorning, we made a rest stop and fell asleep on the side of the road, utterly exhausted.

The Heaven Sapphire rested in my lap, the cigar box having been devoured by the fire. At least Leyla's portrait on the inside of the box got to feed the fire she adored.

The sapphire, too, was dead. I wasn't sure if it had sacrificed its life to stop Asmodel, indeed if the intelligence within it could be classified as "life." For once, I didn't pester Raziel with my many questions.

Once we woke up, Raziel started up the truck again and we drove all the way back to Krasnaya Polyana without speaking. The death of Asmodel, maybe of the sapphire itself, weighed heavily on him, but I sensed that he could not explain the inner life of the sapphire to me, even if he knew.

Now the sapphire was no more than a blue paperweight, pretty, eye-catching perhaps, but inert. It reminded me of me. But I remembered what it had been, and what it meant to my people. "Little star," I whispered. It had been my father's pet name for me, and now I knew why. This was the star that my creed followed.

The Lazarus witches. I the eldest. The second daughter, Gisele, was dead. My magic was dead, and that meant one thing I had not had the luxury to consider until our drive back to Churchill's dacha.

My line too, dead. The Witch of Ein Dor's prophecy had proven true. The lineage of the Lazarus witches, stretching in an unbroken line all the way back to time out of mind. With the death of my magic, the story of the Lazarus witches was ended.

The few people we met on the drive back to the Black Sea were possessed by a boundless elation, almost a madness of joy. The offense at Stalingrad had prevented the Wehrmacht attack on the Caucasus, broken it. The war in the East was over.

Now that Hitler and Asmodel were dead, the rebellions that had been bubbling under the surface in Nazi Germany burst into the open. Aristocratic German nationalists and patriotic army generals, joined by the commander of the Valkyrie Corps, sprang forward to wrest control from the Nazi Party and declare a military dictatorship. Overnight, the Nazi Party was outlawed and high-ranking members summarily executed before they could effectively mobilize their own resistance.

It was prudent for the new, Prussian military leadership to

achieve an accommodation as soon as possible with the West. The hated Communist empire was another matter. Stalin's Red Army had just delivered a crushing blow. The generals didn't have the resources or the inclination to fight the Soviets, not now.

So both Soviet bear and German wolf remained strong after this short, attenuated war of the Caucasus. I couldn't help worrying that another war would soon erupt, one meant to contain Stalin from his own plans for world domination.

But that was not today's war.

The Reich had not unconditionally surrendered. The politicians now had their jobs to do, the postmortem of diplomats and business magnates. But the Reich's Eastern invasion was broken, for a while at least.

And that meant that Gisele's visions no longer obtained. I thought of all that Gisele had told me, the summer before in Budapest. The ovens, the factories of death, the warehouses filled with human hair and pyramids of baby shoes.

None of this would happen now, because Hitler had not gotten the chance to create the death factories, what Gisele called "the concentration camps." The sapphire had immolated him first.

The prophecy of the Witch of Ein Dor had indeed fallen upon us Lazarus witches. But with the intercession of a fallen archangel, and the stubborn refusal of some orphaned girls in Budapest to accept the inevitable, a terrible holocaust had now, somehow, been set aside. We lived in a world free of Gisele's horrifying visions, a world liberated from the fate foretold by the Witch of Ein Dor.

Gisele gladly had traded her life for this state of affairs. So, too, would I, if I only could have brought Gisele back again, the way that I had returned so many times before.

But such violations of the world's way it was not my privilege to make. No longer.

I longed to see Churchill, and Bathory. And dreaded it, too. For now that my war was over, I'd have to find a way to survive the peace.

✳ 30 ✳

Nearly six months had passed since Asmodel had met his end in a remote little dacha near the Black Sea, Hitler and his army vaporized by a mysterious Soviet superweapon. Raziel and I had come to America at Knox's urging, to encourage the Americans to negotiate the Treaty of Baku, despite their minimal involvement in the Eastern European War of 1939.

We came to America on urgent business, but we had time to spend on pleasure, too. Raziel and I were designated members of an unofficial delegation commissioned by Churchill himself to come to America. We had come in order to convince the Roosevelt administration to participate in the ongoing peace talks in Baku, which, predictably perhaps, had encountered roadblocks and tangles. An outside, objective party could remove those barriers and allow the negotiations for a peace treaty to proceed once again, or so Churchill hoped.

The stipend we received from Churchill gave us the luxury of a leisurely trip from New York to the capital, Washington, D.C., to the south.

Once the Treaty of Baku was concluded, our position as unofficial emissaries of the Churchill government would come to an end, and we would have to find another job, somehow, one that paid decent wages for honest, unmagical work.

Raziel had a strong back, and I loved to write and could speak nearly fluent French. But otherwise we were all but unemployable.

I had more immediate matters to attend to, in any case. The butterflies in my stomach started fluttering again, and I pulled Raziel's hand over the spot. "Here! She kicked me."

"She's too little for me yet to feel her foot from the outside, Magduska."

The New York City sun beat down on the top of my head, and my flowered cotton dress stuck to my curves like wet tissue paper. Raziel and I sat on a park bench on the Coney Island boardwalk, and he had just bought me a vanilla custard with chocolate sprinkles, to feed my strange cravings and my growing belly.

I sighed, watched the waves crash to shore, again and again and again, while dirty-looking gulls swooped overhead like tough New York angels.

New York City was loud, grimy, gray, and cacophonous. So different from Budapest in so many ways. But I was falling in love with New York, not at first sight, but bit by bit.

The baby fluttered again under my ribs as I ate the frozen custard—she liked dessert as much as Gisele ever did.

A butterfly, pink and gold, rose above our heads, making its way upside down and backward down the boardwalk, improbably staying aloft despite the gusting breeze, the hungry gulls, and the briny air.

"Ah, Eva," I said, with a lump in my throat that even the frozen custard couldn't soothe. Ever since I had begun carrying this little Lazarus, I had become a weepy, sentimental Hungarian lady. The little butterfly fluttered madly, paused over an overflowing trash can, then continued on its merry, upside-down way.

"Eva," Raziel said, his warm voice gentle and thoughtful as always. He stroked my knuckles with his fingertips.

I sighed, tried to regain my composure. "You'll never guess the dream I had last night, my love."

Raziel leaned closer so he could hear me over the crashing waves and loud Brooklyn voices all along the splintery boardwalk.

I couldn't help smiling. "I know the soul of this child. You'll never guess who it is."

"Gisele," he said, and he cleared his throat. We rarely spoke of my little sister, but I knew he thought of her as often as I did.

"No, Gisi's off to the highest emanations of Heaven. I wouldn't be surprised to find she is learning how to read Hebrew from Yankel Horowitz himself."

"Hm, if it isn't Gisele . . ." Raziel trailed off, wondering.

Sadly, we knew too many people who had died in the war who would gladly return. Most recently, Ziyad Juhuri, the carpet trader of Baku. Long after our final battle with Asmodel, I'd learned of his fate.

When the professor and the Institute had destroyed Ziyad's superweapon, namely me, Ziyad in his despair chose to embrace a final act of rebellion. He sacrificed himself to the fire before the battle of Stalingrad, in order to augment the power of Uzziel and his band of fallen angelic brothers.

But the soul growing a new life inside of me was not Ziyad's. Nor was it Leyla, nor Viktor. Not even Obizuth, the ancient demoness who in the end chose her freedom over power and revenge.

It was not any of these. "My darling Leopold," I whispered, and I couldn't suppress a low laugh of wonder. "He never did leave me, did he. Not even when I couldn't tell he had stayed."

"Leopold!" Raziel said, his eyes widening in surprise.

"He comforted Gisele in her despair at Chartwell, and he comforted me, too. How much merit did he gain? Enough to return as a human child. Kindness is the greatest magic."

"But are you ready?" Raziel said, only half joking. Leo was so much like me that fireworks came with the package, for certain. "Boys can wear their mamas out."

"Oh no," I said, my voice as serene as Raziel's had ever been, emanating from the seat of the second Heaven. "I am carrying a girl. The eldest daughter of the eldest daughter . . ."

And I sighed again, in happiness but also in fear. I had grown into my power as an untrained witch, and look at all the trouble I had caused. This child's mama had no magic left to share—how could I teach this Leo-lah, this little Gisele (for that was going to be her name)?

As if Raziel had read my fears, he stroked my belly again,

and the baby leaped, enough for both of us to see. "David, melech Israel . . . ," he sang under his breath.

David, the King of Israel. I felt the prickle of the Hebrew words all along my forearms. "Okay, while we wait, let's review today's lesson," Raziel said.

I squinted up into the sky. "Oh dear. Aleph, Bet, Gimel, Daled, Hai, er Hai, Hai . . ."

"Vav," Raziel said. "Vav."

I said it again. "Aleph, Bet . . ."

And this time, if I squinted just right, I could see the Hebrew letters shoot into the sky, orange sparks, and disappear into the heavens.

"I'm going to teach you Hebrew if it's the last thing I do," Raziel said. "And you are going to learn it. Your magic is based in words, in the Hebrew language. I will bet you a thousand American dollars that your magic comes back to you, inside the words."

It was more than I could hope for. But I had learned to welcome the impossible. "We'll see," I said.

"You bet!" Raziel said in English, and both of us laughed.

He checked his new wristwatch, a farewell gift from the great Churchill, and grumbled under his breath. "She's late, that girl is late. You'll get sunburn sitting out here."

"My love, I am not a hothouse flower—" But before I could say anything more, I saw them, along the other end of the boardwalk near the roller coaster, and my heart leaped in recognition.

She wore red. Of course, she wore red. And he wore a crumpled white shirt, and tan pants two sizes too big, and he smoked a cigarette.

She saw us and broke into a run. I managed to haul myself off the bench and waddle down the boardwalk toward her, and we met each other halfway, hugging each other and crying like silly schoolgirls do on the first day of a new year.

"Eva, you look more beautiful than ever," I managed to force out, and I held her at arm's length to take a better look at her.

She dazzled like a diamond. And the terrible tension that had knotted her neck, and haunted her eyes when she thought nobody was looking—all of that burden had lifted from her. "In all my travels," she said, "I never imagined we'd meet again, in a place like this. And you with a belly like that! I am going to see first about a proper job for your handsome young man, so you can have your baby in peace."

Eva was always the practical one, bless her.

"And speaking of handsome young men, look at you," I said, turning to look at her skinny yet dapper companion. "Most famous war photographer in the world."

It was Robert Capa, hero of the Spanish Civil War, the man who still grieved over his lost fiancée, Gerda Taro, murdered in Spain, but who had managed to move on, to live, not just to mourn. Eva had met him in Paris, after Hitler was dead and the Reich self-destructed. Robert and Eva were made for each other—maybe not for forever, but for today.

And today is plenty.

So now my belly grows, and the world gropes its way to an uneasy peace. The jewel of Raziel a pawn in government negotiations, among parties that do not realize that it no longer has the power to destroy the world. Only heal it, perhaps, if the world will ever listen to its divine call.

The Nazi regime still retains the subverted *Book of Raziel*, but no one of sufficient magic and will remains to wield it in service of evil. It, too, is an object of negotiations, the secret magical talks conducted in concert with the open, conventional diplomacy over the pending Treaty of Baku.

Germany itself is in the process of repudiating and destroying the subverted, twisted Teutonic magic of the Nazi regime. The wolves, freed from their vow of service to a hideous tyrant, must now discover what they will live for, now that their reason to die in battle is gone.

Despite all the evil that is done in this world, I still believe that love is stronger. And if not, an army of angels, on earth and in Heaven, stands at the ready to do battle against the evil that forever lurks in the hearts of men.

Despite the fighting and dying over the Book and the gem, no mortal has ever succeeded in translating the angelic script within into a human language. After all that has happened, I suspect an angelic scribe, writing the Book over into Hungarian, would write the words that I have set down in service to the dead, intended to console the living.

The secrets of the Book of the angel Raziel are hidden in plain sight, within my desperate tale. Love is the only power that transcends the entire world.

ABOUT THE AUTHOR

Michele Lang is the author of two previous historical urban fantasy novels, *Lady Lazarus* and *Dark Victory*. *Rebel Angels* is the final book in the trilogy. Like her protagonist Magda, Lang is of Hungarian-Jewish ancestry. She and her family live on the North Shore of Long Island, New York.

Learn more at www.michelelang.com.